'Absolutely loved this book ... about connection, kindness and so much more, all mixed in with a kind of sci-fi element but totally relatable' Sally Boocock

PRAISE FOR DOUG JOHNSTONE

SHORTLISTED for the McIlvanney Prize for Best Scottish Crime Book of the Year
LONGLISTED for Theakston's Old Peculier Crime Novel of the Year
SHORTLISTED for Amazon Publishing Capital Crime Thriller of the Year

'An engrossing and beautifully written tale that bears all the Doug Johnstone hallmarks in its warmth and darkly comic undertones' *Herald Scotland*

'Gripping and blackly humorous' *Observer*

'A tense ride with strong, believable characters' Kerry Hudson, *Big Issue*

'The power of this book, though, lies in the warm personalities and dark humour of the Skelfs' *Scotsman*

'A touching and often funny portrayal of grief ... more, please' *Guardian*

'Wonderful characters: flawed, funny and brave' *Sunday Times*

'A lovely, sad tale, beautifully told and full of understanding' *The Times*

'Exceptional ... a must for those seeking strong, authentic, intelligent female protagonists' *Publishers Weekly*

'Keeps you hungry from page to page. A crime reader can't ask anything more' *Sun*

'This may be Doug Johnstone's best book yet ... Tense, pacey, filmic' Ian Rankin

'As psychologically rich as it is harrowing ... one of the genre's premiere writers' Megan Abbott

'A brooding, intensely dark thriller with a defiant beating heart. Evocative, heartbreaking and hopeful ... STUNNING'
Miranda Dickinson

'A noir heavyweight and a master of gritty realism' Willy Vlautin

'The perfect free-range writer, respectful of conventions but never bound by them ... each book is something new in this world'
James Sallis

'Bloody brilliant' Martyn Waites

'Pacy, harrowing and occasionally brutal' Paddy Magrane

'If you loved Iain Banks, you'll devour the Skelfs series' Erin Kelly

'A poignant reflection on grief and the potential for healing ... A proper treat' Mary Paulson-Ellis

'A thrilling, atmospheric book ... Move over Ian Rankin, Doug Johnstone is coming through!' Kate Rhodes

'An unstoppable, thrilling, bullet train of a book that cleverly weaves in family and intrigue, and has real emotional impact'
Helen Fields

'A total delight ... Johnstone never fails to entertain' Gytha Lodge

'Compelling and compassionate characters, with a dash of physics and philosophy' Ambrose Parry

'Balances the cosmos, music, death and life, and wraps it all in a compelling mystery' Marni Graff

THE SPACE BETWEEN US

ABOUT THE AUTHOR

Doug Johnstone is the author of thirteen previous novels, most recently *Black Hearts* (2022). *The Big Chill* (2020) was longlisted for the Theakston Crime Novel of the Year and three of his books, *A Dark Matter* (2020), *Breakers* (2019) and *The Jump* (2015), have been shortlisted for the McIlvanney Prize for Scottish Crime Novel of the Year. He's taught creative writing and been writer in residence at various institutions over the last decade, and has been an arts journalist for over twenty years. Doug is a songwriter and musician with six albums and three EPs released, and he plays drums for the Fun Lovin' Crime Writers, a band of crime writers. He's also co-founder of the Scotland Writers Football Club.

Follow Doug on Twitter @doug_johnstone and visit his website: dougjohnstone.com.

Other titles by Doug Johnstone, available from Orenda Books

THE SKELFS SERIES

A Dark Matter
The Big Chill
The Great Silence
Black Hearts

Fault Lines
Breakers

THE SPACE BETWEEN US

DOUG JOHNSTONE

ORENDA
BOOKS

Orenda Books
16 Carson Road
West Dulwich
London SE21 8HU
www.orendabooks.co.uk

First published in the United Kingdom by Orenda Books, 2023

A catalogue record for this book is available from the British Library.

ISBN 978-1-914585-44-9
eISBN 978-1-914585-45-6

Typeset in Garamond by typesetter.org.uk

Printed and bound by CPI Group (UK) Ltd, Croydon CR0 4YY

For sales and distribution, please contact info@orendabooks.co.uk or visit www.orendabooks.co.uk.

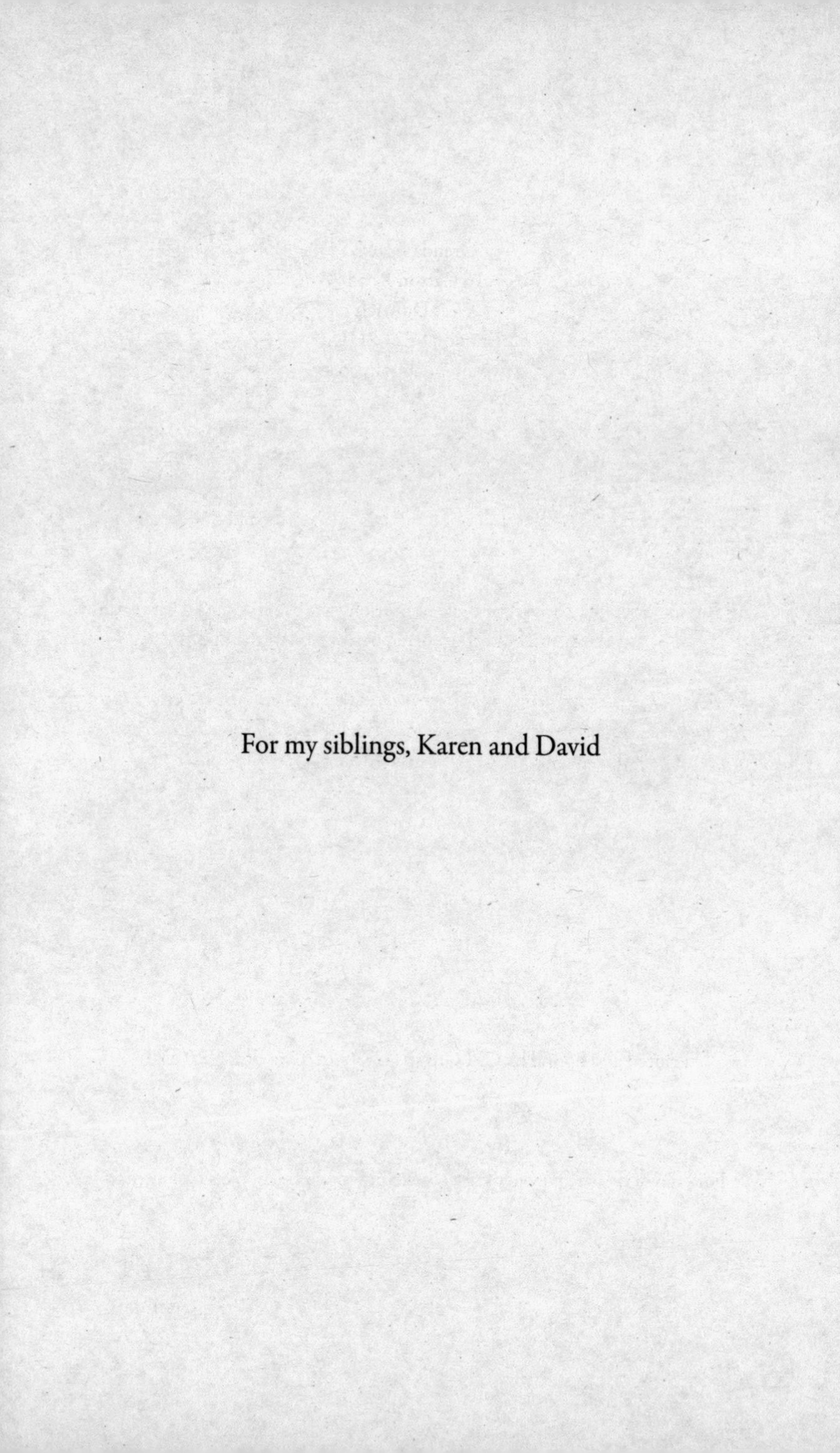

For my siblings, Karen and David

1
LENNOX

He knew they were following him. A shift in the shadows as he entered Figgate Park. He pressed pause on the Self Esteem track he was listening to but kept the headphones over his ears. If he dropped them round his neck they would know he was onto them. He kept his stride regular, changed his grip on the skateboard from the deck to the wheel axis, so he could swing it better.

He heard whispers, the scuff of trainers. He sped up. The path split round the pond and he had to choose which direction. Left was quicker but darker so he went right, into the light overspilling from the railway sidings up the hill. He cut across the grass between trees, then left around the water. The sky was clear, sprayed with stars, full moon like a coin pressed into the dark. Lennox spotted the resident heron standing on one leg on the island, hunched over, waiting for prey. He sensed movement behind him, gripped his board tighter.

He reached the wooden platform for feeding the ducks, saw something ahead to the left, coming round the pond from the other direction. Two guys, and he knew them. He sped up but they were too close. They loped into a casual run to cut him off from the path by the burn. They emerged from the shadows. At the front was Blair, thick neck and shoulders, grey top and joggers. Behind was Kai, one of his simpering minions, taller than Blair, mouth-breather. Lennox turned and saw two more of Blair's gang behind him, Carson and Cal, little and large. Lennox turned back and Blair was only a few feet away, scratching his chin and smiling.

'Sup, Scarecrow.'

Lennox swallowed, didn't speak.

Blair stuck his chin out and tapped at his ear. 'Lose the cans.'

Lennox pushed the headphones down round his neck, felt his hair spring up where the headband had been.

'That's better,' Blair said. 'Let that beautiful mop free.'

He looked at the rest of them and they sniggered.

When Lennox started at high school he was self-conscious about his Afro, kept his hair buzzed short. But he gradually got more confident, helped by some girls starting to notice, and when he turned sixteen he grew it out. Most kids loved it, and girls like to touch it without asking, which made him feel weird. But it also attracted attention from bottom feeders like Blair.

These four were in Lennox's year at Porty High, but not in his classes. Lennox wasn't exactly academic, but he did OK. He liked physics and engineering, how things worked. But these guys were in the bottom classes, treading water until they could leave at the end of the year to become drug dealers or join the army.

'You not saying hello, Scarecrow?' Blair was performing, leading the gang. Without him they were nothing, he made them feel part of something.

Lennox shuffled his feet, looked at the path beyond Blair. 'Hey.'

Blair smiled and held his hands out. 'There you go. And where you off to so fast?'

Lennox shrugged.

'We could hardly keep up with you, right, lads?'

'Just heading home.'

Blair took a step forward. 'Past your bedtime in the Kiddy House?'

The truth was it was hours after curfew at the children's home where Lennox stayed, but he was almost an adult, they didn't give a shit.

'Watch out going through Junkie Town,' Blair said.

This was what Blair called Northfield, which was fucking rich, given the number of junkies around where he lived.

Blair took another step forward and Lennox could smell his breath – weed and energy drinks. Lennox saw Carson and Cal closing in behind, Kai on Blair's shoulder. He was used to getting shit from arseholes because of his hair, brown skin, the poor-little-orphan bullshit. But that didn't make it any easier.

'Leave me alone,' Lennox said, and tried to walk past.

Blair blocked him, the rest closing in. Blair raised his hands like he was affronted. 'We're just talking, Scarecrow. Just talking.' He nodded at the two guys behind.

Lennox began to raise the skateboard but felt a thud of pain in his ear knocking him sideways. His arms were pulled behind him and he dropped the board. Blair threw a fist into his stomach, winding him, then punched his cheek.

'We're just trying to be friendly, fuck's sake,' Blair said, punching Lennox in the gut again.

Lennox wheezed, tried to suck in air.

'You think you're fucking better than us,' Blair said. This was his standard bullshit, anyone smarter or better-looking thought they were some fucking elite. Bullying 101, pick an easy target and find a reason.

Another fist to the face made Lennox's knees buckle, and his shoulders burned as he slumped, still held by Carson and Cal. Kai was leaning over Blair's shoulder, laughing, eyes shining.

Blair picked up Lennox's skateboard and swung it against a park bench, splitting the deck, splinters flying. He threw the pieces on the ground in front of Lennox and grabbed a fistful of hair, pulling his head back.

'Try showing off your fucking tricks now, Darkie.'

'Fuck you, Dick Breath,' Lennox said.

Blair's eyes hardened and he swung his fist hard into Lennox's eye, a burst of pain and light in his mind, tears on his face and blood from a cut on his brow.

Then the light seemed to get brighter. Lennox closed his eyes, sensed brightness against his eyelids, opened them again.

The park was bathed in shimmering blue-green light, odd shadows moving round the trees. It was brighter than daylight, a hundred floodlights in weird colours, like they were underwater.

A crackle came from the west, above them, and Blair let go of Lennox's hair. They all stared at the sky as a fiery throb of light swept over them. There was an enormous hiss, mixed with an underlying scream and rumble, and Lennox felt the air vibrate, the ground shudder. It was shimmering, impossible to say how high, and it was fast, shadows sweeping around the park, making Lennox dizzy. The noise and the blue-green wash faded as it thrust eastward, leaving a trail of colourful sparks which floated and danced in the air.

Everyone was still staring after the ball of light. In the silence the world seemed different, a residual throb in the air.

Lennox stood and Blair turned to the others.

'What the fuck was that?' He was met by shrugs.

Lennox smelled something, like baking or an experiment from his chemistry class, acrid but with an underlying sweetness.

Blair stared at him, shaking his head. 'Where were we?'

Lennox braced himself. But Blair swayed like a sapling, lifted a hand to his temple. He cricked his neck and looked at the others, his eyes glassy.

'What the fuck?' he said, then his knees crumpled and he fell like a bag of sand, cracked his head on the concrete. Kai did the same, keeling over like a comedy pratfall. Lennox turned to see Carson and Cal reach out to each other then faint, falling hard on the ground.

Lennox looked at the four flat-out guys. He stared at the sky where the ball of light had gone then the world started spinning, trees spiralling, the park and the pond racing around him. He leaned over and vomited hard, hands on his thighs, then he slumped to the ground and let the darkness overwhelm him.

2
AVA

She lay in bed and held her breath so she could listen better. Michael lay next to her, his breathing ragged and slow. She wondered about the dosage she'd put in his food. Really, she had no idea. She'd been stealing pills from Rowan's handbag in the staffroom at work, storing them up. She'd experimented with half a pill in his food for the last couple of nights, then crushed up three in tonight's casserole, putting in too much garlic to cover it. He berated her about the food, but that was nothing new.

She stared at the swirling pattern on the ceiling, strands intertwined like the arms of some creature. His breathing slowed even more and she felt the baby kick in her belly. Ava was eight months gone, and the baby was letting her know she couldn't wait much longer. It was one thing for Ava to be controlled and dominated by this monster, another to bring a new-born daughter into this home. That's why she had to do this now.

Michael turned towards her, face slack in sleep. She flinched. How had it come to this, the sight of him making her cower? She was ashamed of who she'd become, coerced and bullied. No more.

She smelled stale garlic on his breath and stomach acid rose up her throat. If she puked now, he would surely wake up. He was normally such a light sleeper, aware of movement in the room even when he was dreaming. Some primal state of alertness, watching for anything that could threaten his world order.

She lifted her side of the covers, pulse beating in her neck. She listened to his breath as the baby pressed against her kidneys and bladder. There would be time to pee when this was over.

She moved her legs, feet onto the floor, rolled her body in a smooth motion until she was standing. Michael was snoring, hands above his head like he was fighting off birds. She stepped to the door, waited, opened it, heard it creak and froze.

Michael snuffled and wrinkled his nose like he was disagreeing with something. He muttered under his breath and fire flowed from her heart through her body. She imagined herself a marble statue, here in the bedroom doorway for hundreds of years, ignored by everyone. She heard a car in the distance, faint rumble of the boiler downstairs. He snuffled again, moved his arm to the empty side of the bed. His hand moved across the bare covers and she was sure it was all over. She began to think of excuses, needing to pee or she had to take another antacid.

He scratched his nose then shifted his weight and went back to snoring.

She watched him for a long time then crept out of the room and downstairs, feet on the outer edges of the steps because some creaked in the middle. She reached the bottom and walked across the hall to the cupboard full of raincoats and boots. She shifted a pile of old jumpers she'd placed there weeks ago, lifted out a small suitcase full of all the things she would need. Change of clothes, money she'd been siphoning from the shopping, toiletries, the passport she'd taken from the locked drawer without him knowing. She could sort everything else once she was free.

She wore loose pyjama trousers and an old St Andrews Uni sweatshirt of Michael's, warmer than she would usually wear in bed this time of year, but she would be outside soon. Her feet were bare. She had trainers in the suitcase, there would be time to put them on once she was out.

She went to his jacket hanging near the door and rifled through the pockets. Keys for his New Town office, ID, wallet. She'd read about human-trafficking cases where women were locked in cages or basements, brought there as sex slaves. She wasn't in that situation but she was still imprisoned by him, by his fucking gaslighting, demeaning her, always making her more reliant on him.

Everyone at the school thought she lived a happy life. Her mum thought she was in love with a wonderful husband. Everything looked good from outside this expensive Longniddry house. How could she be in a prison with a handsome, rich husband and a baby on the way? But that's what had changed, the realisation that it wasn't just her anymore. She'd become used to her situation, excused it and normalised it. But a daughter made everything different and she needed to get out.

She found the car key and took the cash from his wallet. She lifted her case and went to the front door. The alarm was on, he always set it before bed. He changed the combination regularly but she'd found the note on his phone with the most recent number. She just hoped it was up to date. She punched in the numbers, cringing at each beep, holding her breath. Waited a moment, expecting the loud wail. But silence. She glanced upstairs, waited for him to shout out or appear.

Nothing.

She opened the door and walked across the driveway to the Mercedes. She unlocked it and cringed again at the blip of the lock, the flashing lights. She placed the case in the passenger seat then took off the handbrake. She didn't want to start it here with the engine noise, so she heaved at the car, door open, hand on the steering wheel. Eventually the car wheels nudged forward. She leaned her shoulder into the doorframe, felt the baby squirm, did a little pee into her pyjama trousers but kept pushing. She turned the wheel to angle the car through the driveway and climbed in, closing the door as quietly as she could. The car had some momentum on the road and she waited until it was another thirty yards down the street then put her foot on the clutch and pressed ignition. It kicked into life, a ping warning her she didn't have her seatbelt on.

She pulled it on and drove away, expecting something to happen – Michael to run down the street, the police to turn up, lights flashing. She drove past the big stucco houses, everyone safe and warm inside. She looked in the mirror. The street was dark and she laughed, feeling the release, then the baby kicked.

She turned left then left again, looping round to Links Road. She didn't want to take the A1, if he woke and found her gone, it was the first place the police would look for the car. She drove along the coast, Firth of Forth to her right. She saw clear skies, stars bulleting the blackness, the full moon. She thought about the distance to that rock, how far she might need to run to really escape.

She reached the Port Seton caravans, beach alongside, moonlight shimmering across the water. She glanced in the mirror again, nervous, still waiting for him to somehow appear.

A bright light appeared in the sky, blazing an eerie blue-green, streaking overhead in front of her. There was a hiss and a roar, a trail of sparks behind. It seemed to be descending, heading for the sea to the east. She couldn't take her eyes off it. The sound penetrated her skin, the car shuddered and rocked, then she smelled something sweet and salty at the same time, tasted it in the back of her throat. The road in front of her rose up and spun round and she felt dizzy, unable to get her bearings. Bile rose in her throat then she puked down her sweatshirt. She pissed herself as the car drifted and she couldn't control it, didn't know which way was up. The car mounted the pavement and went over the grass verge to the rocky beach where it thumped into the sand and she passed out.

3
HEATHER

She stood with her toes pushed in the sand and tried to make sense of the lighthouses. Just offshore was the Fidra lighthouse, sticking up from the small knuckle of land that inspired *Treasure Island*. Beyond that was the blinking light from the Isle of May, then to her right was the beacon on the Bass Rock, a shadowy lump in the gloom.

She'd spent plenty of time on Yellowcraigs Beach over the years, living up the road in Dirleton. Tonight she was in her usual spot, away from where kids sat and got stoned round campfires. In all her visits, she'd never managed to get the lighthouse signals to synch up. She had a feeling they would mean something if she could just decode their timings and ratios, some great truth would be revealed. She'd looked up their patterns online, but that information didn't correlate with what she saw.

Four flashes spaced out to her left, longer blinks from further away, a more hesitant glimmer from the Bass Rock. She opened her eyes wide, maybe the light would go directly to her brain and solve it. Cure her. But that was a fantasy, nothing would cure what was spreading through her synapses. She'd been offered chemo and radiotherapy treatments, aggressive invasions trying to stop her cells from killing themselves. But she'd seen how that was for Rosie, still felt the visceral sickness at the memory of her daughter, bald and sunken-eyed in a hospital bed, defeated.

She breathed deeply, tried to calm her heart. She had to pull herself back to what she was doing here. She looked at the sky.

This far away from streetlights it was bristling with stars, shimmering freckles above the Firth of Forth, the moon blazing a trail across the water. She spotted Jupiter and maybe Saturn, the peachy tinge of Mars. So beautiful, yet so far away.

The gentle shush of the sea brought her back to earth. She saw the rockpools in the sweep of the Fidra beam, like shadows of sea creatures hunching their way onto land. She turned to the heap of large stones next to her.

She crouched and began placing the stones in her pockets. She wore loose yoga pants and felt stupid as the pockets started to bulge. She tied the waistband tight to make sure they didn't fall down. She stuffed rocks into her hoodie pockets too, then zipped them up. The weight was already making her hunch. Over the hoodie was a fleece, three more zip pockets, one each side and one on the left breast. She filled them in turn, closed them. They would be hard to open in a panic.

She felt stupid with the weight, an ancient lumbering beast, soon extinct. She walked with a cumbersome gait to the water. It wasn't far but each step was slow progress.

She stopped at the edge of the water, heard the ripple and slurp. She looked at the expanse of sea, the yellow lights of North Berwick to her right. She looked behind her at the beach where she'd been most days for the last twenty years. Single, married, pregnant, a mum, a grieving woman, divorced, a terminal brain tumour patient.

Now she was just Heather, ready to go. She'd had enough.

She stepped into the icy water, the material of the trousers clinging to her skin. The shock jolted her chest but she breathed through it, kept walking, felt her trouser pockets enter the water, the weight pulling her down. She was up to her waist, then her hoodie and fleece were soaked. She felt so heavy, like she was a rock herself, part of the rockpool alongside her. She'd been here for millennia, waiting for this. Anxiety rose in her chest but she stepped forward, the sand soft under her feet as she sank but kept going, up to her chest, neck. It got deep quickly in this stretch, that's why she'd chosen it. She instinctively raised her chin to keep her mouth above the surface, kept walking and stretching her neck.

Between the flashes from Fidra, she sensed another light to her left, a glow shifting from aquamarine to teal, getting brighter until it was fierce. She saw a glaring ball of fire streak across the sky, ripping between her and Fidra, a crackle and fizz in her ears, a glimmering trail of sparkles in its wake as it tore into the sea a hundred yards away.

She waited for waves or steam or an explosion, but the night was silent and dark. She stood like that for a long time, the pull of the rocks in her pockets, the push of the water against her body. Then she stepped forward and there was no more sand under her feet. She tried to swim, arms beating the water, but the weight made her head sink under. She thrashed back to the surface, gasped in air, sank again. She stretched her toes, feeling for the seabed to kick against, but there was nothing. She began trying to remove her clothes, but her fingers fumbled. She tried to unzip a pocket, but the zip stuck as she yanked. She heaved her arms and legs in the water and rose for a moment, gasped in air, smelled something like scones which confused her, then sank again.

She opened her eyes underwater and they stung, the sand and seaweed she'd kicked up making it like she was drowning in soup. She felt dizzy, unsure which way was up, then vomited, the bile drifting away from her face as she sucked in sea water against every impulse in her body.

She lost all energy and stopped thrashing, her vision spinning and limbs like lead. Then she saw something in front of her, a tangle of bright seaweed but more solid, the same blue-green colour as the light in the sky. It came closer, arms reaching out and holding her, squeezing her, like a hug from her daughter. Finally she could give up fighting and rest.

4
LENNOX

He dreamed he was underwater but he could breathe. He felt at home in the cold darkness, fish and other creatures swimming around him. He opened his eyes. Throbbing strip light over his bed, scratchy sheets against his skin. He was in a small hospital ward, watery light seeping through the window, four beds with papery curtains pulled back. Televisions hung on robot arms to the side of each bed, playing local news with the sound off. He peeled his tongue from the roof of his mouth, spotted a plastic cup and took a sip of water. He moved his head, it didn't hurt. He remembered blinding pain, sickness, the rest of them collapsing around him at the Figgate.

He cleared his throat and sat up. In the bed across from him was a middle-aged woman, straggly blonde hair, washed-out complexion, eyes closed. To his left was a younger woman, redhead bob, pregnant belly obvious under the bedsheet. He recognised her, a maths teacher from school, Mrs Cross. She was pretty but sad too, ghostly bags under her eyes. She seemed to be sleeping.

He looked at the final bed and his throat closed when he recognised Blair from the park. He got out of bed and walked over. There was a machine on a stand next to Blair's bed, a digital display linked to an air bag, from which a tube ran into Blair's throat, stuck with tape to his cheek.

'Blair?'

He opened his eyes and coughed, gargling like he was choking. He turned and Lennox saw that the right side of his face had collapsed, muscles drooping his eye and mouth. Dribble had formed a wet patch on his bedsheet.

'What happened?'

Blair tried to lift his hand but his arm flopped to the side. The effort made him sink back into his pillow and close his eyes.

'Ah, the dead have arisen.'

Lennox turned at the voice.

A thin guy in a pink striped shirt with a big collar had come in. 'And you are?' he said.

Lennox spotted a nametag, Dr Ormadale. 'What?'

Ormadale waved a hand. 'You had no ID when they brought you in last night.'

'Where am I?'

'RIE, of course. Stroke ward.'

'Stroke?'

Ormadale looked impatient, pointed at the bed. 'Perhaps sit?'

Lennox stared at him then went to the bed. He sat on the edge and noticed that the two women in the other beds were awake now, thanks to Ormadale's foghorn voice.

Ormadale opened a folder, took out some scans, held them up to the dirty window. 'You suffered a severe stroke. A huge haemorrhage in your cerebellum. Very rare, only two percent of strokes are cerebellar haemorrhage. Usually.' He paused and looked around the room. 'Except all four patients in this room had the exact same stroke. Which is impossible.'

'Right.'

He was addressing all of them now. He waved around the room like an actor on stage.

'All four of you suffered exactly the same very rare and serious stroke at the same time in the middle of the night. How do you explain that?'

Lennox looked at Mrs Cross, who was sitting up cradling her

belly. Then at the other woman, wide-eyed. Then at Blair, blinking and breathing through his tube.

'And it gets stranger,' Ormadale said, lifting more scans from the folder and fanning them out. 'Three of you have recovered completely.' He prodded at the pictures. 'Within five hours, before we had a chance to attempt any treatment.'

Lennox glanced at Blair, it was obvious which one hadn't recovered.

'Six impossible things before breakfast,' Ormadale said under his breath.

'What?' This was the blonde woman across the room.

'Lewis Carroll, *Through the Looking-Glass*. "Why, sometimes I've believed as many as six impossible things before breakfast."'

Lennox shook his head, remembered the blue-green light overhead, the dizziness, the smell of burning biscuits. And something else.

'What about the others?'

'What?'

Lennox pointed at Blair. 'The others who were with us in the park?'

Ormadale seemed to deflate, his theatricality gone. 'They didn't make it to the ward, dead on arrival.'

Mrs Cross looked anxious. 'What?'

Ormadale nodded. 'They're not the only ones. There's been a four hundred percent increase in stroke cases in the last twenty-four hours. It's an impossible health emergency. The government have been told, but what do you do about something like this?'

Lennox remembered that he'd not answered Ormadale's question at the start, no one here knew who he was.

'What about us?' Mrs Cross said. She picked at the blanket over her belly.

'That's why I'm here.' Ormadale looked at Lennox and the two women. 'You're free to go once OT and PT have signed you off.

In fact, the sooner the better, we need the beds for other patients. Things are crazy. And you all seem fit and well.'

His phone buzzed in his pocket and he took it out. 'Jesus.' He put the scans back in the folder and turned to leave.

'Good luck,' he said, shaking his head, then under his breath: 'Six impossible things before breakfast.'

Lennox stared at the doorway then the two women. He couldn't bring himself to look at Blair with his tube and drool.

'Put the volume up,' the older woman said, getting out of bed. She was wearing cheap, blue hospital pyjamas.

'What?'

She pointed at the television screen above Mrs Cross's bed. Lennox saw a news reporter standing on a beach. He walked over and lifted the remote, turned the volume up.

The female reporter was talking about some unfortunate creature found washed up on Yellowcraigs Beach in East Lothian. There were rocky outcrops in the background and a stubby lighthouse on an island. Lennox had never heard of it yet he felt sick with recognition, as if he'd been there. He remembered his dream, swimming in the ocean.

The older woman joined them at Mrs Cross's bed.

The reporter talked to a marine biologist who said she wasn't sure of the exact species, but it appeared to be a cephalopod, an octopus, squid or cuttlefish. She'd never seen one this big and it had unusual markings. And it only had five tentacles, but maybe it lost the others in a fight.

Then he saw it. A shot of the creature, long, domed head, blue with green ripples and striations running down its length, darker tentacles splayed out beneath. A feeling swept over him, a nagging in his heart like déjà vu. He somehow knew that the creature was usually thicker and fuller in colour, pictured it in his mind swimming alongside him, scuffling over rocks and shells on the seabed, wrapping its tentacles around him. He felt sick and exhilarated at the same time and wondered for a moment if he was having another stroke. The camera moved to the other side of the creature, then panned out to give a sense of perspective. It was maybe six feet long including its tentacles, waves nudging its body.

There was a final shot of the reporter thanking the biologist then it was back to the studio, and Lennox felt as if he'd been snapped out of hypnosis. He shared a look with the two women.

'What is that thing?' he said.

Mrs Cross shook her head. 'I don't know.'

'I was there,' the other woman said.

'What?' Lennox said.

'Last night.' She looked at her pyjamas as if she'd only just realised she was wearing them. She touched the pockets of the trousers. 'The beach is near my house.'

'Did you see something?' Lennox said. 'In the sky?'

Both women stared at him and he knew.

'You can take us to it?' he said, surprised at his own words.

'Why?' the woman said.

'I don't know.'

'But you have to,' Mrs Cross said, pulling on her earlobe.

There was noise in the corridor behind them then a man in a dark suit strode through the door. He walked towards Mrs Cross's bed like he owned the world.

'Ava.'

She shrunk into herself, gripped her bedsheets.

'I've been worried sick,' he said, sounding anything but worried. 'These morons only just called me. Are you OK?'

She nodded, eyes lowered.

He pulled back her sheets and grabbed her arm, guided her firmly out of bed. She was in the same hospital pyjamas as the other woman.

'Wait,' the blonde woman said. 'Who are you?'

The guy stared at her. 'I'm her husband, who the fuck are you?'

The woman stepped back at the venom in his voice.

Mrs Cross looked panicky while she typed on her phone one-handed. She pushed the phone under the pillow before her husband turned back.

'Come on,' he said.

He spotted a small suitcase next to her bed and paused. Stared at it, then at her. 'Where were you going?'

She shook her head, fringe falling over her eyes. 'Nowhere.'

'That's right.' He lifted the suitcase and took her arm, hustled her towards the door.

She was wide-eyed, resisting. They were halfway to the door when she pulled free.

'Wait, I borrowed the boy's phone.'

She stepped back and pulled her own phone from under the pillow, handed it to Lennox. Their fingers touched as she passed it over, giving him a look.

'Thank you,' she said, nodding at the screen.

Her husband grabbed her arm and they were gone. Lennox touched the phone to wake it up. The Notes app was open, a few typed words:

15 Gosford Road, Longniddry. Help, please.

5
EWAN

Thirty years as a journalist and this is what he'd come to, writing up a dead fish. Ewan looked around Yellowcraigs and grudgingly acknowledged it was beautiful. Nice for walking the dog or playing with your family. If you had a family who weren't on the other side of the planet forever.

A few bystanders were looking at the washed-up thing on the wet sand. Vikki the marine biologist had told him she'd never seen anything like it. Wasn't the whole point of being an expert that you had answers? Four years of university to stand on a beach and declare you have no idea about the octopus that's just washed up. And she wouldn't even speculate how it had died, which made his article for the *Standard* even more boring.

It was gross, for sure. He looked at the cephalopod, a word he'd just learned from Vikki, who was now giving the same non-answers to a woman from BBC Scotland. Ewan stepped closer to the thing, coated in sand on one side. He had his notebook out, thinking of a way to describe it that might paint a picture. Not that it mattered, they would run a photo of it. Words were irrelevant these days. Every social-media post was accompanied by a picture, video or GIF. Imagine reading a piece of writing longer than 280 characters? Being a reporter felt obsolete, but what else could he do?

He watched Vikki chatting to the beautiful BBC presenter. He used to be on television when he was younger and gave a shit. Politics was his beat and he enjoyed the cut and thrust of it, but as he got older and started refusing to work crazy hours for virtually no pay, work dried up.

So here he was, thinking of ways to describe a dead octopus. It wasn't cordoned off yet, the council hadn't decided whose responsibility it was. When a whale beached a few years ago in Aberlady Bay it took days for anyone to take charge. People thought the authorities had rules in place for stuff like this, but in his long experience, no fucker had a clue. No one wanted the ball ache of getting rid of a stinking dead animal. Ewan remembered famous footage of a whale being blown up on a beach in America in the 1970s. The case of dynamite sent whale flesh and blubber for miles, raining down on onlookers, smashing nearby cars.

The octopus was pale green and blue, blank eyes on the bottom of its ... head? Body? He crouched down and was about to prod it with his pen, then remembered he chewed the end of that pen. A wave reached the creature's body, making it rock a little. Ewan thought he saw something else, a movement that wasn't because of the force of the wave. Probably imagined it. A cloud passed overhead and the change in light did something to the octopus's skin, a shiver or ripple of thickness. The more he stared at it, the less he was sure he would be able to describe it properly.

His phone buzzed. It would be Patterson hassling him for copy, even though deadline was hours away. He was so hands-on as an editor he might as well type the thing himself.

Ewan straightened up, felt a twinge in his back. He'd been getting that since he turned fifty. He pulled his phone out. He'd entered Patterson in his contacts as 'Cuntybaws', puerile but it made him smile.

'McKinnon.' Patterson was a hard-bitten cliché and he loved it. Barking was preferable to speaking, and he dispensed pearls of wisdom rather than having conversations. 'Have you finished with the killer squid?'

'Cephalopod,' Ewan said, just to annoy him.

'Fuck your pod.' Which didn't make sense. 'Are you done or not?'

Ewan stared at the thing, looking for another shimmer on its skin. It had a translucent quality, shifting from solid to ghostly as clouds passed overhead.

'I'm just about to type up my notes.'

'Throw them in the bin, I've got something else.'

Ewan sighed. Spiked before he'd even written it. 'Yeah?'

'Get yourself to the hospital. A bunch of people have had strokes.'

Ewan frowned. 'What do you mean, "a bunch"?'

He sensed annoyance down the phone and smiled.

'That's what I want you to find out, dickhead.'

6
AVA

'Well?' Michael stood at the mantelpiece and lifted their wedding picture, young and smiling at Dirleton Castle. It was a small ceremony, he persuaded her she shouldn't invite most of her family. He was cutting her off even then, isolating her so he could have complete control.

Ava looked around their living room. Part of her couldn't believe she was back here, but another part felt it was inevitable, like some Kafka nightmare she couldn't wake from. She felt the baby nudge her inside, wondered how she could keep her safe once she was out in the world.

'Well?'

There wasn't a good answer. Anything she said would enrage him. His silly little wife didn't know what she was doing or thinking. He'd said that so often she began to believe it, let him destroy her confidence, her sense of self.

'I just needed some space,' she said, flinching.

He turned and beamed, a smile she used to love. Now it meant something totally different.

'Space.' He ran a finger across the wedding picture, down the length of her dress, across her face like he was trying to remember something. He rubbed harder, like he was trying to erase her. Then he threw the picture against the marble fireplace, glass shards flying.

'Fucking space.' He walked to the sofa, stood over her with fists clenched. He didn't hit her, that wasn't his way, too easy for her to escape, evidence a doctor could see. He was careful.

'Have you seen our fucking house? There's loads of space.'

'That's not—'

'Is this not enough space for you? It cost plenty. Haven't I fucking provided for you? Haven't I given you everything?'

He stared at her belly. This was his line, he provided everything, gave her the baby she apparently craved. Without asking whether she wanted children or asking permission to fuck her all those times. Rape her. She needed to use the correct term. She hadn't physically resisted but hadn't wanted to either, so it was rape. He was a rapist. She said it in her head while he stood over her. She looked down at her belly, then the ground.

They stayed like that for a long time, then he sat down and took her hand. She jumped at the contact. His hands were warm and smooth.

'It's the baby,' he said. 'Hormones messing you up. You're not thinking right. It's OK, I understand. But you were out in your pyjamas in the middle of the night. I could have you seen by a psychiatrist. Sectioned. You know that I know people. This is dangerous behaviour, Ava. I'm worried about you and the baby. You could've both been killed.'

He squeezed her hand too tight, getting the message across. He could have her locked up. He had enough money to get away with it. Rich people can do what they want. She was endangering the baby, after all. And herself.

'You know you're a nervous driver, especially at night.'

He hadn't even mentioned yet that she'd totalled his Mercedes. But he would hold that over her, despite the fact he still had his precious Range Rover outside.

Michael still held her hand. Her skin crawled. He knew it and was enjoying it. She couldn't work out what his end game was. Intimidate, gaslight and abuse her for the rest of her life? And the baby, his own daughter? She remembered him forcing himself on her and thought of something much darker, something she couldn't let happen. That's why she tried to escape. All she could do was keep her head down and hope for another chance.

'Please don't worry about the Mercedes,' he said, standing up.

She thought about last night, the light in the sky, the smell of burning, dizziness. It was more than just being dizzy, she'd felt like she was outside her body for a moment, inside the burning light, looking down on earth with a sense of excitement and trepidation. The blue-green glow was soothing and she'd felt weirdly calm as the car went off the road.

And earlier today, that thing on the beach on television. She shared something with the boy from her school and the woman too. They'd all seen it and felt it. She didn't believe in supernatural stuff, she was a practical person, but she had an urge to see that creature up close. Or maybe it was just concussion, maybe Michael was right about the hormones.

'You need to lie down.' Michael held out his hand to help her up. She didn't take it. He produced pills from his pocket. 'I got these from the doctor. To help you sleep.'

The doctor was his rich pal Fergus who he went to Gordonstoun with, another over-privileged wanker trying to control the world.

'I don't think so,' she said, rubbing her stomach. 'Not with the baby.'

'It's fine.' He grabbed her forearm and yanked her off the sofa.

An alarm sounded outside, a loud yelp Ava recognised as the Range Rover.

Michael put the pills in his pocket and went to the window. 'What the fuck?'

He ran to the front door and pulled it open. Ava moved to the window. She saw him reach the Range Rover which had a brick embedded in the shattered windscreen and two flat tires.

Michael looked around, walked to the bottom of the drive then back to the car. He got his phone out, no doubt to call one of his cop friends.

She jumped when she heard a tap on the window at the other side of the room. She turned and saw Lennox smiling in her back garden. He nodded towards the rear of the house and raised her phone with the message on it. She glanced out front, saw Michael on his phone, pacing up and down, staring at the car.

Another tap from Lennox. He threw a thumb to the back of the house and shrugged. Isn't this what she wanted?

She walked fast through the house, picking up her suitcase Michael had left in the hall, and out the back door where Lennox was waiting.

'What are you doing?' Ava said.

'Helping.' He took the case from her. 'This way.'

He strode towards a gap between the fence and hedge. It was a way through to next door's garden.

Ava watched him but didn't move. Her feet were frozen to the ground. She could still hear the alarm.

Lennox turned at the fence. 'Coming?'

Ava remembered the thing that passed between them earlier. A sense of connection. But she couldn't run off with a teenage kid, for fuck's sake. Then again, she'd done it her own way and ended up back here. Then she felt something, her daughter pushing her feet against the wall of Ava's womb, letting her know she was there. She needed help as much as Ava.

She followed Lennox through the gap in the fence, away from her home, her husband and her life.

7
HEATHER

She stood in the hallway in her hospital pyjamas, holding a Sainsbury's bag with her clothes in it. The clothes were still wet and smelled of seaweed. The bag also contained the stones from her pockets, so the handle was straining. The nurse who handed her the bag earlier at the hospital had raised her eyebrows. She asked if Heather needed a referral, but Heather just shook her head and took the bag, stones and all, glad to get an ambulance ride home.

She stared at the hallway. She'd walked out last night presuming she would never return. But here she was, tumour still eating her brain, apparently, and she'd suffered and recovered from a massive stroke in the meantime. None of it made sense. She dropped the bag on the floor with a clunk and walked to the kitchen, filled the kettle and switched it on.

Nice cup of tea.

She should be dead, twice over.

How the hell do you process that? Tumour, attempted suicide, stroke. She put a teabag in the Best Mum in the World mug, the one she used to remind herself that her daughter was dead. She was never meant to use that mug again, never supposed to take milk from the fridge again, taste tea and feel it warm her up.

Fucking hell.

She walked to the living room with a swish of her cheap pyjamas. She sat at the table where she used to eat meals with Rosie and Paul, when they played happy families, before everything went to shit. Saw the scratch on the table where, as a toddler, Rosie had gouged at it with a plastic knife. Those early years were exhausting, the constant demands, but she would give anything to have that tiredness back. She was exhausted now but it was different, soaked into her bones.

But she wasn't dead.

She rewound last night. She was in the water, struggling to keep her head up, then the light, sparkling tracers, the smell, then she seemed to enter a dream. She'd presumed she was drowning, but now she wasn't sure. She pictured something pressing against her body, wrapping her in a hug, pushing her back to shore.

According to the nurse, she was found on the beach by two teenagers who'd sneaked away from a bonfire down the coast. They called an ambulance for her.

She wanted to die last night. Had that changed? She didn't believe in fate, and she was still dying. She drank tea and thought about the others in the ward. What was going on with the redhead and her husband? Heather would've told him to fuck off. But then it wasn't as if her marriage to Paul had survived. The boy and the woman had recognised each other. And something had passed between the three of them when they saw that thing on the beach. She felt a tingle in her body, a frisson of recognition. Her dream from last night. It had washed up on Yellowcraigs, didn't take a genius to realise some weird shit was happening.

She put her tea down and picked up her phone. It was still here on the table where she left it last night. She scrolled through the news until she found it. She skimmed the story, it didn't say anything she hadn't heard earlier. The council were trying to work out the best way of removing it. No one knew what species it was. She thought about that. The light in the sky.

She zoomed in on the photograph, looked at the smooth surface of its head. Two blank eyes at the front. What were the parts of an octopus called? She felt she ought to know, given she'd worked at SEPA for two decades, but all she'd dealt with were bacteria, parasites and pollution. She looked at the tentacles, striped skin, suckers underneath. She zoomed until the image was pixelated, narrowed her eyes, remembered her dream, felt the tentacles envelop her, imagined suckers against her skin. It felt good.

She looked out at her back garden, short grass, trimmed hedge. Why had she bothered? She was going to die, suicide or cancer, who the hell needs a tidy garden? She looked at her tea cooling on the table, rug recently vacuumed, fireplace dusted. She'd barely been alive yesterday, if this was all her life amounted to. Now it felt like there was something else, something bigger calling to her.

She went upstairs, pulled clean clothes from a drawer and got dressed. She went back downstairs then out the door towards the beach.

8
EWAN

'How many?' Ewan stared at Theresa in her charge-nurse uniform, blue scrubs with the NHS logo. He wasn't sure he'd heard correctly.

'Eight,' Theresa said, stirring her coffee. She had one of those reusable flask things, chrome and black, saving the planet. He looked at his own Costa takeaway and felt guilty.

'Eight strokes or eight dead?'

'Eight dead. Sixteen strokes in total.'

Ewan shook his head and looked around the hospital café. It was neutral and bland, open plan and high ceilings, swathes of broken humanity hobbling and wheeling past to get x-rays, treatment, bad news. Visiting families with teddies, chocolates, balloons, trying to cheer up someone's stay.

He looked at Theresa. He'd known her for twenty years, half of being a journalist was your contacts. He first met her working on a clinical-waste scandal before this new site existed, when she was a young nurse in the old place at Lauriston. She didn't know everything that was going on, of course, but she knew someone who did. He'd called ahead and asked what she could find out about a sudden increase in strokes and she'd come up trumps. All it cost him was a coffee and the occasional withering look.

'Let me get my head around this,' he said. 'Sixteen strokes came into RIE last night, and eight of those are already dead?'

'Correct.'

'What are the normal rates?'

Theresa was an attractive woman, early forties but she looked younger, despite her black hair greying at the temples. Green eyes, strong jaw, happily married to a cop.

She shook her head. 'One or two admissions a night, if that.'

Ewan had his notebook out, scribbled down the numbers. Theresa wouldn't be quoted on the record, more than her job was worth.

'That's crazy.'

Theresa nodded. 'The stroke unit is overwhelmed. They've grabbed beds in other wards.'

Ewan sipped his coffee, tasted like burnt water. 'What's going on, T?'

'There's more,' Theresa said, leaning forward. She was a gossip at heart, all good contacts were. She wasn't in it for a payoff. Most of her tips were moral, she wanted people to know about some NHS bullshit. But this was just sharing weirdness for the sake of it.

'Most stroke patients are old men with high-risk factors. Morbid obesity, diabetes, high cholesterol, smokers, heavy drinkers. But none of these new admissions had any risk factors.'

'None?'

Theresa spread her hands on the table. 'Teenagers, young women, middle-aged.'

'No old people at all?'

'One guy out walking his dog when he couldn't sleep, but he was fit as a fiddle. That's the other thing.'

Ewan was writing this down, waving his fingers for her to carry on.

'They were all outdoors.'

'What?'

'Every one of them was outside when it happened. And all within around twenty minutes of each other.'

'This is…'

Theresa leaned in. 'I know, right? And that's not even the weirdest thing.'

Ewan shook his head. This was big, but he was already worrying how he would persuade Patterson of it. Newspapers didn't like unexplained mysteries, those were for true-crime podcasts or ghost stories.

'They all had exactly the same type of stroke. Strokes are either ischaemic, haemorrhagic or transient. They each had a severe haemorrhagic stroke, all in the same part of the brain, the cerebellum.' She tapped two fingers against the back of her skull. 'Very rare.'

Ewan stopped writing. 'What does this mean?'

She leaned back, sipped from her flask. 'You tell me.'

'It's not just a coincidence, right? So maybe there's some outside agent involved. Poison?'

'Poison doesn't cause stroke.'

'Radiation?'

Theresa smoothed her scrubs and placed her flask on the table. 'The doctors haven't had time to worry about it, they're just trying to treat all the new patients.'

Ewan rubbed at the back of his head, trying to imagine what his cerebellum looked like. Would he miss it if it was gone?

'One last thing,' Theresa said. 'Three of them recovered.' She cleared her throat like that was nothing.

'You mean they're getting better?'

Theresa smiled, she loved sharing secrets. 'No, completely recovered. As in, they were absolutely fine just hours afterwards. Second scans this morning revealed that the haemorrhages had completely cleared. They've already been discharged.'

'What?'

Theresa lifted her shoulders in a shrug.

'Have you ever heard of that before?' Ewan said.

'Nope.'

'Is it possible?'

Theresa looked coy. 'I'm not a stroke expert, Ewan.'

'In your opinion?'

She waited a moment, building her own wee drama. 'It's not possible.'

Ewan tapped his pen on the table. 'Have you got details for those three, names and addresses?'

Theresa pouted. 'I shouldn't give out that information, you know that.'

Ewan angled his head, as if to say that's why they were both here.

Theresa pressed her lips together. 'Check your inbox, I already sent it.'

He pulled his phone out. Three names, ages, addresses. Northfield in Edinburgh, Longniddry and Dirleton. He pictured the three places on a map, they were roughly in a straight line. Then he remembered he'd already driven past Dirleton today, it was just along the road from Yellowcraigs Beach where that thing washed up. He didn't believe in coincidences, years of journalism had drilled that into him. This was something. He read the name, Heather Banks, and checked the address. This was definitely something.

He looked at Theresa, who was smiling, and he smiled back. 'Thanks.'

9
LENNOX

The road passed through a golf course, manicured fairways either side of them, old guys dressed like boring clowns clacking their balls into the air. It was only ten minutes since he took Mrs Cross from her house in Longniddry. Lennox had never been to East Lothian before, it looked rich and exclusive, not for the likes of him.

He slowed the car as they entered Gullane, a high street of boutiques and big old houses. He glanced at Mrs Cross in the passenger seat. She was holding her belly and Lennox thought about the baby inside. Then he felt weird for thinking about Mrs Cross's womb. She saw him looking then glanced behind them, but there was no way her husband was driving that Range Rover, Lennox had done a job on it.

'Are you old enough to drive?' she said as they left the village.

'I can drive.'

'That's not what I asked.' She smiled. 'And whose car is this?'

'Geoff's.'

'Who's Geoff?'

'Runs the children's home.'

'I didn't know you live in a children's home.'

Lennox didn't want to say anything about that.

She looked out the window. 'Does Geoff know you've got his car and are driving it underage?'

They passed a turnoff for Dirleton, but his phone said to keep going.

'Not exactly.'

This was all weird. The stolen car, a pregnant teacher, criminal damage. But then everything that had happened since last night was weird.

He hadn't thought twice about it when she gave him her phone in the hospital. He went back to the children's home in Northfield, where Geoff gave him a bollocking for being out all night, not realising he'd spent it in hospital. Lennox didn't bother telling him. Then when Geoff was distracted with some other shit, Lennox walked out with the car key, headed to the address in Longniddry.

'Where are we going?' Mrs Cross said as Lennox signalled left.

He gave her a look. 'I think you know.'

She went pale and rubbed her stomach.

'Mrs Cross, are you OK?'

She swallowed. 'It's Gallacher, Cross was my married name.' She touched his arm. 'But call me Ava.'

'Ava.'

Her hand was still on his arm. 'And thank you. For back there.'

Lennox took the turn, the road running through wheat fields, heading towards some pine trees. The sun was low to their left, giving the air a golden shine. They drove in silence until Lennox saw the grassy car park, a few cars and campervans around. The road ended at a sign for Yellowcraigs Beach pointing through the trees.

Lennox parked and they sat there, engine ticking as it cooled, crows flapping in the trees.

'You felt it too,' Ava said eventually.

Lennox looked at her. Her red hair was striking against her pale skin. He touched his frizzy mop and nodded.

Ava touched the back of her own head. 'What's happening to us?'

Lennox sucked his teeth. 'I don't know.'

'Last night.' Ava looked out the window, up at the sky. 'Did you see it?'

He didn't have to ask what she meant. 'Yeah.'

'Where?'

'Figgate Park. It saved me.'

Ava held his gaze. 'How?'

Lennox rubbed at his wrist. 'I was in trouble. Some dickheads.'

'The boy in the other bed?'

'And others.'

'The ones the doctor said were dead.' Ava rubbed her neck. 'Why aren't we dead?'

Lennox held his hands out. 'You're asking as if I know what's going on.'

'Sorry, I just...' She trailed off and stared at the sign for the beach.

Lennox nodded at it. 'Maybe we should find out.'

It was easy to spot where the creature was. A handful of short wooden posts were stuck in the sand near the water's edge, tape strung between them. A woman stood behind the barrier. Even from here Lennox could tell it was the woman from the ward. He looked at Ava as they trudged over the sand. She huffed at the effort, waddling with her extra weight.

He took in the rest of the beach, dog walkers in the distance, a family with two kids in the rock pools. It was as if this didn't matter. A creature washed up on the shore and everyone moved on.

The woman turned as they got closer and didn't seem surprised to see them. Somewhere inside him, Lennox had expected to see her too. There was something connecting them and he needed to find out what.

'Fancy seeing you again,' the woman said.

Ava smiled. 'Yeah.'

'Heather.'

'Ava. This is Lennox.'

'So,' Heather said, nodding at the creature.

Lennox walked past her and stared at it. It looked the same as they'd seen on television, but somehow different too. The screen hadn't really conveyed its colours, he wasn't sure if it was blue or green or something else with no name. When he looked from one part to another it seemed to shift colour like swirls of paint were running under its surface. The head was around two feet from the rounded dome to the fringes below, where five long tentacles stretched out, each about four feet long. They were darker in colour but still not quite definable, light circular suckers lining them from top to bottom. Its eyes were closed, one side of its body covered in a thin layer of wet sand.

'Why are you here?' Ava asked Heather.

'Why are *you* here?'

Ava folded her arms. 'Lennox saved me.'

Lennox blushed and didn't look round.

'From that shit of a husband?' Heather said.

Ava laughed nervously. 'Yeah.'

'Good.'

Lennox looked at them now. 'We should all be dead, that's what the doctor said.'

Heather looked down and shuffled her feet. Ava hugged her shoulders against a breeze coming off the firth.

Lennox turned back to the creature. He ducked under the flimsy tape and stepped closer. Crouched down and stared, soaking it up.

'What are you doing?' Ava said.

He reached out and touched its smooth head, it wasn't exactly warm, but not cold either. He stroked it from the top to its eyes.

'Be careful,' Heather said.

He moved his hand to the tentacles, touched one. And

suddenly he was flying through darkness, unimaginable distance, dots of light scattered across his vision. He somehow sensed it was brutally cold but he didn't feel it. He spotted a blue-and-white ball in the distance which grew in size until he could see jets pluming from its underside into the surrounding blackness. It seemed like a planet or moon, pockmark craters along the top hemisphere and icy-blue tiger stripes or giant claw marks across the south pole. He shot towards it, avoiding the streaming jets, but close enough to feel heat from them. He flew so fast he couldn't breathe, yet it felt effortless as the moon grew to occupy his field of view. He caught a glimpse of a large brown planet with rings before he plunged through jets of hot vapour, then layers of thick blue ice, then he was underwater in dark blue, flashes all around him, glowing blue and green and white, and larger throbbing red lights down below, and he looked down at his body and he wasn't human, he was the creature, tentacles shivering in delight as he propelled through the water, head expanding and contracting like bellows, body talking to him, his limbs alive and sending messages, agreeing, arguing, resolving, and he felt like he was half a dozen creatures combined.

Then suddenly he was hauled back out of the water, through the ice and into black space, hurtling through nothing, a small blue-green ball in the distance getting larger. He felt a voice inside him, somehow recognised it, a voice that was part of him already.

<Help us.>

Then everything went black and he was lost.

10
HEATHER

They must've looked crazy. A fifty-year-old and a heavily pregnant woman carrying an unconscious teenage boy between them across the beach, kicking up sand through the dunes as they headed back to the car. What the hell was she doing? She was supposed to be dead already.

Luckily they didn't pass anyone on the way, it would've taken some explaining. Yeah, he touched an octopus and fainted. When he held its tentacle, the tentacle gripped back, two other limbs slowly curling around his arm, a shiver of light passing from the top of the creature's head to its limbs and back again. It was only when she and Ava pulled Lennox away that the light display stopped. Maybe it had stung him, that's why he was still unconscious. An ambulance would take forever and his pulse was strong, so they'd decided to take him back to the car. They could take him to Heather's house up the road to recover.

'That one.' Ava pointed at a grey Renault that had seen better days.

They carried Lennox between them, Heather fishing in his pocket for the key. They opened the car, laid him in the back seat. Heather checked his breathing then jumped in to drive. In five minutes they were at her house on Main Road, the ruined castle across the street. It suddenly seemed very exposed here, the houses circling the village green, curtains would be twitching. Dragging an unconscious young man into your house was definitely noteworthy.

It was a struggle to pull him out the car. She was doing most of the work, Ava could barely bend over enough to help. But they got him upright, then Heather opened the front door, and they shuffled him onto the living-room sofa.

Heather grabbed a blanket and put it over him, checked his pulse and breathing again, went to get a glass of water from the kitchen.

'Is he going to be OK?' Ava said when she returned.

Heather remembered being pregnant with Rosie, the trepidation at what's to come, parenthood anxiety off the scale, how would she cope? How could she keep a baby warm and fed?

'He'll be fine,' she said, kneeling at Lennox's side. She wanted to believe that and wanted Ava to believe it too.

She cradled Lennox's head and held the glass to his lips, but water just dribbled down his chin. She dried him with a tea towel and put the glass down. She examined his arm where the thing's tentacles had been, no red marks or raised areas, no sign of a sting. She remembered she had some old smelling salts in the kitchen and stood up to fetch them, just as Lennox gasped in air and bolted awake, eyes wild.

'Jesus, are you OK?' Ava said.

Heather tried to regulate her breath, thought about Rosie, the other teenager she was supposed to take care of.

Lennox wrapped his arms around himself like he was cold and Heather put a hand on his arm, lifted the blanket around him.

'Where am I?' he said.

'My place.'

He looked at the two women, then around the room. 'How did I get here?'

Ava laughed, releasing her nerves. 'With difficulty. How do you feel?'

He lifted his hands to his face and looked at them as if he was holding something.

Heather placed the back of her hand to his forehead, checking his temperature. Then she remembered she barely knew this kid and removed it.

Lennox shook his head. 'OK, I think.'

'Have some water.' Heather held the glass out.

He took it and stared at the tiny ripples on the surface. He stuck a finger into it, watched as more ripples spread out, then swirled his finger so that some spilled and ran down the outside.

'Are you sure you're OK?' Ava said with a frown.

He looked at her, then at the water. 'They need our help.'

'Who does?' Heather said.

But she knew what he was talking about, felt a trill in her stomach.

'At the beach,' he said.

'It spoke to you?' Ava said. 'How? I didn't hear anything.'

Lennox shook his head. 'I don't know. What happened down there?'

Ava scratched her ear.

Heather rearranged herself on the end of the sofa. 'You touched its tentacle. And it, I don't know, reciprocated. It held your arm.'

Ava frowned at Lennox. 'I thought it was dead. I thought *you* were dead. Did it hurt you?'

Lennox looked puzzled. 'No, they didn't hurt me.'

Heather couldn't get her head straight. '*They*?'

Lennox shrugged. 'It feels like ... more than one thing.'

'What?' Ava said.

Lennox blinked and looked around the room. 'I was flying through darkness, then swimming. I was one of them, we were all together. It was warm but there was lots of ice, a whole planet of ice.'

'What does that mean?' Ava said.

Heather played with her hands in her lap. 'I think we know what it means.'

They looked at her.

'Something happened to us the other night. And it wasn't from Earth. Right?'

'No, no, no,' Ava said, touching her face. 'This can't be happening.'

'Come on,' Heather said. 'The fireball in the sky, the strokes, the recovery, this thing on the beach. How we're feeling. It's all connected. And now Lennox has spoken to it.'

'Not exactly,' he said, removing the blanket. 'They showed me stuff.'

'Where's it from?' Heather said, as Ava began pacing up and down.

'I don't know, but they've come a long way.'

'Is there anything else?'

Lennox looked at the two women, and Heather caught the seriousness. 'They need our help.'

Ava stared at him. '"They" as in this creature, or "they" as in there's a whole load of them?'

The doorbell rang and they all jumped.

Heather got up. 'What the fuck?'

11
EWAN

He rang the doorbell and waited. Stepped back and looked up. Nice end cottage of three, old brick, small dormer windows amongst the rickety slates of the roof. He looked to his right, thought he saw movement behind the curtains. An old Renault was parked in the overgrown driveway. Most of the cars in this street were expensive family saloons. He checked the address on his phone. Maybe Theresa got it wrong or maybe the woman had given the wrong address to the hospital.

Ewan walked towards the living-room window. The front door opened. She was about the same age as him, bags under her eyes. Slim and tall, shoulder-length blonde hair, a mix of concern and confusion on her face. She was beautiful and looked strong, in control.

'Heather Banks?'

She folded her arms. 'Who are you?'

'Ewan McKinnon, I'm a reporter with the *Evening Standard*.'

'I've got nothing to say.'

Ewan narrowed his eyes. 'I haven't told you why I'm here yet.'

'Doesn't matter.'

He held his hands out in supplication. 'I'm just trying to write a story.'

She began to close the door in his face.

He stepped forward. 'Don't you want to know what story?'

'No.'

The door was almost closed.

'Do you know Lennox Hunt and Ava Cross?'

The door stopped and she glared through the crack. 'No.'

Ewan angled his head. 'Look, I need to write this or my editor will have my bollocks.'

'He's welcome to them.'

'What I mean is, I'm writing it with or without you. Wouldn't it be better to have your say?'

'There's no story.'

Ewan stuck his chin out. 'Really? Three people miraculously recover from catastrophic strokes on the same night that many others die of the same thing.'

She stared at him. He considered himself a good judge of people, you had to be in his line of work, but he couldn't work her out.

'There's no story.'

Ewan thought he heard something from inside the house. 'Your husband home? Would be good to speak to him too.'

Heather ran her tongue around her teeth. 'Divorced.'

Ewan nodded at The Open Arms up the road. 'How about I buy you a drink and we have a chat?' He put on his boyish face, had no idea if that still worked these days. 'Then I promise I'll leave you alone.'

'You promise.'

Ewan nodded.

Heather left the house, closed the door and walked towards the hotel bar without looking back. Ewan smiled and scuttled after her.

When he caught up she was at the bar ordering a double Laphroaig. He added a pint of San Miguel and looked around. The décor was ornate and plush, purple flock wallpaper, heavy curtains, tartan and thistles everywhere. It was almost empty, two elderly guests sharing a sofa and sudoku.

The drinks came, hers with a small jug of water which she splashed into her dram. Ewan paid and she walked to an armchair by the fireplace and eased herself in. He sat opposite and lifted his pint.

'Cheers.'

She drank but didn't speak.

Ewan got his phone out. 'Mind if I record this?'

'Yes.'

He stared at her. Some people claimed they didn't want attention but they usually played along in the end. A subconscious desire to have their stories told, for their lives to matter. And if she really didn't want to talk to him, why was she here? He thought about how quickly she'd left the house, without taking anything or looking back. Like she was leading him away from something.

He got out his notebook and pen.

'So can you tell me what happened to you the other night?'

'No.'

'Then why are we here?'

They both took a drink, a break after some light sparring.

Ewan held his notebook up. 'Will I tell you what I know?'

Heather shrugged and sipped her Laphroaig. He could smell the peat and seaweed from her glass. She drank it without flinching.

'You were taken to A&E in the early hours of this morning, having been found on the beach by two teenagers. Soaked through, pockets full of stones.'

That made her flinch. Ewan felt sorry for her but ploughed on. 'They diagnosed a massive stroke, you know the details. They presumed you would die. But a later scan showed that all evidence of your stroke was gone. They had to double-check they had the right patient.'

'How do you know this?' Heather said, leaning forward. 'Patient records are confidential.'

'I find things out, that's my job.'

'Muckraker is not much of a job.'

It was true and he knew it. He'd started as a journalist for altruistic reasons, pursuing the truth, holding those in power to account. But look at him now, harassing a suicidal woman who had cheated death twice, by the sound of it. She didn't drown, her stroke disappeared, and here she was drinking whisky with some idiot.

But he had a sniff of something here that he couldn't let go, it wasn't in his nature. He sipped his lager.

'Here's where it gets interesting,' he said, watching her. 'One medical miracle is a short paragraph on page nine, but three identical miracles at the same time, a few miles apart, that's front-page news.'

'You've lost me.'

'When I said Lennox's and Ava's names before, you reacted. You were in the stroke ward together.'

Heather stuck her lip out like she was thinking it over, but it wasn't convincing. 'Oh, those two. We never really talked.'

Ewan smiled and shook his head. 'You had the same miracle recovery in the same ward at the same time, but you never spoke.'

She drank, rolled her shoulders.

'I have their addresses,' Ewan said, picking up his phone. 'And there's something interesting.'

He opened Google Maps and showed her. He'd plotted the route from Northfield to Longniddry then Yellowcraigs. Taking the road it was a crescent shape around the coast from Edinburgh to North Berwick, but you could draw a pretty straight line between the three points as the crow flies.

She didn't take the phone but did glance at it. 'What am I looking at?'

'Did you see something, Heather? When you had your stroke?'

She stared at the phone for a long time, and he thought he saw her grip on her glass tighten. 'Like what?'

'You tell me.'

She handed his phone back and finally looked at him. 'I didn't see anything.'

12
AVA

Christ, she was hungry. Everyone knew stories of pregnant women with cravings, peanut butter, sauerkraut, even coal, but for her it was just tons of carbs. She rummaged through Heather's kitchen cupboards, found a packet of bagels and pulled one out, started chewing it. She leaned against the kitchen cabinet to take some of the weight off but she couldn't get comfortable whichever way she stood. And she needed to pee again.

She went to the toilet, struggling to get her trousers down then struggled to get them back up. Everything was a struggle. She couldn't wait for her daughter to be out. But, given her current situation, she also wanted her to stay in as long as possible. At least with the baby in her womb, Ava could offer some protection.

She went to the living room, chewing the bagel. Lennox was on the sofa, headphones on, checking his phone, which was charging. She tried to remember him from school. The kids were mostly a blur, if she was honest, boys in white shirts and with flick haircuts, girls in tight skirts and elaborate make-up. But Lennox stood out with that hair and skin colour in a mostly white and Asian school. She always thought he looked cool, that's all that registered, but now he held a totally different place in her life. She was amazed he'd come to help her. She wouldn't have had the balls if the situation was reversed.

She went to the window, no sign of Heather. Ava had listened to the doorstep conversation. Given her situation with Michael, the last thing she needed was a journalist sniffing around.

Her baby kicked against some organ near her pelvis. What does an itchy spleen feel like? Then she rolled around and Ava traced the bulge on her stomach with her fingers. She felt heartburn through the chunks of bagel she was swallowing, went to her bag and dug out the Gaviscon. She chugged it like juice.

'You OK?' Lennox said, looking up from his phone.

She put the Gaviscon away. 'Yeah, just one of the joys of pregnancy.'

She'd discovered how overfamiliar people became when she got pregnant, sharing stories of their own nightmarish experiences, offering unwarranted tips, touching her belly without asking.

Lennox nodded. 'Sounds tough.'

Ava eased onto the sofa. Up close she could see he would be a handsome man in a few years, but he still had some teenage uncertainty, not sure who he was yet. That was a laugh, none of us really know who we are, she didn't and she was almost thirty. Whoever she was with Michael, she didn't want to be that person anymore.

She looked at him and he glanced away.

'I never really said thank you properly,' she said. She didn't feel confident, hadn't done in a long time, but the tricks of being a teacher in a room full of kids still worked. Fake it till you make it.

'You did,' he said, removing his headphones.

'I don't know what I would've done if you hadn't come along.'

Lennox pouted. 'You would've got out.'

'No.' Her cheeks reddened. 'I don't think I would've. I've been in that prison for years and never did anything about it.'

'You always seemed so together at school,' Lennox said, flicking his phone between his hands. 'Confident.'

Ava swallowed. 'Just an act.'

'I get that.'

Silence for a moment. She wondered about Heather in the pub along the road. What was she telling that guy?

'Why did you come?' Ava said eventually.

Lennox brushed that off like it was nothing. 'You asked.'

'Come on, a woman gives you her phone with a message on it. That's enough to steal a car and rescue her?'

He looked around the room then down at his hands in his lap. Cleared his throat. 'I feel like we're … connected.'

The swell of emotion in her stomach rose through her chest to her face. 'Because of that thing.'

Lennox ran his tongue under his upper lip. 'Sandy.'

'What?'

'That's what I call them.'

'They told you their name was Sandy?'

He smiled. 'Na, they were just sandy, like, on the beach. I thought it suited them.'

Ava smiled at how daft the idea was, and how perfect. 'Sandy, I like it.'

She'd felt drawn to Lennox and Heather in hospital, but she'd pushed that down when Michael arrived, self-preservation kicking in. The thing with the phone was last-minute panic but it paid off. They should all be dead but they weren't. That meant something.

'What about you?' she said.

Lennox pressed his lips together. 'What about me?'

'Won't they miss you back home?'

Lennox snorted a laugh. 'They'll barely notice.'

'Come on, the children's home can't be all that bad.'

Lennox thought about that for a moment. 'It's not bad, it's just … It's a job for them, right? They don't have enough staff, funding, anything. And I guess the kids there don't exactly make it easy for them. Folk are always bunking off, missing curfew, running away.'

'But you stole a car.'

Lennox sucked his teeth. 'Yeah, I feel bad about that, Geoff is a decent guy. Tries his best.' He nodded at his phone. 'I have eleven missed calls from him, so he knows it was me. I guess he's contacted the police, so I can't go back there. I mean, I was done with the place anyway, I'm sixteen. I could join the army, right? Kill people or get married. They wanted rid of me.'

'I'm sure that's not true.'

Lennox laughed again. 'This isn't Tracy Beaker.'

'How did you…?' She realised how rude that was after the first three words, when she saw his eyebrows raise. 'I'm sorry, it's none of my business.'

He took a beat to think it over, kindness in his eyes. 'It's OK, I don't mind. I was taken from my mum as a baby, or maybe she gave me up willingly. I don't know. That's something about our fucked-up care system – you can't try to find out about your birth parents until you're eighteen, and even then they have to agree to the contact. I have a feeling my mum wouldn't.'

'Do you want to find her?'

Lennox shrugged. 'What difference would it make?'

Ava felt her baby kick, and a twinge of guilt. 'It might give you some answers.'

Lennox cricked his neck. 'There are no answers. I'm on my own.'

Ava put on a smile. 'Not anymore. You have me and Heather. And Sandy.'

He didn't seem convinced.

She took a bite of bagel and chewed. Lennox's phone pinged. Her own phone was in her bag, switched off. She'd disabled the Find My Phone app but she was sure Michael had some other way of tracking her. And he had friends in the police, he always reminded her.

She nodded at his phone. 'What's happening in the world?'

She wondered if they'd made the news. The strokes, the recovery. The thing in the sky, the animal on the beach. It was all one story, but maybe others hadn't made the connection yet.

Lennox turned his phone over, unlocked it. After a few moments his face fell. 'Shit.'

'What?'

Lennox ran a hand through his hair and handed his phone over. A story on the BBC. Photograph of Ava smiling, it was from a picture that sat on her mantelpiece back home. Then a picture of Lennox, some officially posed headshot. She scrolled through the text, detailing how they were both missing, some suggestion that Lennox was responsible for Ava's disappearance. Then at the bottom of the article was a large picture of the Renault, the one parked right outside. The car that the journalist had looked straight at half an hour ago.

13
LENNOX

He felt something in his forearm where Sandy had touched him. Itchiness and pain but a sweetness too. He was in the driving seat of the Renault, having just parked it in Heather's garage, down the lane to the side of her house. When Heather came back from the pub they showed her the news, decided to hide the car. First, Heather backed an old brown campervan out of the garage, then Lennox drove the car in.

The tingling in his arm increased as he got out the car and Heather shut the garage door. It spread up his arm and across his chest. He pictured electric worms swimming through his blood. Then the sun dimmed for a moment and he was underwater or in space, somewhere impossible. He heard their voice, panicky and urgent. He leaned against the garage for a moment then opened his eyes.

'They're in trouble,' he said.

He was amazed the campervan worked, it was an ancient relic. He watched Heather drive, Ava in the seat between them. It was only five minutes to the beach car park, then they walked through the trees, over the dunes and Lennox's breath caught in his chest as they came over the final rise.

A council flatbed truck was backed up next to Sandy, three guys in grey overalls negotiating a pallet onto the sand. One of the guys went back to the truck and lifted out three shovels.

'Shit.' Lennox sped towards them, the women behind.

The wind picked up swirls of sand from the beach, complicated patterns, dancing like the grains were alive. As he reached the waterline he could see choppy waves out to sea, white edges on the breakers, the island solid amongst the wash.

'Hey,' he shouted.

The workmen turned, each with a shovel in hand.

'What are you doing?'

He reached the flimsy barrier fluttering in the wind. He stared at Sandy, they were paler than before, grey lines on their skin, which had lost its sheen. He thought for a moment they were already dead, but then who messaged him back at the garage?

The nearest council guy nodded. 'What's it to you?'

He was in his forties, squat and solid, tattoos on his neck. The two other guys behind him were younger, baggy overalls making them look like kids dressing up.

Lennox looked at Sandy. 'Leave them alone.'

Tattoos guffawed theatrically. 'It's a fucking dead octopus.'

'They're not dead.'

Tattoos shook his head, tapped the handle of his shovel. 'Kid, we're just doing our job. Loading this thing up and taking it to some guys at the university.'

'Shame,' said the lanky guy behind, nudging his shorter mate. 'Would be nice fried up with salt and vinegar.'

Ava and Heather arrived and Tattoos gave them the once over. 'What is this?'

'Just hang on,' Heather said.

Ava was catching her breath.

Tattoos glanced at his watch, shook his head. 'We're already late for the next job. What's this got to do with you?'

Lennox felt his arm tingling again, saw a faint ripple of light run up Sandy's body. 'They're not dead.'

Tattoos rolled his eyes. 'Fuck this, come on, lads.'

The three of them slid the pallet alongside Sandy's body. Shorty dug out some sand from near Sandy's head.

'Stop.' Lennox ducked under the tape and started dragging the pallet away.

'The fuck,' Tattoos said, dropping his shovel and pushing Lennox away.

He was twice Lennox's weight. Lennox ran to Shorty, grabbed the head of his shovel and yanked it out of his hands. He gripped it over his head like a weapon.

'Lennox, wait,' Heather said.

He couldn't let this happen, had to protect Sandy.

Tattoos put his hand out. 'Take it easy, lad. You don't want to do something you'll regret. Maybe we need to get the police.'

Lennox glanced at Ava, who shook her head. That was the last thing they needed. He felt the weight of the shovel across his shoulders as it wavered in the air.

Tattoos ran at Lennox like a rugby player and barrelled into him, knocking him towards Sandy and the two guys, the shovel flying from his hands into the waves. They staggered back together, Lennox's lungs empty. They were about to land on Sandy but Lennox managed to lurch to his left, knocking Lanky's legs as he thudded into the sand with the weight of Tattoos on his chest. Lanky lost balance, tried to stay upright, but fell face down on top of Sandy and began convulsing like lightning was passing through him, arms and legs flailing, torso shuddering.

Shorty watched in horror. Lennox was on the ground with Tattoos still on top of him, Ava and Heather wide-eyed behind the tape. Eventually Shorty grabbed Lanky's ankles and dragged him clear, turned him onto his back. Tattoos untangled himself from Lennox. Lennox saw Lanky's face, burn marks on his cheeks, his overalls scorched and discoloured.

Shorty pressed fingers against his neck. 'No pulse.'

'What?' Lennox said.

Tattoos turned to him. 'What the fuck did you do?'

'Me?'

Tattoos scuttled over to Lanky, pushed Shorty out the way and checked for himself. He shook his head and began CPR, pushing hard on Lanky's chest. He turned to Shorty. 'Call an ambulance. Now.'

Shorty had his phone out.

Tattoos glanced at Lennox and the women as he kept pumping Lanky's chest. 'And the police.'

Lennox looked at Sandy, saw another faint wave of brightness and shadow move along their body.

Shorty was on his phone.

Lennox looked at Ava and Heather, then they turned and ran towards the car park, ignoring the shouts behind them.

14
EWAN

He watched through binoculars as the ambulance and police car drove slow over the sand. They reached the council truck and two paramedics got out and started treating someone on the ground. The cops talked to two workers, lots of waving and pointing towards the dunes on Ewan's right.

He lowered the binoculars and hunkered down in case they spotted him. He'd been following Heather since The Open Arms. He watched the three of them hide the car, then drive the campervan to Yellowcraigs to see his friend the octopus. He followed from a distance, watched the argument, the fight. And now this.

He lifted the glasses again, watched the workers. The older one was doing all the talking, angry, threatening. The cops didn't take that too well, but one was making notes, then spoke into her radio. Ewan tried to see what the paramedics were doing, but he couldn't make it out.

He tried to think. The council guy was obviously blaming Heather and the others for what happened. A middle-aged woman, a pregnant woman and a gangly kid with an Afro? Didn't seem likely. Why were they even together, and why on octopus beach? There was something big here but he couldn't put it together yet.

His phone rang in his pocket. 'Cuntybaws'. He answered.

'Where are you with my stroke follow-up?'

Ewan had written the basics of the story, the number of dead, just the facts. He'd talked Patterson into letting him write a follow-up on the ones who recovered.

'I'm working on it.' Ewan knew that was ridiculous, this wasn't the *New York Times* in the seventies, weeks of time and resources to break the big scoop. This was local news, bin collections and vandalism, school-run bust-ups and council backhanders.

'Don't bother, I've spiked it,' Patterson said. 'We've rejigged the pages, going big on this Bonnie and Clyde thing.'

'What?'

Patterson sighed. Ewan could hear the eye-roll down the line. 'Fuck me, McKinnon, for a newshound you don't know much about the news, do you?'

Ewan resisted the urge to tell Patterson to fuck off, because this was his only paid gig. 'I've been busy working on the story you told me to. What Bonnie and Clyde thing?'

'I don't have time. Google is your friend, as the kids say.'

Patterson hung up.

Ewan looked at the beach. The paramedics were lifting someone on a stretcher into the back of the ambulance. Two seagulls whirled above them. The ambulance and cop car left, followed by the council truck. The tape around the octopus fluttered in the breeze as the seagulls landed along the shore, pecked at the sand.

He checked the news on his phone and almost dropped it. The lead story was two missing persons, Lennox and Ava, possible kidnap or abduction and a stolen car, the Renault he saw them hide in Heather's garage.

He rang the doorbell. The curtains were drawn this time, and the campervan was parked in the lane. He rang the bell again, waited. Nothing. He leaned forward and opened the letterbox.

'I know you're in there,' he said. 'All three of you. And I know you were just at the beach.'

Waited. Silence.

'I want to help.' Was that true? He wanted to know the truth, that wasn't the same thing. But there was something about Heather.

'I just want to know what's going on,' he said, realising how weak it sounded.

No answer, no surprise.

He looked up and down the street. 'You need help, right? Especially Ava and Lennox.'

He hoped using the names would give them a jolt.

'I'm sure there's some kind of misunderstanding. But the longer this goes on, the worse it's going to be for everyone.'

He wondered if this was worth it. But he still had that nagging feeling of being a real journalist, tracking down a story. He spoke into the letterbox again.

'You know, as a good citizen I should really contact the police. But I don't necessarily *have* to do that, you understand.'

He straightened up, felt a twinge in his back. Heard the bolt slide across and the door opened. Heather stood there, arms crossed again. She gave him a narrow stare for a long beat, then glanced each way along the street.

'Get in.'

He followed her to the kitchen at the back of the house, where Ava and Lennox were sitting at the scuffed wooden table. There was tension in the air and he presumed they'd been arguing about what to do.

'He shouldn't be here,' Ava said.

Heather held her hands out. 'What else can we do?'

'Run.'

'Where exactly?'

Ewan tried to sense the dynamics. There was no kidnap here, obviously, so why was that the news line? Someone wanted Ava back, his guess was her husband. And Lennox's address was the children's home in Northfield, where the car was stolen from. Heather, found unconscious on the beach with pockets of stones. And here they all were, best friends, wanted by the police.

'What happened at the beach?' he said.

'What do you mean?' Heather said.

'I followed you.'

Lennox shook his head. 'They think I hurt that guy, but it wasn't me.'

Ewan frowned. 'Then who was it?'

'They didn't mean it.'

'Lennox,' Heather snapped. 'Enough.'

Ewan stared at her.

'This was a mistake,' Ava said. 'You should go.'

She had both hands on her stomach, legs stretched out.

'Wait,' Ewan said. 'I can find out what the police know.'

'How?' Heather said.

'I have a contact, Nina Pearson, she's a DI now. We keep each other informed sometimes.'

Ava sat upright. 'You can't tell her anything about us.'

'No worries.'

Lennox tapped his foot under the table. 'Find out what they're going to do to them.'

Ewan frowned. 'Who?'

Lennox got a glare from Heather.

'The creature,' she said.

Ewan looked at her for confirmation, but she stared stony-faced. Lennox scratched at the tabletop as Ava went to the sink for a drink of water.

He pulled out his phone. Listened to it connecting as he tried to figure out what was going on here. He put the call on speaker-phone, maximum transparency, trying to win their trust.

'Ewan.' It was amazing how Nina managed to imbue those two syllables with world-weary resignation. 'What do you want?'

'How are you, Nina?'

'Can it, you only call for favours.'

'That's not true.'

'Get on with it.' But he could sense a smile. It sounded like she was in a coffee shop, scooshing noises and cutlery clanking in the background. She was the same age as him but had managed to keep her marriage together.

'Love you, too,' he said.

'Ewan, you've got until they finish making my latte.'

'I'm just writing up this abduction in Longniddry.'

'You and everyone else.'

'It sounds off, what's the inside on it?'

'What do you mean, off?'

Ewan watched Ava sit back down as Heather poured tea from a pot with a knitted cosy. Nice wee domestic scene.

'Why would a teenage kid take a pregnant woman?'

'Why does anyone do anything?'

'You're a cop, Nina, you're supposed to find that out. The boy doesn't seem like the type.'

Silence for a moment, chatter in the background. 'How would you know?'

'Just from what I've read.'

She chewed that over. 'Right.'

'Maybe the woman went freely?'

'Not according to the husband,' Nina said. 'And he knows people in the force. This came from high up.'

'Maybe the husband has other motives,' Ewan said. He saw Ava turn and look out of the window.

'Abuse? He's an upstanding member of society.'

'Come on, this is the twenty-first century.'

'Sure, it could be coercive control, abuse. But we won't know until we find her. We can protect her. She'll be safer with us than some random kid.'

Ava shook her head.

'But if the husband has connections, she might *not* be safe with you.'

'I'll personally vouch for her,' Nina said. 'Anyway, we'll find out soon, we've got a lead.'

Ewan looked around the room. Heather stopped fussing with the teapot, Lennox's legs became more twitchy.

'What lead?'

'As if I can say.'

'Off the record.'

'Not even.'

'You mean Yellowcraigs.'

Silence down the line. He heard Nina's name being called by the barista. Waited a long moment. The three of them stared at him. He wanted to explain that they were already in the shit, the council worker would've described them to the police. It wasn't as if they were anonymous, a mixed-race kid with an Afro and a pregnant redhead.

'I don't know what you mean.'

Ewan smiled, he had her on the hook. 'Come on. I know.'

'Ewan, you don't know what you're getting into.' Nina's voice had changed. 'This is potentially a murder case now.'

'The council worker?'

Shocked faces around the room. The guy was dead, however it happened. Shit, meet fan.

'How the fuck do you know all this?'

'I keep my ear to the ground.'

'Your instincts were never this good. Let me give you some advice, stay away from this, OK? It's not just the kid and the woman. There's other stuff.'

'Like what?'

Nina sighed. 'Other interest.'

'What sort of interest?'

'From down south. Some task force. They've asked us to keep them in the loop about everything, including the fucking octopus.'

'What?'

'God knows, it's above my pay grade. Speaking of which, I'm late for the office and you're out of time.' She sipped her latte. 'But I mean it, don't get involved, there's trouble here we don't even know about yet.'

She hung up and the air was sucked out of the room.

'You'd better leave here and hide,' he said, waving his phone. 'The cops will trace my call.'

15
AVA

Ava sat in the campervan and stared at the road barrier. The van was parked under pine trees down a lane to the side, hidden in shadows. The lane ended with large green storage sheds and skips, piles of wood, trailers, mowers. It was used by the greenkeepers at Archerfield, a golf course through the trees. So much of East Lothian was given over to exclusive activities and access, thus the road barrier. It glowed red in the gloom, a beacon of privilege. Ava was amazed you were allowed to block off roads for residents only, but with enough money you can buy whatever peace and quiet you want.

Heather was in the driver's seat, Lennox out amongst the pines, crouched and waiting. This was crazy but she was dragged along by his confidence and determination. They were going to rescue Sandy under cover of darkness, and they needed to get the van down this private road to do it.

She had to pee. She always had to pee. Her daughter squirmed in her womb as if she was nervous, which spread through Ava. She wondered about Michael, how outraged he must be. He didn't love her, hated her, in fact, it was all about control. Get the police on her tail, the media involved, do whatever you can to get back what was stolen from you. The idea of Ava having agency was alien to him. And to be honest, it felt alien to her too. She was shocked when Lennox and Heather had asked her opinion of the plan. She just shrugged and they took that as agreement. But that's what she'd done for years with Michael. She had to break that habit.

'Look.' Heather nodded down the road. A black Mercedes like

Michael's slowed as it approached the barrier. For a moment Ava thought it was his, then she remembered she'd smashed it up and smiled. Michael would love to live in a place like this, but there were always levels of society out of reach, if that's the kind of bullshit you were into.

The car slowed and the barrier lifted smoothly. The Mercedes sped through onto hallowed ground. The barrier began descending and Lennox darted out from behind a tree and grabbed the arm and held it above his head. He walked to the fulcrum, levering the arm vertical, as Heather started the van engine and put it into gear.

There was a chance the barrier would be alarmed so they had to be quick. Ava touched the dashboard as they drove under the barrier then pulled over on the grass verge. Lennox walked the arm back down calmly, his headphones still over his ears on top of his hoodie, then he lay the barrier to rest in its cradle. He jogged to the camper and got in the back.

'Brilliant,' Heather said.

Lennox shrugged as they drove off, past millionaires' sprawling houses, large gardens carved out of the woods, houses more like American suburban mansions than Scottish homes. The road ended in a cul-de-sac of five houses. Heather drove round checking for security-camera blind spots, then parked between lampposts and killed the engine. No one spoke, just the ticking of the van's engine. An owl hooted somewhere in the trees. Shit, being rich bought you better nature too.

They left the van, Lennox with the paddleboard under his arm. They walked away from the houses and skirted the golf course, went across a fairway, past two bunkers, then through a copse of pine. A construction fence blocked their way to the beach but Heather led them to a hole ripped in it, and they were on the sand. Judging by the flashes from the Fidra lighthouse, they were a little northwest of Sandy.

They walked along the waterfront. The tide was in, that was part of the plan. As they got closer Ava could see the tape around Sandy, two cops sitting in a police car alongside, the interior light on. The car was pointing towards Yellowcraigs car park. Of course, that's where anyone approaching would come from. Ava smiled, that's why they were coming from the opposite direction.

Heather held up a hand and they stopped. Lennox dropped the paddleboard and began undressing. Underneath his clothes he was wearing the wetsuit Heather gave him. She didn't explain why she had a wetsuit that fitted a teenager and Ava didn't ask.

'Are you sure about this?' Heather said.

They'd finally agreed this after a long conversation in the campervan earlier. Lennox said he had to rescue Sandy whatever it took, and both women agreed. But then the logistics. With the cops on the beach, Heather had the idea to come from the west, go into the water, lift Sandy onto the board and float them back. Then keep them in the van until they worked out what to do next. But Heather couldn't swim, which made the paddleboard and wetsuit more mysterious. Lennox said he would do this on his own but Ava wanted to help. She was used to sea swimming, had gone with a few members of staff from the maths department for a while before Michael shut it down. And being in the water was one of the few times she didn't feel like an elephant lugging a bowling ball in her belly.

She stripped to her underwear. No wetsuit for her, it wouldn't have fitted her stomach anyway. Her pants and bra were like scaffolding for her outsized ass and boobs, thanks, baby. She saw Lennox glance at her. She looked down at herself, her stomach looked like a full moon.

Lennox lifted the board and waded into the water. He was different from a lot of the teenage boys at school, not performative, just getting on with things. She followed him, felt the cold water on her legs then crotch. Her breath caught in her throat but it was always the same for the first moments. You can learn to live with anything. She went in over her belly and felt the baby flip, then she launched into the wash and swam, followed Lennox who was pushing the board in front of him.

The lighthouse ahead blinked. She saw the police car lit up, North Berwick in the distance. Stars were sprinkled overhead, sparks of life in the blackness. They swam a few hundred yards then Lennox headed for shore. Ava followed. She thought about what she did two nights ago, sneaking out of the house in the darkness. It was supposed to be a new life, but not like this.

She felt sand under her feet and started wading. Lennox crouched as he walked ashore. The police car was at an angle, so the nearest officer might see them if he turned and looked closely, but who would suspect abduction by sea?

She caught up with Lennox. Sandy was in six inches of water, the wash running over their head and tentacles then back out. Lennox brought the paddleboard alongside.

'Ready?' he said.

She glanced at the police, no movement. She looked along the coast but couldn't see Heather, even in the moonlight and lighthouse flicker. Good. They both wore rubber swimming gloves, in case touching Sandy made them pass out like Lennox earlier. Ava nodded at Lennox then pushed her hands underwater and dug into the sand around Sandy's head with her fingers. Lennox collected the tentacles together.

Ava lifted Sandy's head and felt the strangeness of their skin through the gloves, then her hands seemed to pass through the surface into softer tissue and suddenly she was surrounded by Sandy as if she was in the creature's womb, safe and warm despite the cold North Sea. She felt welcomed into another entity, this must be what it was like for her own baby, they were a nest of Russian dolls, Sandy keeping them all safe. Suddenly Ava was out of the water, still inside Sandy, flying towards the moon, streamlined and easy. She breathed deeply, could sense the cold but couldn't feel it, and she had a sense she was going to meet her family, never worry again. They reached the edge of the earth's atmosphere and something shimmered, a giant arc of black nothingness that reacted to Sandy's arrival, welcomed them into a chasm of love. Just as they were about to reach it she was back standing in the sea with her cold hands holding Sandy's head.

Lennox stared at her. 'They showed you something.'

Ava didn't know what to say. Something deep had happened, something that made speech superfluous. They had been inside each other.

Lennox frowned. 'Are you OK?'

She nodded then lifted Sandy's head and slid it onto the paddleboard as Lennox did the same with the tentacles.

The flash from the lighthouse was like a search beacon trying to find them behind enemy lines. The cop car on the sand seemed pathetic all of a sudden, they had no idea what they were dealing with.

'Let's go,' Ava said, pushing the paddleboard as she headed back into the cold sea.

16
HEATHER

She walked into Dirleton trying to breathe normally. It was early morning, low sun making her squint. It had been easy to dump the Renault. She'd taken the car from the garage, drove to Archerfield, turned off along a farm track between fields and woods, then driven it between the trees into a ditch. It wouldn't stay hidden for long but it bought them some time.

She crossed the green and saw the police car outside her house. Thought about running, felt her cheeks flush and tried to calm them, opened her eyes and mouth wide to oxygenate herself. She wondered if Ewan had spoken to them, but she thought not. He told them to hide, after all.

The two officers at her door spotted her as she got closer. Both were half her age, a man and a woman.

'Mrs Banks?' the woman said.

'Is something wrong?' Heather was surprised her voice sounded calm.

'Can we maybe talk inside?'

Her badge said De Vries, the other officer was Fisher. Heather pictured Sandy in the campervan in Archerfield, sprawled in the sink full of water, tentacles dangling over the side. They'd shown no signs of life since last night. Maybe they needed to be in the sea, or wherever they came from.

'What is this about?'

'Can we go inside?' De Vries was young and pretty, black hair, sharp blue eyes.

'I'd rather get this over with.'

De Vries and Fisher shared a look. De Vries held out a tablet. 'Do you know either of these people?'

It was the pictures of Lennox and Ava they used on television. Heather swallowed. 'I met them in hospital.'

'Lennox Hunt and Ava Cross, you were in the same ward together, right?'

'Two days ago, yes.'

'You all had strokes.'

'That's right.'

Fisher butted in. 'You look OK for someone who just had a stroke.'

De Vries glared at him.

Heather smiled. 'Thank you.' The sarcasm was obvious.

De Vries tried to pull things back. 'But you haven't seen them since hospital?'

Heather pretended to think about it. 'I did see them on the beach yesterday.'

De Vries' eyebrows went up, although she knew already, that's why she was here. 'Really?'

Heather nodded. 'I was out for a walk along Yellowcraigs, my usual exercise. I saw something happening by that thing that washed up, went to take a look. The two of them were arguing with some council workers, I think.'

De Vries narrowed her eyes. 'You didn't go there with them?'

'Goodness, no, I told you, I don't know them.'

The 'goodness' was a mistake, she was overegging it. Calm yourself, fuck's sake, you're not Miss Jean Brodie. It seemed obvious that she was lying, but if she'd learned one thing from Rosie's suffering and her own marriage, it was that people don't see what's really going on.

'What were they arguing about? De Vries said.

Heather stuck her lip out. 'They were going to remove the octopus and the boy didn't want them to.'

'Why not?'

Heather held out her hands. 'No idea.'

'And they were together, Lennox and Ava?'

'They were standing together, that's all I know.'

De Vries was shorter than Heather but she had a steeliness to her.

'I have to tell you, Mrs Banks, that doesn't tally with other witness statements.'

'I'm just telling you what I saw.'

Fisher had wandered off for a look around the side of the house. De Vries watched Heather for a reaction.

'We also traced a phone call to this area,' she said eventually.

'OK.'

'A journalist called Ewan McKinnon. He spoke to my boss about these missing people.'

'He came to see me, yes.'

'Why?'

'He asked about my stroke. Said he was working on a story for the paper.'

'Did he ask about the others?'

Heather chewed her lip like she was thinking. 'He never mentioned them.'

'But all three of you had the same stroke and recovery. How do you explain that?'

Heather shook her head. 'I'm not a doctor.'

Fisher appeared back from the side of the house. 'Can we see inside the garage?'

'Sure.' Heather led them round the corner, opened the garage door, just a few cardboard boxes around the walls.

'Do you have a car, Mrs Banks?'

She shook her head. They could check this, of course. They might have already.

De Vries looked back along the lane. 'Have you seen a grey Renault around here recently?'

'Is this to do with these people?' She deliberately didn't use their names.

Fisher was annoyed. 'Just answer the question.'

'No.' She lowered the garage door without checking it was OK, fuck it, time to be a bit bolshie.

Fisher's radio crackled and he stepped away to answer.

De Vries lowered her voice. 'Mrs Banks, this will go much better for you if you cooperate.'

'I am.'

De Vries stared at her. She knew.

'We have to go,' Fisher said, getting off the radio.

'What's up?'

Fisher looked at Heather. 'Those clowns at the beach have lost the squid.'

'What?' De Vries looked flustered. She handed Heather a card. 'We'll be in touch. Don't go anywhere.'

Heather watched as they walked away.

When they were around the corner, she leaned over and put her head between her knees, breathed heavily, gulping in air, trying to feel normal. She stayed like that for a long time. Then she heard an engine and straightened up as a Range Rover turned into the lane. It skidded to a halt a few feet away and she saw the windscreen was a spider's web of cracks.

A man in a suit jumped out and she recognised him as Ava's husband from the hospital. He strode towards her. 'Where the fuck is my wife?'

'Who are you?'

He punched her face and a bolt of white pain sliced through her nose, tears in her eyes, adrenaline coursing through her as she began to shake. He grabbed her hair and yanked her head back then threw his fist into her stomach. She tried to suck in air. Her knees buckled but the guy's grip on her hair kept her upright.

'Don't play the daft cunt,' he said. 'My wife, Ava. You know where she is. If you don't take me to her right now, I will make you wish you'd never been fucking born.'

17
LENNOX

Lennox sat in the van and stared at Sandy. He hadn't been able to sleep since he heard Heather creep out to ditch the car. Sandy's body filled the sink, tentacles sprawled out, two on each side and one hanging to the floor. Their skin looked healthier, a darker mix of blue and green. Eyes still closed. He wanted to see lights rippling across the skin like before.

He steeled himself then reached out and held the hanging tentacle. Waited to lose himself in whatever was thrown at him. But nothing happened. He squeezed his fingers against the suckers, felt them squeeze back and his heart raced. But maybe it was just an automatic response. He lifted the tentacle to his face and examined it. He saw something under the skin like blood vessels, a network of narrow black lines connecting small nodules.

He squeezed again, nothing. Sandy's tentacle was warm, and he wondered about that. And what about their brain? How had they shown him all that shit earlier?

'What are you doing?'

He turned to Ava, sitting on the fold-out bed at the back of the van. She'd crashed out straight after they got back last night. She pushed her hand through her hair now. It was weird seeing a teacher like this, in old pyjamas of Heather's.

He felt self-conscious about holding the tentacle but didn't want to drop it.

'I was just seeing if they were OK.'

'Did they ... talk to you?'

He shook his head and let go of the tentacle.

Ava looked round. 'Where's Heather?'

'She went to hide the Renault.'

Lennox thought about the guy on the beach. If he was dead, that was murder. But if Sandy was just an animal defending themself, that couldn't be murder, right?

'When did she leave?' Ava said, easing herself up.

Lennox stood and looked out the window. They were parked in the golf-course maintenance area, under trees and behind a shed. The sun was up and dew shone on the grass.

'A while ago.'

Ava joined him at the window. She smelled salty from the sea. She held her breath for a moment, glanced at her stomach.

'You OK?' he said.

She smiled and he felt himself glow. 'Fine. She's just kicking against my kidneys, I think.'

'Must be weird.'

She laughed through her nose. 'For sure.'

He glimpsed two deer between the trees, a doe and her fawn, alert to danger, close to each other. They disappeared into the shadows.

'What now?' Ava said.

'How do you mean?'

Ava waved around the van. 'This is crazy, you have to go home.'

His chest tightened. 'What?'

'You're sixteen, Lennox.'

'So what?'

'If you're worried about the police, I'm sure we can smooth things.'

'I don't care about the police, I care about Sandy.' His voice was high and he felt his cheeks flush.

Ava stared at him for a long time.

'What are we doing?' she said to herself.

The door clattered open and Heather stumbled into the van,

banging her head on a cupboard. Behind her was Ava's husband Michael, waving a golf club.

'What the hell?' Ava ran to Heather who was holding her head.

'You piece of shit,' Michael said to her. 'You think you can run away? You realise what you've put me through, what you made me do?'

He was manic, looking around the van. Lennox thought about rushing him.

'What the fuck?' Michael pointed the club at Sandy in the sink.

He laughed too loud and took a step closer. Lennox blocked him. Michael was the same height but three stone heavier. 'I presume you're the cunt who fucked my car.'

'Leave us alone.' Lennox hated his voice, so boyish and unconvincing.

Michael grinned. 'What are you going to do?'

Lennox lunged at him with his fists up and felt the golf club pummel his face, knocking the breath from him and throwing him to the floor.

'Come on,' Michael said to Ava, cowering by the cupboard. He grabbed her wrist. 'Fuck the lot of you.'

He dragged her out of the van. She kicked at him as she tumbled down the steps.

'Let's go home, love,' he said.

'Fuck you,' Ava shouted.

She tried to scratch his face but he ducked out of the way, swung the club at her head, connected with her temple. Only his grip on her arm stopped her falling over.

'Don't make me hurt you,' he said softly. 'Think about our baby.'

Lennox followed them towards the Range Rover.

'Stop,' he shouted, but it was useless. He was useless.

Ava looked back with tears in her eyes. 'Don't, Lennox.'

Then her gaze switched to something behind him and he heard a high-pitched humming noise. He turned and there was Sandy, upright on their tentacles, six feet tall, head distended and glowing green and blue. They walked on their tentacles with a rolling gait, suckers coming up from the ground, five limbs switching seamlessly, moving forward steadily. The noise was a whistle mixed with a hum, a deep throb underneath. Their eyes were open, black orbs that sparkled in the sunshine.

They approached Michael and Ava. Michael gawped then raised the club to strike Sandy but they shot out two tentacles, whipped it away from his hands and threw it into the woods. The tentacles reached for either side of Michael's head, stuck to his temples and he crumpled to the ground. Sandy eased him onto the dirt as Ava staggered back. Michael looked asleep as Sandy removed their tentacles and turned to Lennox.

<Hello, again,> they said in Lennox's mind.

18
EWAN

Ewan stood in the woods between some storage sheds, his car back along the road. He'd turned up at Heather's house in time to see her getting strongarmed into a Range Rover by a guy in a suit. He followed. He saw the guy rush into the campervan and drag Ava out. And he saw that thing come out and disarm him then knock him out without hardly trying.

The creature was still standing in the middle of the clearing, using three tentacles as legs, two more waving in front of it as it looked at the kid, Lennox. Heather staggered out of the van and went to the other two, her eyes on the octopus thing. It was tall, its head extended more than when it was on the beach. He'd presumed it was dead, but here it was saving Ava and assaulting a wanker.

He stepped out of the woods. 'Hey.'

Ava jumped then relaxed when she saw it was him. She looked at the guy on the ground. He seemed like he was sleeping. Lennox didn't turn round, just stared at the octopus, which was waving at him. Heather saw Ewan and smiled. The look on her face made his heart warm.

'What are you doing here?' she said.

He held out his arms to take in the whole scene. 'Following the story.'

He reached the guy on the ground, knelt down and checked for a pulse. It was faint but regular.

'I saw him take you from your house so I followed to make sure you were OK.'

Heather looked behind her at the kid and the octopus. 'I'm fine.'

'Want to tell me what's going on?'

'I wish I knew.' She nodded at the guy on the ground, drool dribbling from his mouth. 'Is he dead?'

'No.' He nodded beyond Heather. 'Whatever it did to him, he's still alive.'

'You saw that.'

'Yeah.' He stepped closer to her. A bruise was appearing under her left eye. A thin crust of blood at her left nostril. 'Are you OK?'

She touched her eye. 'I'm fine.'

'Was that him?'

She nodded.

Ewan glanced at the body. 'In normal circumstances I would say call the police.'

Heather touched her nose and shook her head. 'These are not normal circumstances.'

'No.'

He walked towards the creature. Lennox and Ava were together five yards away. Lennox had his hand out, eyes closed.

'What is it?' Ewan said.

The thing was shimmering, patterns irradiating its surface. Blue and green and shades between, flashes of orange and yellow like lightning along its tentacles, its head changing colour all the time like the northern lights. And its head was changing shape, from a long oblong to a fatter sphere, then narrowing at the bottom and enlarged on top. There were crenellations above its eyes, ridges shifting across and back again.

'Sandy,' Heather said.

Ewan frowned. 'Sandy?'

Heather shrugged. 'Lennox named them. Because they were sandy on the beach.'

'They? Like a non-binary thing?'

Heather looked at Lennox. 'No, like a plural thing.'

'How does he know?'

'They talk to him.'

Ewan laughed and Lennox's eyes snapped open. The colour drained from Sandy's body and their limbs went pale, then they slumped to the ground, kicking up dust. Lennox looked drunk and swayed. Ava put out an arm to steady him.

Sandy looked like they had on the beach, and Ewan wondered if they were exhausted from stunning the guy.

'What do ... they want?' he said eventually.

Lennox looked at Ewan and took a moment to recognise him. 'They want to be ... reconnected.'

'What?'

Lennox ran a hand through his hair, then down his face. 'It's impossible to explain. It's feelings and images, mostly. They want to be reconnected ... to themselves.'

'What does that mean?'

Lennox shook his head. 'I don't know. But I need to help.'

The sun was higher now, the golf course would be busy soon. The guy on the ground hadn't moved, dust covering the side of his suit.

'What about him?' Ewan said.

Ava pressed her lips together. 'What about him?'

'You can't just leave him there.'

Ava looked at the others. 'We're already wanted by the police for what happened on the beach. We can't go back now.'

Ewan turned to Heather. 'What do you think?'

Heather stared at him and he thought about the stones in her pockets that night on the beach.

'I'm with them,' she said eventually.

'Hey.' The shout came from the trees.

Ewan saw a guy in a groundskeeper's polo shirt, canvas trousers and work boots. He was young and solid. 'You can't be here.'

Lennox moved to hide Sandy, Ava and Heather stepped back.

The guy spotted Ava's husband on the ground. 'What the fuck?' He turned to them. 'What's going on here?'

He ran to the body and pulled out his phone.

'We have to go,' Lennox said. He turned and grabbed Sandy's head, heaved it and staggered towards the van, the tentacles trailing in the dust.

Ava walked backward towards the van, keeping an eye on the groundskeeper, covering Lennox.

The groundskeeper stood and shouted over to them. 'Why haven't you called an ambulance?'

Ewan felt Heather tug his sleeve.

'Come on,' she said.

He tried to clear his head. He'd spent his life following shitty stories, pretending he wanted the truth, but really he mostly just exploited people's misfortune. He didn't want to do that anymore. The story here was in the campervan, but he had a better idea.

'I'll stay,' he said, and Heather's face fell. 'I'll deal with this. Give you the chance to get away.'

Heather frowned. 'Come with us, we could use your help.'

'I'm more help here. I'll stall the cops, mislead them.'

He dug in his pocket and pulled out an old business card. 'Call me here. Let it ring twice then hang up and I'll call back.'

The groundskeeper was talking to the ambulance service, then requested police.

Ewan turned to Heather, saw a look of something in her eyes.

'Go,' he said.

19
HEATHER

She threw the campervan round the bend and accelerated. They were exposed here, large grassy area to the left, practice greens next to the first tee. But a brown campervan stuck out like a sore thumb anywhere. She glanced back. Sandy's deflated and shrunken body was squeezed into the sink, limbs hanging down to the floor. Lennox was slumped on a seat staring at Sandy. Ava was in the passenger seat, rubbing her arm where Michael grabbed her.

Heather felt her mothering instinct kick in. Mothering was just crisis management, avoiding catastrophe, keeping your kid free from harm. She hadn't managed that with Rosie, but she could do it here.

She turned left at a junction.

Ava noticed. 'What are you doing?'

'I need to get some things from the house.'

'What if the police are there?'

Heather shook her head. 'They've visited once today already, and they just got a call from the greenkeeper. But I'll check first, if they're there, we leave.'

She turned into Dirleton, past Rosie's old primary school, past The Castle Inn where she'd spent lazy summer afternoons in the beer garden with Paul, Rosie chasing bees between flowers. Past the castle and trees that dominated the village. This might be the last time she would see any of this.

She slowed the van outside The Open Arms, checked for police. She turned and parked out of sight from the main road.

'Wait here.'

'What if someone comes?' Ava said

She handed over the van keys. 'Run.'

She went to the house, worried she would see a neighbour, the police, or Michael suddenly risen again. But there was no one. She went in and grabbed a backpack, threw in money and jewellery she could sell, bank cards, though they could be traced. Clothes, blankets, first-aid kit. Water bottles and basic food. She tried to imagine it was a last-minute camping trip, but she'd never been outdoorsy, never had proper rainproof gear or hiking boots.

She kept waiting for the door to be hammered open, police officers pointing guns at her. She stood in the living room and looked round. She gazed at the picture of Rosie on the mantelpiece. She was eleven in it, goofy grin, wearing a swimsuit on the beach. She was long-limbed, beautiful and free, not yet weighed down by teenage angst, by chemo, by fucking death. Heather slid the picture out of the frame, touched Rosie's face with her thumb, then folded it and put it in her pocket.

She felt pain across the back of her skull and neck, recognised it as one of the symptoms of the tumour. She'd been getting these flashes more and more recently. She put a hand out to steady herself, then felt bile rise up her throat. She dropped the bag and ran to the bathroom, vomited watery sick into the sink, felt more rise up, her head pounding in time with her retches. She stayed there for a few minutes, eyes watering, spitting and rinsing her mouth from the tap, washing away the evidence. Eventually she straightened up, checked herself in the mirror, then went back to the living room.

She took a last look around then left, checking the street before she stepped out. As she passed The Open Arms she saw staff prepping the dining area for service. She didn't catch anyone's eye. She reached the van and no one had moved. She wondered briefly if the universe had frozen.

'You guys OK?' she said.

Ava nodded, then Lennox.

'We need a plan.'

Ava looked out of the window. 'Let's just go.'

'Where?'

'We can work that out on the road.' She handed the van key back to Heather.

Heather turned the engine on then drove out of the village towards Drem, avoiding the main coast road. Back roads were easier to get lost in.

They drove past fields of wheat and potatoes, the Lammermuir Hills a ripple on the horizon. The road was narrow and windy, and Heather drove carefully, no point looking like you're running away.

She glanced back. 'Lennox, what happened back there?'

He had his hood pulled up, arms folded. 'How do you mean?'

'After Sandy attacked Michael. It was pretty obvious they communicated with you.'

Long silence. Heather shared a worried look with Ava.

'Kind of,' Lennox said.

Heather curbed her instinct to yell at him. Another part of mothering she remembered, bite your tongue if you want results.

'What do you mean?' she said, voice even.

'They didn't speak much, just a few words. I think it takes a lot of effort if we're not touching. But they showed me stuff.'

'What kind of stuff?' This was Ava using a calm teacher voice.

'They're part of something like a family, but not quite. They want to be together again. I felt that.'

'Reunited, makes sense,' Ava said.

Lennox shook his head. 'Not reunited, more than that. Something bigger.'

Heather swallowed. 'Bigger?'

Lennox shrugged and pushed his hands into his pockets. 'That's what I felt.'

'And where is this ... bigger thing?' Heather was in two minds about doing what the creature wanted. Who's to say it would be best for them?

Lennox pointed out the window. 'Northwest.'

Heather frowned. 'Anything more specific than that?'

Lennox put his hands back in his pockets.

They'd passed through Drem and Athelstaneford, the roads nice and quiet.

Ava checked her phone. 'I have a place.' She showed Heather the screen, a Scotland map with a wiggly line across the country, ending near Skye. 'Ratagan. It's remote and we can use smaller roads.'

Heather slowed the van as they passed through East Linton.

'What's in Ratagan?' she said.

Ava pressed her lips together. 'My sister.'

20
LENNOX

There weren't many Google hits for 'telepathic octopus'. Shocker. Lennox looked up from his phone and stared at Sandy. He felt like a different person to the one who walked through the park two days ago. Now he was wanted for murder and kidnapping, sitting in a cheesy brown van with an old woman and a pregnant teacher, and getting psychic messages from a telepathic octopus.

He looked out of the window. A small loch on one side, a tight slope packed with trees on the other. Everything was green and blue and the sun was shining. He turned back to Sandy in the sink, tried to untangle what had happened. He'd had two messages from them on two different occasions, plus two mind-melting trips. They showed him things, more than showed, they made him feel what they were feeling.

He returned to his phone and read about octopuses. Regular octopuses were small, especially around Scotland, nothing like Sandy's size. And they only lived two or three years. He'd felt that Sandy was a lot older than that.

He pulled his headphones over his ears and played some HalfNoise, chilled-out beats that nobody knew about, his secret. But nothing like the secrets he was accumulating since he met Sandy.

Back to his phone. Normal octopuses had three hearts and nine brains. Two hearts pumped blood to the gills, the third moved it around the body. They had one central brain but most of their neurons were spread through their bodies, collecting in eight nodes in their arms. So they could taste and feel things independently of the central part. Lennox looked up as they went through a village, the road winding over a low bridge. Maybe that's why Sandy was plural, like a collective of mini-brains. But what about being part of something bigger? Were they part of a hive mind or some shit?

Regular octopuses didn't have tentacles, they were arms, apparently, something to do with the number of suckers. And they had blue blood. At least, normal, Earth-based ones did. He was trying hard not to think about what Sandy had showed him. He'd moved through space to a different planet, blue and green ice, striped and pockmarked, then into some crazy jets and under the ice into an ocean.

He closed his eyes, listened to the music slide over itself, tried to think of nothing. But memories flashed into his mind from years back, like they often did, the bad old days. It was weird, having spent his life in the care system, he didn't have a fucking clue who he really was. The policy preventing you finding out about your birth parents until you were eighteen was strict, and even then, the chaotic system of records meant you might never find out. Shit just got lost. So he'd drifted rudderless through his early life, with no sense of community or belonging anywhere.

He'd been shunted between six different children's homes over the years, and he'd been fostered twice, both times ending in disaster. It was always the wives in the relationship who wanted to look after a mixed-race kid with cute hair, then the husbands would realise it wasn't plain sailing, and would start trying to impose their own backward kinds of discipline. Shit they learned from their own fathers.

Dave in Wester Hailes had beaten him with a shoe for talking back at the dinner table. Fergus in Corstorphine made him lie in the sheets he'd wet himself in, teach him a fucking lesson. The only lesson he'd learned was that Dave and Fergus didn't give a shit, loved to control, bully and abuse. And he'd also learned that it was possible to piss in a kettle and for your foster father not to be able to tell that his coffee was made with watered-down urine.

He'd run away both times, spent a couple of cold nights on the streets, nervous and scared of anyone passing by, before turning up at his previous children's home, begging to be taken back. As far as he knew, Dave and Fergus were still fostering unsuspecting kids with their well-meaning wives.

And that shit spilled over into school. Bullies have a sixth sense when it comes to the vulnerable, and they could spot him a mile away. Cheap-ass clothes, crazy Afro hair – anything different was an excuse to get stuck in. Teachers sometimes tried to intervene, but that only made things worse. You were the teacher's pet and punished accordingly. Primary school was less obvious but still the same – not invited to birthday parties, ostracised in the playground. The ages of twelve to fourteen were the worst – everyone was trying to find their tribe, often at the expense of loners. Now at sixteen, there were enough outsiders at school to give a little herd immunity, and the worst bullies had already fucked off to join the army or police.

But he still got it sometimes from the likes of Blair and his pathetic minions. He thought about him back in hospital, drooling and unable to speak. He was surprised to feel a tiny bit of sympathy for him. And the others were dead, holy shit. They didn't deserve his sympathy but he felt it anyway. For some reason, Sandy had chosen *him* to recover and not them. Or maybe it was all random, a pure fluke that he was here and one of them wasn't. But the way he felt about Sandy, he didn't want to believe that was true.

He drifted off to sleep, dreams of swimming through an endless sea of ice, happy at last to have found his tribe.

'I need to stretch my legs,' Ava said in front.

He jolted awake. The album had finished and the landscape outside was different, no trees, just brown mountains on all sides, the narrow road threading through them like a vein. They slowed at a sign for the Glencoe Mountain Resort and turned off. Hillwalkers in expensive gear everywhere. Mountain bikers, tents, cabins and a wooden lodge at the end of the road. The car park was full of RVs, caravans and minibuses.

'Is this too busy?' Ava said.

There were several campervans similar to theirs in the car park.

'No, we can get lost in the crowd,' Heather said.

She threw Ava a hat with earflaps to cover her red hair, and Ava put on sunglasses she found in the glovebox. She looked like a pregnant spy as she stepped out of the van, hands at her back as she straightened up.

'How are you doing?' Heather said to Lennox. She sounded like she cared and Lennox wasn't used to that. Her voice was like honey.

'Fine,' he said, taking his headphones off.

'You fell asleep, must've needed it.'

There was so much Lennox wanted to talk about but he didn't know where to start.

'Is this the Highlands?' he said, looking out. The mountains made him feel small.

'Have you never been before?'

Lennox shook his head. He didn't like Heather's look, she felt sorry for him. He got enough of that in the care home, at school. He didn't want it following him here.

'Maybe you should go and check on her,' he said, pointing at Ava.

She was at the large cabin, looking at signs for tubing and off-road biking. She was pretty conspicuous.

Heather stared at him for a long time and he felt naked. 'You want to join me, get some air?'

'No.'

'OK.' She shuffled out the van and looked at him. 'Back in five.'

He turned to Sandy, thought he saw slight movement in their head. Were they breathing? That was another thing he'd read, normal octopuses don't spend this long out the water.

He touched their tentacle.

Nothing.

He touched another tentacle with his other hand. And he was suddenly flying or swimming, he wasn't sure, viscous stuff around him blurring his vision of millions of stars. He had a sense they were all connected, like veins in his arm or Sandy's tentacle, but he was the blood molecule, a tiny and insignificant traveller in a giant system. He was dizzy and nauseous, but felt Sandy next to him, all around him like last time, like he was inside them or part of them, and there were others like them but much bigger, wider, more tentacles and massive splayed heads, light displays and shape changes until his head swam and felt like it might explode.

<This is too much for you,> Sandy said in his mind.

<No.> He hadn't said it, but thought it.

<Your ... system cannot support it.>

<I don't understand.>

<Your biological vessel is basic. Receptors not designed for this. We're surprised, we expected you to be able to speak.>

<I can speak.>

<Sound communication is very ... rudimentary.>

Lennox felt Sandy's tentacles moving around his waist and across his back. They were signalling colours and patterns up and down their body in time with what he heard in his head. An image of him swirling through a star-studded sky crept in and began to overwhelm him.

<Do I have your permission?>

He felt Sandy's tentacles reach around his head, one on his neck. It felt like a hug. The light display on their body intensified, ripples down their tentacles and back, switching to hoops around their body then pinpoints growing and shrinking, giving the impression their body was throbbing.

<Permission for what?>

<To communicate more effectively.>

<How?>

A tentacle circled his right ear, the tip of it touching the curve of his skin.

<We can place a small ... part of us. A device. In your receptors. We will communicate better over distance.>

Lennox thought of all the times people wouldn't leave him alone because of his background, his colour, his fucking hair. How he'd always felt apart from others.

<I give permission.>

The tentacle entered his ear, changed to a sharp point, delved deeper until it was against his ear drum.

<Be calm.>

He squirmed. It felt like his brain was being tickled, his senses all firing at once, a swampy ringing sound, the warmth of Sandy's tentacles around him, the smell was something he couldn't describe. They felt like they were inside him, part of what made him.

'Hey,' Heather said, opening the van door.

Sandy's tentacles retracted and slipped across Lennox's body. But something was left inside him, something had changed.

'Are you OK?' Heather said.

Lennox tried to stop his head from swimming.

'Fucking hell,' he said.

21
EWAN

It wasn't his first time in a police interview room. They were nicer these days, more like a place for a job interview, white walls with crime-prevention posters, a solid desk, a view of Arthur's Seat out the window. The chairs were cheap but comfortable. They'd brought him to St Leonard's in Edinburgh rather than the local East Lothian station, which suggested this was a big deal.

Nina came through the door, latte in hand. She looked good, brown hair in a bob, kind eyes, if a little tired, sharp features, trim figure. She sat down.

'I told you not to get involved in this.'

Ewan waved at her. 'Hi, Nina, how are you?'

She smiled. 'Don't. Jesus.'

'You look great, have you been going to the gym?'

She smoothed her skirt. 'I do look great, don't I? But Christ, the gym's hard work.'

Ewan shook his head. 'Not my thing.'

She sipped from her cup and leaned forward. 'No, your thing is getting mixed up with fugitive teenagers, kidnapped women, mysteriously injured and dead people.'

'How is Michael?'

Nina raised her eyebrows. 'First-name terms?'

'Not exactly.'

She narrowed her eyes, tried to see something inside him. He wanted to tell her. His whole life had been about telling stories, exposing the truth, such as it was. But he couldn't tell her this. Where to start?

'Enough dicking around,' Nina said. 'This doesn't look good for you.'

'How so?'

She sat back and glanced out of the window, put her coffee on the table. 'You've been seen with two people wanted by police, Lennox Hunt and Ava Cross. You called me from nearby an address in Dirleton belonging to a third person of interest, Heather Banks. All three were together on Yellowcraigs Beach yesterday when a council worker died. He had a girlfriend, mum and dad, two brothers, all distraught.'

She paused. He let it sink in, Christ, this was a mess. But he thought of Heather, Ava and Lennox. They weren't trouble-makers.

Nina brushed her hair away from her face. 'And now we have Michael Cross injured.'

'You never said how he was.'

She stared at him. 'He'll live, unconscious but stable. Do you want to tell me what happened?'

He thought about it. A fucking giant octopus knocked Michael out. Sandy, they called it. Or them. Plural. Whatever that meant.

'He just passed out.'

'What?'

'He was rough-housing the redhead.' He didn't want to use their names, seem too familiar. 'Dragging her to his car against her will. Maybe he had an aneurysm or something. He just keeled over.'

The tip of Nina's tongue was jammed between her teeth. She shook her head. 'You're not a good liar.'

He turns his hands palm-side up. 'That's the truth.'

'I told you already, Mr Cross has high-up friends. You couldn't have got involved in anything worse, honestly. I'm getting so much grief.'

'It's true, Nina.'

The door opened and two men walked in wearing the sharpest suits Ewan had ever seen. These were bespoke motherfuckers, top to toe. The guy in front was thin, with a long face, tousle of wavy hair in a fringe. Behind him was the muscle, taller, bulked out, blond buzz cut. The bulge at his breast pocket was probably a gun. What the fuck?

'Is this him?' the first guy said to Nina. She looked annoyed by his air of superiority. He had a smug manner and posh English accent like a fop actor. Nina had said something on the phone about other interest, not just the police.

'Ewan McKinnon,' Nina said.

Ewan threw on a smile and held out his hand. 'Pleasure, and you are?'

'Oscar Fellowes.' He stared at Ewan's hand until he dropped it.

'Can I see some ID?'

'No.'

The other guy stood at the door, hands folded. Ewan wanted to feel cool about that but his fingers and toes were tingling.

'Which division of the police are you guys from?' Ewan said.

'None of your business.' Fellowes leaned over the table as he spoke to Nina. 'Where had you got to?'

Nina's face was sour but Fellowes didn't care.

'His presence at the two incidents and his connection to the missing trio.'

Fellowes rolled his shoulders as he turned back to Ewan. 'Never mind that. Mr McKinnon. Ewan. How's your health?'

'What?'

'Fit and well?'

Ewan frowned. 'I guess.'

'No dizziness, fatigue, loss of coordination.'

'No more than usual.'

Fellowes pulled up a chair. 'This isn't a laughing matter, Ewan.'

The first name thing felt so fake.

'Is this to do with the strokes?' Ewan said.

Fellowes pulled at his earlobe. 'Did you see a light?'

'What?'

'Three nights ago, blue-green, in the sky. And a smell.'

'Are you serious?' Ewan glanced at Nina, who widened her eyes.

Fellowes leaned back. 'Did you?'

'No lights in the sky.'

Fellowes glanced at the other guy and Ewan stared at the bulge in his jacket.

'Yet you're connected to these people,' Fellowes said.

'By coincidence.'

Fellowes nodded to himself. 'I don't believe in coincidence.'

Ewan wondered what it must be like going through life as this guy. Fellowes pulled his phone out of his pocket and scrolled. Held it out to Ewan. It was a picture of Sandy at Yellowcraigs, half in the wash, pale compared to the most recent time Ewan saw them.

'You've seen this,' Fellowes said.

'On the beach, yeah.'

'And at the second incident.'

Ewan had wondered if the groundskeeper spotted Sandy or if he was too distracted by Michael. That answered the question.

Nina looked confused. 'The octopus?'

So she wasn't in the loop with Fellowes, interesting. Who was this guy?

Fellowes ignored her, looked at Ewan. 'Well?'

Ewan thought about what was to be gained from truth or lies. And Nina was right, he was a shit liar.

'Yes, I saw it there.'

Fellowes smiled. 'Did this thing attack those two men?'

'I don't know.'

'I think you do.'

Ewan shrugged.

Fellowes sat back. 'I think you saw this creature in both instances, and that it hurt those men in self-defence, a self-preservation mechanism.'

Ewan remembered Sandy with their tentacles on Michael's head, how he collapsed like a sack of tatties.

Fellowes looked at the picture on his phone.

'Remarkable,' he said under his breath. 'Truly remarkable.'

He looked up at Ewan. 'One last question. Did it speak to you?'

22
AVA

Ava glugged Gaviscon from the bottle as they turned up the Old Military Road and went over Shiel Bridge. Heather was careful behind the wheel, if the camper blew a tyre or the exhaust fell off they were screwed. Ava looked out of the window. The mountains of Glencoe had been replaced by smaller hills covered in pine and fir. Low cloud hung over the peaks as they drove round the head of Loch Duich. Across the water was the main road to Skye they'd just left, lots of trucks and cars. But this road petered out further along the banks of the loch, empty apart from them.

Her heartburn eased but she felt anxiety rise in her chest. She hadn't spoken to her sister in five years and hadn't warned her they were coming.

'There,' she said to Heather, pointing to a turn-off.

They drove along the edge of the loch on the narrow lane, a strip of spread-out houses on their left, flat expanse of peaty-brown water on the right. The houses were a mix of new builds, older crofts and fishermen cottages, mossy pebble dash and pine panels, steep roofs for snow in the winter. She tried to remember what Freya's place looked like. She'd only been here twice before she was married, and afterwards Michael had her locked down.

'That's it.' She pointed for Heather to pull in opposite a bus stop. Ava tried to imagine a bus coming this way, it would barely make it along the lane.

She undid her seatbelt, turned to see Lennox asleep in the back next to Sandy. He'd slept the whole way from Glencoe.

'Let him sleep,' Heather said.

They got out. The smell of seaweed and the smirr hanging in the air made Ava feel like she was underwater, the low cloud like the underside of a thick ice floe.

Heather stretched her shoulders after the drive.

'I'd better speak to her myself first,' Ava said.

'I thought this was a safe place for us?'

Ava shrugged.

Heather tilted her head. 'Everything OK between you and your sister?'

'I'm about to find out.'

She went to the front door. It was gloomy but still daylight and the house was dark. She looked for a doorbell then knocked. Felt a squirm from the baby, a flush of indigestion. She took a swig of Gaviscon and a deep breath.

She knocked again, glanced at Heather who was examining the timetable on the bus stop. She looked at the campervan and thought of Scooby Doo's Mystery Machine. It wasn't quite as conspicuous as that but not far off. The police had put out a picture of it. She wondered about Michael, if he was in hospital, if they were looking after him. Then she checked herself. He didn't care about *her*.

The door opened and Freya stood in the doorway. She was shorter than Ava, curvier than she used to be. She had the same red hair but curly and thick, grown out since Ava last saw her. She wore a long-sleeve *Animaniacs* sweatshirt, faded and worn, and she smelled of weed. Ava's stomach tightened.

'The prodigal daughter,' Freya said, staring at Ava's belly. 'Bearing a grandchild, no less.'

'You don't seem very surprised,' Ava said, glancing behind. Heather stood watching from the van.

Freya raised her eyebrows. 'I watch the news. I thought you might come.'

'Why? We haven't spoken in years.'

'Because you're on the run and I live in the middle of nowhere.' She chuckled. 'I almost shat myself when I saw your picture. On the run with a teenage schoolboy. Is this a Mrs Robinson thing?'

'It's not that.'

Freya nodded at the van. 'Is he in there?'

'Sleeping.'

'Who's the frazzled housewife?'

'Heather.'

'Are you solving mysteries now?'

Ava laughed. 'Actually, maybe we are.'

Freya looked confused. 'How are you connected to these people?'

Ava pictured Sandy inside the van, what they'd done to Michael. 'It's hard to explain.'

'Try me.'

Ava felt the baby kick and straightened her shoulders. 'I left Michael.'

Freya chewed her lip and stared at Ava for so long that she had to look away.

'So you finally figured out what a piece of shit he is.'

Ava swallowed. 'I always knew, deep down. But I couldn't…'

She was dismayed to feel herself welling up, her breath catching in her throat.

'Hey,' Freya said.

Ava brought her hands to her face as if she could hold the sobs inside. She felt her daughter stretch, had a flash of panic at the thought of being responsible for someone else in the world. That made the crying worse.

She felt Freya's arms around her, grabbed her sister and hugged. She remembered Freya coming out to her when they were teenagers. How she fancied Grace in the year above, but they couldn't tell Mum, she wouldn't understand. Freya had been the one crying then, and Ava hugged her until it stopped. It felt so comforting to be in her sister's arms after all this time.

'It's OK,' Freya whispered in her ear. 'You're safe here.'

And Ava did feel safe, for the first time in years.

23
HEATHER

Heather sat in the bus shelter and watched the light fade from the glen. The cloud had lowered since earlier and the hills across the loch had vanished. She imagined what it was like to be above the cloud line, nothing to worry about.

But here she was in a bus shelter covered in cigarette burns, staring at the house that was their refuge tonight. Ava hadn't said much about her sister but she seemed welcoming enough. Freya didn't know everything, obviously, they'd left Sandy in the camper. But she knew they were on the run and didn't ask any more than that. They'd moved the van to the back of the house, out of sight from the road, roused Lennox and taken him inside. He was very quiet and Heather wondered about his last conversation with Sandy. Had things changed? It had been a long time since she'd had to negotiate teenage hormones with Rosie, and she was out of her depth.

Ava was relieved that her sister welcomed them, and they'd spent some time catching up in the kitchen. Heather couldn't help chewing over everything, so she decided to step outside to get some air. The mizzle hanging in the air was a veil across the world, suspended in time. Freya's house had the lights on, smoke coming from the chimney.

Heather raised a hand to her head and thought about what Michael had done to her. Several punches to the face and body, that left its toll at her age. And she'd knocked her head in the van. She wondered about concussion. How could you tell? She felt out of sorts, but then she'd left her home forever and gone on the run with a pregnant woman, a teenager and a seemingly telepathic octopus. Two days ago she'd tried to kill herself. She pictured the tumorous cells in her brain munching their way through her central processing and nervous systems. She felt dizzy and sore. Then she thought about the stroke, the blood clot which had miraculously disappeared. She pressed her lips together and thought about Sandy, what powers they might have.

She pulled Ewan's card from her pocket. Scratched her ear and took out her phone, punched in his number and pressed call. It rang twice then she hung up. Looked at the dripping pine trees that lined the lane, the living-room windows glowing between them like woodland sprites, tiny signs of life amongst the vast gloom. It was hard to live here, far from the idyllic idea of London Sunday supplements.

She jumped at her phone ringing. A different number. She hesitated. But what were the chances of a random call right now? She answered.

'Heather?'

She exhaled at Ewan's voice, only then realising she'd been holding her breath. She remembered him sipping his beer in The Open Arms. She was shocked to realise that was only yesterday. Now here she was on the other side of the country, surrounded by hills, on the run.

'Hi,' she said. 'What's this number?'

'An old one,' Ewan said. 'The police had my phone while I was in the station. They could have bugged it.'

'The police station?' Heather pictured a television cop show, overbright interview room, sweating criminal. She looked around the gloomy loch, heard the soft slap of the water on the shore.

'They were just shaking me down for information.'

'Aren't you friends with a cop?'

'She warned me to stay away from you.' There was a smile in his voice. 'Said you were trouble.'

'Me specifically?'

'You're obviously the ringleader.'

'How do you figure that?'

'You're the only one who looks like you know what you're doing.'

'I'll take that as a compliment.'

'It was meant to be.'

So this was her life now, flirting on the phone with a middle-aged man, on the run, fresh from a failed suicide attempt, a miraculous stroke recovery and a mysterious octopus encounter. Fuck it, she'd felt like an old woman, a husk, since Rosie died. Maybe some harmless flirting was what she needed.

'How are you?' Ewan's tone was concerned. She liked it.

She touched her sore face. 'I'm OK.'

'I saw the way that prick treated you,' Ewan said. 'All of you. He got what he deserved.'

'Is he dead?'

'He'll live. I thought maybe because Sandy touched him, he might have what the others had, the council worker, the stroke victims who didn't recover. But he's just unconscious in hospital.'

'I'm glad.'

'Ava's well away from that prick.'

Heather wondered if Ava was free, if any of them were free. She wished Ewan didn't know about the stones in her pocket that first night.

'I won't ask where you are,' Ewan said. 'But are you safe?'

Heather looked at the glowing windows in the gloom. She hadn't seen a car since she'd come out here. 'I think so, for now.'

'Do you have a plan?'

Heather thought about Sandy asleep in the van, Lennox drowsy all day, Ava relaxing with Freya. 'Not exactly. We're trying to help Sandy.'

'I'd like to help.' Ewan paused. 'I mean, I'd like to see you again. But I don't know how.'

Heather sighed. 'No.'

Silence down the line, just the lapping of water in the darkness. She pictured all the creatures under the surface, scurrying along the bottom of the loch, darting through the murk, scything after smaller prey, hiding in the blackness. Life carrying on.

Ewan cleared his throat. 'Won't you be missed at home?'

Heather smiled. He was fishing about her private life, as if she had one.

'You mean by a husband or boyfriend?'

'No, I didn't...'

She was glad to hear his embarrassment down the line. 'I'm messing with you.'

'Fuck.'

Heather looked at the darkness around her. 'No, I won't be missed.'

'What about a job?'

Heather shook her head, even though Ewan couldn't see. She snorted a laugh. 'The irony is, I used to work at SEPA dealing with rivers and coastal seas. This is like a busman's holiday for me.'

'What did you do?'

She waved a hand around. 'Pollution control, checking companies weren't breaking the law, pumping shit into the sea. We tried to protect the environment and the creatures that live in it.'

'Like Sandy.'

She laughed again. 'In twenty years, I never came across anything like them, that's for sure.'

'You're not there anymore, did you retire?'

He was a journalist, couldn't help punting for information. She didn't want to tell him she got signed off long-term because of her tumour. Then when her sick leave ran out, she was dropped like a stone. Now all she had to do was wait for the end.

'Kind of,' she said.

She wondered what she was doing here, talking to a man as if it could mean something. She had no future, this was selfish and pointless.

'There's something else,' Ewan said eventually. 'Someone else is interested in you, not just the police.'

'What do you mean?'

'Another guy interviewed me.'

'Not a cop?'

'He must be connected, it was at the station. He seemed powerful, bossed my contact around. He was different.'

'Different how?'

'He wasn't interested in the council guy or Michael. He asked about Sandy.'

'He knew about them?'

'He asked if I'd seen them. If they spoke to me.'

Heather swallowed. 'Shit.'

'Exactly.'

24
LENNOX

He was back in the Figgate Park, surrounded by Blair and his minions. But this time he was a giant octopus, his tentacles sending him messages, the taste of the air, the boys' distinct scents on the breeze. He sensed warmth radiating from their bodies as they approached, felt a strange kindness towards them. They were all about to die and there was nothing he could do. He could see into the future, the others were all cremated except Blair, lingering in a hospital bed until his body and mind gave up. He rose into the air and hung over their heads, began spinning, his tentacles brushing their outstretched hands. They crumpled to the ground. He kept spinning, feeling the breeze against his skin, sensing the possibilities of a new home.

He woke on the sofa in the back room of the house, light leaching through the curtains. Checked his phone, 5am. He lifted his hands to check they weren't tentacles, felt anxiety from killing the boys in his dream.

He tried to shake the weed fog from his brain. He'd stayed up late smoking a skunk pipe with Freya, swapping small talk about experimental indie, skaters, gaming. It felt weird to talk about that shit with Ava's sister. He wondered if anything would feel normal again.

He raised a hand to his ear, where Sandy had inserted whatever it was. That side of his face was a little numb. He rubbed it and got up, walked through the house and out the back door.

He'd never been anywhere like this, the emptiness. Hills, trees and birdsong. It was a Scotland he'd only seen in adverts. He stepped onto the wet grass with bare feet. He flashed back to the dream where he'd had more sensations all over his body. Signals everywhere. Christ, that skunk was strong.

He walked to the campervan, dew like sprinkles on the windscreen and bonnet. He opened the side door and went in.

Sandy was gone.

He ran to the sink, checked the rest of the van, not a lot of hiding places. He felt his heart in his throat as he looked around again.

He jumped out and stared in each direction. He jogged to the front of the house, feeling the gravel under his feet.

He stared at the loch, the expanse of it unsettling. He looked at the hills on the other side.

<We're here.> Clear as anything in his mind, like a whisper from a friend.

'Where?' he shouted.

No reply.

He thought for a moment, closed his eyes.

<Where?>

<Here.>

Somehow he sensed what Sandy meant and stared at the loch. He crossed the road and stepped onto the beach. It was pebbly and slippy with seaweed.

Then he saw them, floating in the shallows a few metres from the shore.

He hobbled over the stones until he was alongside then sat down and breathed deeply.

<I was worried,> he thought. He didn't know how he was doing it.

They looked larger in the water. Full head, pulsing green stripes running down their tentacles, which moved around the rocks, feeling the way.

<We are recovering well.>

<Recovering?>

<Our journey here was not as planned.>

<What journey? What plan?>

Lennox glanced up. The sun hadn't fully risen over the head of the loch, but to the west the uppermost peaks were blazing in sunshine. He glanced along the road and beach, no sign of movement except two boats bobbing on their anchors.

He turned back. Sandy's eyes were open. He stared and seemed to get sucked in, felt a darkness coming for him. <Where are you from?>

<Home.>

'Fuck's sake,' Lennox said. <I don't understand that answer.>

He wondered if his impatience was apparent in his thought-speech.

The green flashes turned blue, then magenta and red-orange, all in a split second.

<Wait, we are touching your tribe-story.>

<What?>

<The information bank for your tribe. In your story-network. How we learned your language.>

'I don't understand, Sandy.'

Silence for a moment, and he wondered if he'd offended them.

<Sandy?>

Lennox sighed. <That's the name I gave you.>

The light show changed tempo and shape, bands across the lower head, almost like neon smiles.

<Partial-identifier Sandy. We are happy.>

<You understand emotions?>

Their skin dulled for a moment. <Of course, we are emotions. Touching tribe-story.>

Lennox shook his head. He almost preferred the visions to this. They made just about as much sense. <What's a tribe-story?>

<Your story. All around.> A tentacle came out the water and

did a quick swirl then pointed at Lennox's pocket. <You taste with device.>

Lennox took his phone out of his pocket. <The internet?>

He somehow knew the increased light display on their skin was agreement. <Tribe-story. Human earth. Our home is a place you call Enceladus. Orbiter of god Saturn.>

<You mean planet.>

<Planet-god, yes.>

'Enceladus.' Lennox took a deep breath and lifted his eyes to the horizon. The moon hung faint over the hills, waiting to go to sleep.

He was itching to look up Enceladus online. He felt nausea spreading from his right ear, lifted a hand to it. Sandy raised a tentacle out of the water and pointed.

<Are we well?>

<What did you put inside me?>

<We are connected. New partial Sandy-Lennox.>

<Was it a part of you?>

<We are together now.>

Lennox didn't know how he felt about that. <Why are you here?>

<Accident. Separated from ourselves.>

<What does that mean? I don't understand.>

<We are in darkness, awaiting signal.>

<What?>

Sandy's skin dulled, water lapping over their tentacles.

Lennox felt faint, a cold, dripping feeling spread along his jaw and down his neck, as if his veins were filling with jelly.

Sandy shifted towards him, touched his foot with a tentacle.

<Your receptors are not ready. We must stop for now.>

They slunk away into open water. Lennox watched ripples play out from their body as they slid through the loch, and wished he could be out there with them.

25
AVA

She stood on the front porch and sipped espresso. She wasn't supposed to have caffeine but at this stage of pregnancy, surely the baby was cooked in the oven, nothing she did would have much effect.

She watched Lennox on the beach, staring at the loch. He hadn't moved in a long time. What must it be like for him? She tried to remember being sixteen. She was a rebel, fighting her parents, who tried to control her and Freya. At the time it felt like typical teen-angst stuff, how every generation fights the one before. But looking back she recognised patterns of coercion by her dad. He'd never abused them, not physically, but he needed to control what happened in his house, couldn't stand the chaotic energy of teenage girls in his space. He tried hard to bring them to heel, curfews, locking them out, embarrassing them at every turn.

She started dating Michael three months after her dad died of a heart attack. It was so obvious with hindsight that she'd fallen into another controlling relationship because of her grief. He was charming to start with, of course, that's how they do it. But even then he'd chipped away at her confidence. She wondered if it was deliberate, using her pain about her dad to dominate her. Or if it was an instinct for control, like her dad. How do men end up like that, what's the psychology? Angry at their own impotence, they take charge where they can.

They'd been maths students together at Edinburgh Uni, met in a statistics class. He was so much more confident than she was, easily took control from the start. It was her least-favourite class but he loved it. She preferred the abstract, non-practical stuff of algebra and calculus, the pure maths. He liked everything practical, was doing a joint degree with economics. But for so long he hid their countless differences and she willingly ignored them. As their relationship went on, she became less of an individual, more like an appendage to his ego. Her own social group shrank, his gang of boorish, right-wing mates with trophy girlfriends became the replacement.

She had half an inkling to go into research when they graduated but he talked her into teaching. That was all women were fit to do, apparently. By then, he'd already chipped away at her confidence so much that she acquiesced pathetically, even apologised for having ideas above her station. He got a job at a hedge fund which suited him perfectly. She never felt comfortable in front of a classroom of kids but she struggled on, thinking it must be her fault, that everything was her fault. She cringed now at the memories, how she'd allowed him to manipulate her at every turn.

She sipped her coffee and wondered about Lennox. The pressure teenage boys were under, it was a miracle any of them turned out right. Not that girls had it any easier. Ava had done her best in school to create a respectful environment but she was always firefighting petty power plays, girls denigrating each other, boys projecting macho bullshit. She'd never had Lennox in her class, but he didn't seem like that. She thought about how he saved her. It felt weird to have her freedom because of a teenage kid.

She felt a hand on her back as Freya joined her holding a large mug of tea.

Freya frowned at Ava's espresso cup. 'Did you sleep OK?'

'Best night in months.'

Freya nodded at her stomach. 'How's the wee one?'

'Quiet. But definitely still in there.'

She watched Lennox straighten up and walk along the beach.

'He seems like a good kid,' Freya said.

'He is.'

'It's quite the weird surrogate family you've got yourself here.'

Ava laughed. Freya didn't know the half of it.

Freya nodded. 'It beats what you had with that psycho.'

'Yeah.'

Ava always loved Freya's bluntness. They'd stayed up last night clearing the air, reminiscing about the not-so-good old days. They danced around the topic of Michael's abuse, talked about Freya's string of short-term girlfriends, how they were both dealing with the aftermath of their upbringing in different, fucked-up ways.

A noise made Ava look up. A low rumble and whine came from the east, behind the hills at the loch head. It quickly got loud, a fierce energy to it. She glanced at Freya, who smiled. The noise exploded as three fighter jets came over the hill and banked, dropping to skirt low over the water, heading west to Skye and open sea. The noise of the engines tore the air as they swept in formation down the loch. Then they were gone, engines growling and singing as they disappeared beyond the horizon.

'They use the glens for practice,' Freya said.

'Practice for what?'

Freya shrugged. 'War?'

Ava thought about Sandy in the van, the ball of light overhead when they arrived a few nights ago. A different universe to million-pound jets lumbering through the air like rocks.

Another noise, this time shouty fem-punk coming from Freya's pocket. She pulled her phone out. When she saw who was calling she held the phone like it was infected.

'Mum,' she said.

'When's the last time she called you?'

Freya shook her head. 'Maybe a year ago.'

'This isn't a coincidence.'

'It is not.' She lifted the phone up. 'Should I answer?'

The song kept playing on the ringer.

Ava stared at it.

'Sure,' she said eventually. 'Knowledge is power.'

Freya pressed answer and put it on speaker.

'Mother,' she said. 'To what do I owe this honour?'

'Do you have to, Freya?'

Ava shivered at her mum's voice. She was scared to breathe in case she gave herself away.

'Well, it's been a while.'

'Please park your attitude today. Have you seen the news?'

Freya glanced at Ava. 'The political shitstorm?'

'Your sister.'

'What about her?'

'You really don't know?'

'Enlighten me.'

'She's been abducted, taken from her home by a violent youth.'

Freya raised her eyebrows and Ava glanced at Lennox on the beach. But the anxiety in their mum's voice was real.

'Really?' Freya was trying not to smile.

'Michael is beside himself with worry. He had to go to Accident and Emergency, you know, attacked by that hooligan.'

Ava tensed at his name.

'I'm sure he'll cope,' Freya said. She was clearly itching to say more.

'You don't sound very concerned.'

Freya looked at Ava, who shook her head.

Freya stared at her phone. 'We don't know what the story is, that's all. It might not be like it seems.'

'What do you know?'

'Nothing, Mother, but I know Ava. And I know Michael.'

'Whatever do you mean? He's been a wonderful husband. Gave her the finest life, looked after her.'

Ava rolled her eyes. Freya raised her eyebrows and Ava shook her head again. Mum had always been blind to Michael's behaviour, he kept her sweet. She'd spent her own marriage blind to her husband's bullying, or internalising it, and now she was doing the same with Michael and Ava. Ava had tried to talk to her about it, but Mum deflected the conversation from anything uncomfortable. It made sense that she was now focusing on Michael's concern over Ava's wellbeing.

'I'm sure Ava is fine,' Freya said.

'Michael is going mad with worry. I've had the police here. And others...'

Ava stared at Freya and her sister understood.

'What others?'

'I don't know, they showed me IDs.'

Ava pressed mute on Freya's phone. 'Ask if they're still there.'

Freya unmuted and asked.

Their mum hesitated. 'Of course not, they just asked a few questions then left.'

The hesitation was enough. Mum was an expert in self-delusion but she was a piss-poor liar.

Ava reached over and ended the call.

'They were still there,' Freya said.

Ava stepped off the porch to get Lennox. 'We have to go. Now.'

26
EWAN

Trinity was an affluent enclave of north Edinburgh sandwiched between Pilton and Newhaven, the old harbour of Granton separating it from the sea. Primrose Bank Road was lined with large Victorian houses, oaks and horse-chestnut trees reaching over the high walls. There were plenty of cars parked in the street which made it easier for Ewan to stay unnoticed.

Yesterday he'd waited in his car outside St Leonard's until Fellowes and his entourage of three goons left. He followed them to luxury flats in Cumberland Street, where they spent the night. He slept in his car outside, woke this morning as they left in comically sinister SUVs with blacked-out windows and drove to this house. They'd been inside for an hour.

He couldn't get a handle on Fellowes. He wasn't a regular cop, obviously, but he was able to boss Nina around. She wouldn't take that shit unless her job depended on it. Which meant he was serious despite his supercilious manner and plummy accent. His armed muscle backed that up. Ewan had tried to call Nina a couple of times but she wasn't answering.

His phone rang on the passenger seat and he jumped. Another call from Patterson at the *Standard* so he diverted to voicemail. That ship had sailed. He'd missed a couple of deadlines and you only diverted calls from Patterson for a very short time before he never called again. Ewan thought about what he was doing. His car smelled of piss from the bottles he'd been urinating in overnight. He stank of sweat and anxiety and he'd just lost his job, but none of it mattered.

In a weird way he felt young again, chasing a story like journalists were supposed to. Following leads until he worked out what the fuck was going on. But it was more than that. He felt connected on a personal level. He didn't have the connection the other three had with Sandy but he was still invested. This was the biggest story in the country, maybe the world, he had to stick with it.

The front door of the house flung open and Fellowes and the other three strode to their SUVs. They put flashing lights on their roofs and sirens filled the air, then they screeched off with spinning tyres. He considered following but there was no way his rust-bucket Honda could keep up. They'd be going through red lights and into oncoming traffic, he couldn't follow without being noticed or killed.

He sprayed his armpits with deodorant, got out the car and walked to the house, getting a pad and pen out of his pocket. He walked up the drive. Christine Gallacher had done all right. He wondered if that coloured her opinion of Ava running away from her rich husband.

He rang the bell and waited. He'd done his share of doorstepping, it wasn't a part of the job anyone liked, bothering victims or the bereaved, but he'd swallowed it just like he swallowed a lot of shit. Now he was trying to do something for the right reasons and it felt good.

The door opened and a small, compact woman with dyed blonde hair looked surprised at him.

'I thought you were...'

'Oscar Fellowes?' Ewan said. 'My name is Ewan McKinnon, I'm a journalist writing a story about your daughter.'

Christine went to shut the door. 'They told me not to speak to—'

'The press, yes. But they don't have Ava's safety in mind, Christine.'

'How do you know my name?'

He'd visited several neighbours under a chatty cover story of collecting for charity, got the gossip on the Gallacher house from an old woman neighbour. The dad had been a banker, died of a heart attack too young, apparently. He was strict with the girls, Christine too. She hadn't blossomed since his death, kept his memory alive, had mostly lost contact with the girls. One of them, Freya, 'played for the other team', while Ava was married to a nice young man like her father. Didn't take Siggy Freud to work out this psychology.

'Ava told me,' Ewan said.

'You spoke to her?'

'I was there when Michael was injured.'

That widened her eyes. 'The boy assaulted him, it's a disgrace.'

Michael was obviously the golden son-in-law. Some people don't want to see the truth.

'I didn't see what happened exactly, but I know Ava is worried.'

'Why did she run?'

'She doesn't feel safe, Christine.'

'What do you mean? She's not well, the stroke and everything.'

'I'm saying she didn't feel safe *at home*.'

'What about the baby?'

'Did you hear what I said?' Ewan wanted to say more but didn't want to destroy his chance of information.

'She must be due any day and Michael is distraught.'

The way she looked behind her suggested he was inside the house. Ewan straightened his back. 'He's here?'

'Resting upstairs,' Christine said. 'This has taken so much out of him.'

Maybe a different tack was needed. 'Christine, your daughter is in trouble.'

'She just needs to go home.'

'Those men,' Ewan said, waving behind him, 'they don't care about Ava.'

'They said they were going to find her and bring her home.'

Ewan didn't know how to explain, but the way Fellowes spoke and the presence of armed agents didn't bode well for anyone's safety.

'With guns?'

'She was taken against her will.'

Ewan saw curtains twitching next door. 'How do you know that?'

'I just know.' She touched her hair, scratched her neck. She was sounding more unsure as the conversation went on. She glanced behind her again. Maybe Michael was pulling his old shit with the mum now, dominating her like her husband used to.

'I've spoken to her,' Ewan said. 'I'm telling you, she's acting under her own free will.'

He thought about Sandy, the strange connection they had with Ava and the rest.

'I don't believe you,' Christine said.

Ewan paused, looked in the direction Fellowes had gone. 'Why did they leave so quickly?'

'I don't know.'

'They had information, didn't they? Did you speak to Ava?'

Christine looked around for help. She wasn't used to making big decisions like this. 'Michael said not to say anything.'

'Michael is not your boss, Christine.'

She swallowed hard enough for Ewan to hear and picked at the beds of her nails. 'I didn't speak to Ava, exactly.'

'Then what?'

She glanced round and Ewan thought he heard footsteps.

'I spoke to her sister. I think Ava was there.'

Definite footsteps down the stairs. Ewan didn't want to see Michael again.

'Where?' he said under his breath.

'She lives in Ratagan.'

27
HEATHER

The worst thing was not having a plan. Heather wasn't super-organised but years of being a mum made her realise you needed focus if your life wasn't going to go to shit. The campervan grumbled along the road. A truck overtook them, making the van wobble in the downdraft. Heather gripped the wheel like she wanted to crush it.

They'd left Ratagan forty minutes ago, having taken a distressing amount of time getting their shit together. While Ava was inside saying goodbye to Freya, Heather stood on the front porch and watched in amazement as Lennox and Sandy walked together from the beach, across the road and into the van. Part of her hoped this was a weird trip, a side effect of the stroke and the tumour. But even if all this was made up, she still had to go along with it.

Once they were on the road they had to make decisions. Lennox was still unclear where Sandy wanted to go, and none of them knew what Sandy's motivation was. A rendezvous point or safe haven of some kind? Lennox just said 'north'. Nobody else had serious input so Heather had to choose. Heading further west took you to Skye and that was a dead end. So they doubled back east for a short time, hoping they wouldn't see a bunch of police cars coming round the bend.

Then they turned north and joined the west bank of Loch Ness at Invermoriston. At least now they were heading further away from Edinburgh. Ava hadn't been clear about the call, just that she sensed someone was with her mum on the other end of the phone. Heather felt the urge to call Ewan but it was more important to make some distance for now.

Lennox was in the back of the van, Sandy spilling out of the sink, Ava up front next to Heather.

'Wow,' Ava said, nodding out the window.

Loch Ness was massive and ominous, a huge expanse. Heather had been this way as a backpacking student three decades ago and had the same impression then. It was too big to make sense of, the water a dark blue that was almost black.

'It's creepy,' Heather said.

'It's beautiful,' Ava said.

Heather glanced behind. Sandy was more animated than before, tentacles waving, colour streams spiralling across their body. Lennox was captivated by the display. He'd become much closer to them, like a best friend he never knew he needed. Sandy was communicating with him, obviously, but it wasn't as straightforward as giving them a postcode. And what would happen if they got to where Sandy wanted to go? What was left for the three of them after that? There was no going back, yet they couldn't run forever.

'Do you believe in Nessie?' Ava said, looking at Sandy.

Heather laughed. 'Up until a few days ago, the idea of mythical creatures living in the water would've seemed like total crap. But a prehistoric monster in Loch Ness is not the craziest thing I can think of anymore.'

They drove for a while, patchy white cloud, beams of sunshine slicing between and hitting the dark water. On the other side of the road was a sheer rock face sprinkled with hardy trees, gripping for all they were worth. Heather wanted to relax but every time they passed a lorry going the other way, the shudder from the slipstream made her imagine the van veering into the cliff or swerving through the barrier into the water.

'Do you want me to drive?' Ava said.

Heather shook her head. 'I just need to relax.'

Ava nodded. 'So tell me something about yourself, maybe that'll take your mind off things.'

Heather laughed. 'I don't think that'll calm me down.'

'Your story can't be any worse than mine.'

'Want to bet?'

Ava was quiet.

Heather sighed. 'I'm sorry, it's not a competition. It took a lot of balls to leave Michael like you did.'

'What about you?'

'What about me?'

'Coming away like this,' Ava said. 'Looking after us all.'

Heather waved a hand around the van. 'I'm not exactly doing a great job.'

Ava smiled. 'You're doing a better job than you think. You're a natural mother.'

Heather felt tightness in her chest. 'No, I'm not.'

'I don't know how I'll look after this one,' Ava said rubbing her stomach.

A large Tesco truck passed them the other way, making the van shake. Then an Audi overtook them on a thin stretch of straight road. Heather swallowed and tried to calm herself. The road had risen away from the loch, trees along the verge strobing the view.

'You'll be fine,' she said. 'Everyone is scared beforehand, but they're so worth it.'

'Sounds like you're speaking from experience.' Ava said this softly, dipping a toe in the water.

'Yeah.' Heather felt bad about shutting this down but she couldn't deal with it just now.

The road climbed and as they got higher there was more perspective on the size of the loch. It stretched to the horizon and Heather felt tiny in their wee camper. Their engine rattled with the steep incline. She had the accelerator on the floor but they were barely managing uphill, a string of vehicles queueing behind. Eventually the road levelled out at a high summit, then began to slope slightly downhill.

'It might help to talk about it,' Ava said.

'I don't think—'

A bang shook the van and they swerved into the middle of the road before Heather righted them. A metallic grinding shook them so much she couldn't think. Black smoke began billowing from the bonnet.

'The power's gone,' Heather said, glancing in the mirror.

She threw on the hazards and was about to pull onto the verge.

'Look.' Ava pointed at a large car park nestled down a slight slope amongst the trees to the right. They freewheeled past a sign for Urquhart Castle. Heather saw several campervans in amongst tourist coaches. It was more anonymous than sitting on the road in full view.

She signalled and turned, using the momentum of the van to slide into a space behind some bushes which hid them from the road. She pulled on the handbrake and stared at the smoke still pluming from the bonnet.

'Fuck.'

Ava stared at the smoke. 'What now?'

Heather knew this was coming. She'd been avoiding thinking about him, but she'd also been heading towards him all along. She'd always known they were leading to this.

'I can call a guy,' she said.

'Who?'

'My ex-husband.'

28
LENNOX

He watched the two women from inside the van. Ava had both hands on her back as she walked down the hill to find a toilet. Heather was pacing back and forth on the phone, brow wrinkled, her hand running through her hair.

<What's that?>

He jumped at the voice in his head, turned to see Sandy standing at the small side window, shimmers of light up and down their body. He felt a shiver at their voice, like an ASMR video, the sound too close, sitting inside his brain.

He walked to the window. A castle was perched on a low cliff looking over a huge expanse of water heading north as far as you could see.

'Loch Ness?'

The pattern accelerated across Sandy's body, spots appearing and disappearing. Lennox could watch that all day.

<The largest loch by volume in the British Isles. Best known for alleged sightings of the cryptozoological Loch Ness Monster, also known affectionately as Nessie.>

What the fuck? Lennox made a conscious effort to think, not speak. <Is that from Wikipedia?>

Sandy's head turned so their eyes were looking right into Lennox's. <Human tribe-story. Earth story-network.>

'Have you got broadband in your head?'

Silence for a moment. <Yes. Do you not?>

'Fuck me.'

<Meaning unclear. Reproduce?>

<No, sorry.>

Lennox had spent plenty of time since Ratagan on his phone checking out Enceladus. He'd never heard of it before. Sixth largest moon of Saturn, covered in ice but with oceans under the surface, thanks to underwater volcanoes and something called tidal heating, to do with Saturn's gravitational pull. It even had geysers around the south pole that shot material into space, stuff that made up one of Saturn's rings. Crazy. A spacecraft called Cassini had flown through those plumes trying to work out what was in them. Lennox stared at Sandy and realised all the scientists in the world would lose their shit if they could see what he saw now, hear what was in his head.

<We would like to enter Loch Ness. New partial Sandy-Lennox.>

Lennox laughed. <You want to go swimming?>

<Very much.> Sandy climbed down from the window and scuttled across the floor, reached for the door handle.

'Wait.' Lennox held the door closed. <You can't just go out there, folk will see you.>

<Not desired?>

Lennox shook his head, realising he had no idea whether Sandy knew what that meant. <Not right now.>

Sandy looked around the camper, tentacles waving like they were smelling the air.

<Put me in the sack.> They glided to a seat and pulled out a backpack.

Lennox stared at it. <You won't fit in there.>

Sandy began to climb in, squeezing their body, shrinking down to a fraction of their normal size, whipping tentacles in after them and hunkering down. Lennox thought of some YouTube footage he'd watched of an octopus squeezing through a tiny hole to escape from the deck of a fishing boat. Sandy zipped the backpack half closed with two tentacles, eyes still visible in the opening.

Lennox smiled. <OK.>

There was a large ticket office at the castle entrance so Lennox walked the other way until he was in the shadow of some pines. He made sure the backpack was secure then jumped the wire fence. He landed on a carpet of pine needles then walked towards the water. He'd seen on the map in the car park that there was a jetty to the left, best avoided, tourists all over it. He went past a low *Private* sign then turned, further away from the castle ruins. There was no path so he scrambled through thick woods, branches whipping him in the arms and face.

<Home tastes good.>

'What?'

<Tastes good.>

He was so distracted by Sandy's voice that he nearly went over a sudden cliff. He stumbled and grabbed a branch, steadied himself and stared down at the brooding water. He looked both ways along the cliff. They were round a small headland from the castle, couldn't be seen. In the other direction was just water and cliffs into the distance.

He felt the weight on his back reduce as Sandy opened the backpack and climbed out sinuously, expanding to stand next to him.

<Home.>

Lennox shook his head. <But how do we get down?>

Sandy turned to him and he sank into their eyes, big black orbs, eyes that had seen oceans on a moon millions of miles away.

<Do I have your permission?>

Lennox remembered last time he was asked, now he had this thing in his ear.

<For what?>

<Protect new partial Sandy-Lennox.>

Lennox thought about Sandy's powers. <I give permission.>

Sandy wrapped their tentacles around him, then stretched and ballooned to twice their normal size. Lennox felt their skin envelope him, it was warm and cool at the same time, as extra pieces of tentacle or flesh emerged from Sandy's body and hugged as tight as cellophane. They held his head and surrounded it then he felt pressure against his face like sinking into a cool pillow. His mouth was covered and he wondered if he could breathe but his breath came, sweet and salty at the same time. He couldn't make out where Sandy stopped and where he started, his eyes still worked but all he could see was opaque blue-green light, as if looking out from inside them.

<OK?>

He was soothed by their voice. <OK.>

He felt himself being moved to the edge of the cliff then over, dropping to the water, the large dark mass approaching, then a splash and they were under, moving faster than he thought possible, thrusts of power from Sandy's tentacles pushing water behind them, propelling them into the loch.

His vision cleared, the coloured sheen vanished and it was like he was just swimming through the water himself. He sensed Sandy's joy as they swept left then right, down then up, rolled over and over in a forward spiral, making him feel dizzy. They stopped and swam straight as if sensing his discomfort, then dropped deeper into the gloom.

Lennox glimpsed fish in the dark and wondered what Sandy ate, if they would snaffle some up and he would taste the raw flesh through Sandy somehow. He thought about Nessie, imagined seeing a prehistoric colossus emerging from the gloom, long neck, giant body shifting through the currents.

But all he could see was water. They rose up and reached the surface faster than he thought possible, then they breached, his head above water. He instinctively tried to breathe then realised he'd been breathing all along. He saw the castle ruins two hundred metres away, tourists scuttling across the land like mites. He wondered if any were looking out right now with binoculars, hoping to catch a glimpse of Nessie. If he and Sandy would be spotted. They dived back under the surface with hardly a splash.

Lennox grinned. <This is fucking crazy.>

They slowed a little.

<Meaning unclear. Bad?>

Lennox closed his eyes then opened them, wondering if this was a dream. <No. Not bad at all.>

29
AVA

Ava looked around as they walked. Castle ruins on the banks of a massive loch was picture-postcard Scotland. This was what people in America, Siberia or Hong Kong pictured when they thought of the country. Tartan and haggis, whisky and shortbread. Not the millions of ordinary people living their lives, taking kids to school, working shitty jobs, living in poverty, getting abused and coerced by their husbands until they couldn't take it anymore.

She breathed shakily and Heather looked at her.

'OK?' Heather said.

'OK.' Ava felt the baby push against her bladder again. She'd not long gone to the toilet, but her life was constant toilet breaks and heartburn, the majesty of motherhood. She waved at the castle walls and turreted tower. 'All this is too much, you know? Like, too perfect. Maybe five hundred years ago I could've been a perfect princess living in that tower.'

Heather smiled. 'You think women had it easy in the 1500s? They were possessions, chattel.'

'What's changed?'

Heather swept a hand around the view. 'We're here of our own free will, aren't we?'

'We're in deep shit, is where we are.'

Heather's ex-husband was coming to help. He apparently lived in a remote croft in the hills near here, and he had a truck and a tow bar big enough to take the camper to the nearest garage. So that was the immediate problem addressed but what about all the other shit? The creature, the people after them, Michael out for revenge. She felt despair at what kind of life she could make for her baby. What sort of start was this?

She stopped walking and burst out crying.

'Hey.' Heather guided her to a bench looking over the loch. Tourists in waterproofs drifted past, a chatter of different languages. Ava wondered if her daughter would travel, learn languages, fall in love with a beautiful Argentinian scuba diver with a ponytail who was entirely wrong for her. She felt dizzy at the infinite strands of possible lives spreading out in front of her daughter, infinite ways to fuck up, infinite dangers as soon as she was outside the womb where Ava would have no control. But that was bullshit conditioning from years with Michael, it wasn't about control.

Her breathing calmed. She wiped at her tears and sniffed. 'Fucking hormones.'

Heather shook her head. 'It's not hormones, you're right, we're in the shit.'

Ava laughed. 'What are we even doing?'

Heather took her hand. 'We felt something with Sandy. We're connected. This is huge. Do you realise what we're dealing with?'

Ava shook her head. 'I just want to be safe.'

Heather squeezed her hand. 'We all want to be safe but we can't bury our heads in the sand. We're involved now, the police are after us.'

'Maybe if we just explain.'

'And go back to Michael, is that what you want?'

'I'm just so tired.'

'I know.' Heather said it with such weight like she felt it in her bones.

'Tell me about your ex, why didn't you mention him before?'

'Paul. He's a good man, there aren't many of them around.'

'So why is he an ex-husband?'

Heather was silent for a long time. 'I'm not sure you want to hear about it.'

'I wouldn't have asked.'

'I hope you never find out what it's like.' She glanced at Ava's stomach. 'To lose a child. When our daughter Rosie was diagnosed with Hodgkin's lymphoma, I felt like my guts were ripped out.'

The baby squirmed and Ava felt sick, pressed her hands together.

'Afterwards, it's hard to explain,' Heather said. 'We didn't fight or argue, we'd agreed about all the treatments and procedures. But our lives, our marriage, were hollowed out. It was impossible to remember life before Rosie and impossible to imagine living together without her. I couldn't even look at him without getting so angry about what had happened. And he was the same with me. We had to destroy ourselves, start again, it was the only way to survive.'

Ava felt heartburn rise up her throat. 'Yet he's coming here to help you.'

Heather ran her tongue around the inside of her cheek. 'I haven't spoken to him in three years. But I knew where he was, and he's always been the kind of man who could get things done.'

The fondness in her voice was mixed with such sadness that Ava felt herself well up.

'Rosie would've been eighteen this year,' Heather said, voice low. 'She was smart, I guess she would've been leaving us for university now. Empty nest. What I would give for that.' She breathed in and out, stretched her neck. 'It's the death of possibility, isn't it? It's the death of all her possible futures.'

Ava was shocked at the resonance with what she'd been thinking earlier, all the possible harm coming her baby's way.

'I just fucking miss her, here,' Heather said, pressing a fist into her gut. 'It just hurts.'

'I wish I knew what to say.'

'There's nothing *to* say, that's the problem.' Heather swallowed. 'There's something else.'

Ava stayed silent, gave her hand an encouraging squeeze.

'I'm dying.' Heather tapped the back of her head. 'Brain tumour. Inoperable.'

'Oh my God.' Ava had a rock in her stomach, couldn't take this in.

Heather stuck her lip out. 'The night we met Sandy, I was trying to kill myself. I walked into the water with my pockets full of stones.'

'Jesus.'

'Sandy saved me. But I'm still going to die.'

Ava didn't know what to say. Words were meaningless, but she had to say something anyway. Wasn't that what humans did? 'I'm so sorry.'

Three Scandinavian tourists walked past – a tall, beautiful family, blond hair and tanned, like a different species.

They sat in silence for a long time.

'What about Lennox?' Heather said eventually.

'What about him?'

'Why is he closer to Sandy than us? It feels like they chose him.'

'Maybe because he's younger, less stuck in his ways.' Ava looked at the loch, the water so dark and deep she could imagine giant beasts lurking below. 'Do you think they're all right?'

Lennox had left with Sandy in a backpack, saying they were going for a walk. Ava was jealous, wanted to know Sandy better. But the closer she got, the more danger her baby was in.

Heather glanced at Ava. 'You saw what Sandy did at the golf course. I think they're fine.'

Ava waved at the expanse of land and water. 'What's our goal? So far we've just been running from things. Where are we running to?'

Heather shook her head.

Ava stared at the ripples on the loch, shifting patterns of light and shade from clouds above. She imagined Nessie's long neck breaching the water and towering into the sky.

Heather's phone rang and she dug it out.

'Paul?' Ava said.

Heather shook her head. 'Ewan.'

30
EWAN

'Ewan?' Heather's voice filled the car. It was good to hear.

'You need to get out of Ratagan,' he said.

'What?'

'They know you're at Ava's sister's. They're on their way.'

'The police?'

'The other guys.'

The traffic on the A9 was shit as always. The overtaking lanes were no use in his shitty Honda so he was stuck in the slow lane with the supermarket trucks and low-loaders full of logged trees. He imagined the black SUVs way ahead, lights flashing, almost at Ratagan.

'We're not there,' Heather said. 'Ava realised something was wrong when her mother called.'

Ewan was always one step behind and he didn't like it. But he was relieved they were OK. 'Where are you?'

He sensed hesitation. He hit an open patch of road, cars zipping out to overtake. Around him were the low edges of the Cairngorms, a river rippling over a stony bed to his left. Big sky everywhere. The Highlands were full of space and he wasn't used to it.

'If you don't want to tell me, I get it,' he said. He was an outsider, didn't have the connection that the rest of them had. But he cared about them, especially Heather. 'As long as you're safe.'

He heard some muffled chat, another woman's voice.

'We're at Urquhart Castle.'

Ewan frowned. 'The tourist trap? Aren't you supposed to be hiding?'

'The van broke down, we had to stop.'

'Are you OK?'

'We're fine, someone is coming to help.'

'Like a garage?'

'Kind of.'

'What about Sandy?'

More silence. He wondered what he would do in their shoes, realised he didn't have a clue.

'We'll look after them,' Heather said.

The road narrowed and a BMW swerved in front of him. This road was a death trap, had been for decades. His pulse quickened.

'These guys after you,' he said. 'The main one is called Fellowes and he has three guys with him, armed.'

'What?'

'They're very keen on finding Sandy. As long as you're with that thing you're in danger. Maybe you should give Sandy up.'

'No.'

'OK, but let me help you, please.'

His phone beeped, incoming call from Nina.

'Shit, I've got another call from my police contact. I should get it, could be important.'

Heather cleared her throat. 'I'll call you once we know where we are with the van.'

He wanted to say more but didn't know how. He answered Nina's call.

'Where the fuck are you?' she said, but with a laid-back lilt in her voice.

Ewan turned off at Dalwhinnie. The new road would be slower and more windy but quieter too. He wondered how far ahead Fellowes was.

'I'm at home.' He tried to keep his voice flat.

'No, you're not,' Nina said, 'because I've just rung your doorbell.'

'Why are you at my place?'

'Because you're a person of interest in a murder investigation, in case you'd forgotten.'

'Come on, Nina, you know I'm not a murderer.'

'Don't fucking Nina me. You might not be a murderer but you're not innocent in all this either.'

'Why are you really at my flat?'

She sighed. Ewan wondered how many times he'd made a woman sigh in frustration over the years. Didn't bear thinking about.

'I came to warn you, a wee chat off the record.'

'About Fellowes?'

'You have no idea what you're dealing with.'

'You said that already.'

'I know a little more now.'

'He told you?'

The road stretched across a wide flood plain, hills in the distance, scraggy fir trees on the roadside. He imagined the blacked-out SUVs pummelling through the quiet.

'Not exactly. I did some digging.'

'And?'

'These are the big guys, Ewan. MI5 or similar.'

'OK.'

'You don't sound surprised.'

'I'm shocked.'

A small laugh came down the line. 'Domestic terrorism? What the fuck are you mixed up in?'

He thought about what he'd seen. 'It's not terrorism.'

'Then what? These clowns only get involved if there's a threat to national security.'

Ewan thought about Heather and the others wandering around a castle on the banks of Loch Ness.

'This isn't a security threat.'

'Then what's going on? I tried a friend of mine with security services. Pretty chatty when it suits him. Clammed up when I mentioned Fellowes. I got the impression this is a different league, like Fellowes is on some lunatic fringe of the organisation.'

'OK.'

'My point is, he doesn't sound like the most accountable guy. A wee bit rogue, like yourself.'

'Kindred spirits, then.'

'Except he's running around with a small gang of armed men.'

Ewan swallowed.

'Sounds like you're in the car,' Nina said. '*Following your story.*' This was dripping in sarcasm, a hint of affection too.

'No, just heading to the shops.'

'If you know where your friends are, you should tell me. Now.'

Ewan slowed the car then overtook a tractor pulling a trailer of hay.

'It's better if we find them before Fellowes, trust me,' Nina said.

'But you can't guarantee their safety.'

'I can try.'

'I saw how that prick railroaded you in the interview room, Nina.'

That was cruel and he regretted it.

'Well, nice talking to you.'

'I'm sorry, Nina, it's just...'

'What?'

'I can't explain right now. You wouldn't believe me anyway.'

Nina sighed. 'OK. But if you meet Fellowes and his pals, don't say I didn't warn you.'

She hung up and Ewan felt alone in the sudden silence.

31
HEATHER

She stood in the car park, armpits damp with sweat, anxiety fluttering in her chest as she watched Paul's flatbed truck turn towards her. The sunlight through the trees flickered across the windscreen so that she only got a glimpse of him behind the wheel. He'd phoned five minutes ago to say he was nearly here and had described the truck. She gave a shy wave and pointed at the campervan. He pulled in just past the van. She reached into her pocket and touched the photo of Rosie there, pictured her long legs in the surf.

Ava had gone to find Lennox and Heather was glad, she wanted to meet Paul on her own. It felt weird enough already and her hands were trembling. Italian tourists drifted into a tour bus along the way, and the murmur of their language was like honey.

Paul got out of the truck and walked over. He wore a checked shirt and scruffy jeans, black Adidas. He'd lost a little weight and his hair was grey at the temples now which suited him. He looked older, but so did she. She touched her hair as if for him and wondered about old patterns. His smile was warm and sad, and she felt a flutter in her stomach. She hugged him and he hugged her back, a brief awkwardness then she sank into him, felt his hands on her back, smelled his familiar scent. She squeezed and let go, stepped back.

'Thanks for coming.'

He spread his arms. 'No problem.'

'I feel stupid.'

'Why?'

'We haven't spoken in three years.'

'Seems longer.'

'It does.' Heather shifted her weight, rubbed her arm. 'Then I call you out of the blue asking for help.'

Paul nodded and looked around the busy car park. 'It wasn't exactly out of the blue, I half expected it.'

'What do you mean?'

Paul looked round again. 'Are you sure you're OK here? You might be recognised.'

Of course he knew, he'd seen the news like everyone else, seen her face in the story about Ava and Lennox. She hadn't checked recently, didn't know how they were spinning it, but it wouldn't be good.

Heather looked over her shoulder. 'I suspect tourists aren't glued to the Scottish news.'

'You'd better hope not.'

He held an arm out and guided her to the other side of the van, in the shade of the tree and away from the coaches. She caught a hint of his scent again.

'You don't have to tell me what this is about,' he said.

Heather shook her head. 'I want to, honestly, but it's complicated.'

'I'm happy to help, regardless.'

'You were always good in a crisis.'

Paul frowned. 'I don't believe I was.'

He'd been a rock all through Rosie's cancer. Taking her to the hospital, pushing her in her wheelchair. Emptying out the sick bucket at home, dabbing her brow when she was drowning in sweat. To begin with they talked about it together, felt comfort from the shared pain and worry, but they both hardened as things got worse. What use was talking? It didn't solve anything. It didn't help Rosie, just made them feel worse, chewing over the unfairness, the lack of options as she slipped further from them.

He kept up that stoic dependability after she died. He dealt with the funeral and all the other shit when Heather was unable. She'd been grateful but also resented him like crazy. How fucking dare he keep his shit together in the face of this, when their lives were destroyed? It was stupid but she needed someone to lash out at and he was there. Of course, she knew all about the stages of grief but that just made it worse. She was a fucking cliché, her daughter a statistic. They were just another couple who split after their kid died.

Paul reached over now and touched the campervan. 'So this old thing is back on the road.'

'Well, it was.'

Paul laughed. 'We had some fun in it though.'

'We did.'

He patted the side of the van. 'Smoke from the bonnet is probably just the coolant system. It never worked well.'

'Can you fix it?'

'There's a garage down the road in Drumnadrochit. Good guys. They'll do it quick.'

'And quiet?'

'I trust them. They don't need to know the details.'

He took a step back to give the van the once over, then looked at her.

Heather felt her face flush and hated herself for it. 'What?'

'You look good.'

She pulled on her earlobe. 'I do not.'

'More at peace with yourself.'

She laughed. It had been three days since she tried to kill herself. And now here she was with a surrogate family, chatting to her ex-husband in a Highland beauty spot.

'I don't look at peace at all, but thank you.'

Paul lifted his chin. 'The news said you'd been in hospital. A stroke.'

'It wasn't that serious.'

Paul narrowed his eyes. Of course, he knew she was lying, they'd been together for twenty years. She thought about her tumour. With everything else going on she'd forgotten about it. When you spend all your time looking after other people, you forget about yourself. You vanish into nothing and that's how she liked it.

She imagined telling Paul she had terminal brain cancer and had attempted suicide. She wanted him to know it all, to know her as deeply as he used to. When they were first together they told each other everything, but that never lasts. No one can ever know you. Paul was the person she knew best in the world and she couldn't say a thing to him.

'Come on, Heather, it's me you're talking to.'

'I'm fine, honestly.'

He didn't say anything.

'Hey.'

Ava's voice made Heather jump. Ava was out of breath, Lennox at her side with the backpack on, glassy look on his face.

Heather introduced them to Paul, then he rubbed his hands on his jeans.

'Well, I better get the tow bar fitted, get this baby to the garage.'

Heather watched him walk to the truck and remembered a time they were on holiday on a beach between Wick and Cape Wrath. She was pregnant with Rosie and they were happy, their future ahead of them. Nothing to do but be happy in love and wait for things to go to shit.

32
AVA

The smattering of wooden tables were round the back of the hotel bar, out of sight from the road. But still, should they really be sitting outside, in broad daylight? She felt the baby tumble in a loop between her pelvis and ribs. She sucked some fresh orange and lemonade through a straw and scuffed her feet in the gravel. The wee river behind her was babbling away.

The four of them sat at a table. Heather and Paul were chatting, low and serious, as if they had a lifetime to catch up on. Heather had a large bowl of gin and tonic, Paul sipped a pint of craft lager. Lennox was across from Ava with a can of Coke. They'd dropped the camper at the garage round the corner, where they were working on it out of sight. Paul and the garage guy had an understanding, as if unofficial shit often happened here and authorities never needed to know.

While Paul negotiated at the garage, Lennox, Heather and Ava decided it was best to leave Sandy in the van, hidden in a compartment under the bed. The mechanics wouldn't go into that part.

The pub was the Loch Ness Inn. The logo on the wall had turned the word 'inn' into Nessie, 'I' for the head, two 'n's for the body. Tourism was crucial in the Highlands, the place depended on it. The tables were full of hikers and cyclists, one young family, local lads near the bar. Midges swarmed down by the river. The sun streaked the garden, shadows growing longer.

'Are you OK?' Ava said to Lennox. He was too quiet, and she wanted someone to talk to.

'Fine.'

'What were the two of you up to at the castle?'

'We went swimming.'

'In the loch?' Ava glanced at Nessie on the outside of the pub.

Lennox nodded.

'How did you get down to the water?'

'We jumped.'

'That must've taken guts.'

Lennox shrugged. 'We did it together.'

'How do you mean?'

He sipped his Coke. 'They kind of wrapped themself around me. Absorbed me into them.'

'What?'

Lennox stuck his lips out and angled his head. 'Then they swam with me, like, inside them?'

Ava watched a wasp flirt with her drink, waved it away. 'What are we involved with?'

Lennox stopped fidgeting and looked straight at her. 'They're an alien, obviously.'

She'd assumed as much, of course, but it was still shocking to hear the word out loud. Ava glanced at Paul, still in a confab with Heather. How could they explain this to outsiders?

'I have so many questions,' Ava said. 'How did they get here? Why? What's their planet like?'

'Moon.'

'What?'

'Sandy comes from a moon not a planet.'

'They told you?'

Lennox looked sheepish. 'Enceladus. One of Saturn's moons.'

'And you're only telling me this now?'

Lennox shrugged. 'I Googled it. It's covered in ice but has oceans underneath. Heated by volcanoes.'

Ava ran a hand through her hair and laughed. 'Christ. Anything else you forgot to mention?'

Lennox stayed quiet.

'Why us?' Ava said. 'Why contact us?'

Lennox shuffled his feet under the table. 'I don't think there's anything special about us. That part's just an accident.'

'What did Sandy do to us? Why did we pass out, what happened to our brains? Can't you ask?'

'It's not like that. They communicate when they want, other times I don't get through. They're confused. This is all new to them.'

'Are we infected? Sandy already caused us to have strokes.' Ava touched her stomach. 'What if they harm the baby?'

'They wouldn't do that.'

'Maybe not deliberately, but the strokes weren't deliberate either, or the guy on the beach.'

'Self-defence.'

'And Michael at the golf course.'

'Sandy protected you.' Lennox's voice was raised and Paul looked round.

Ava spoke under her breath. 'I appreciate that but I'm worried, OK?'

A breeze rippled the edges of their sunshade, a buttery scent came from the trees on the riverbank.

Ava scratched at the table. 'What does Sandy want, Lennox? Where are we taking them?'

'I've asked, but their geography isn't right. They're not used to land. They showed me the place but they don't understand maps and roads.'

'What does it look like?'

Lennox shrugged. 'A Scottish town on the banks of a loch.'

'Are there others there?'

'Maybe. They talk like they're part of a collective or something.'

'What happens when we get there?'

She didn't expect an answer, just needed to vent. This was all so frustrating.

'Hey.' She recognised the voice and turned to see Ewan beside Heather and Paul. He was sweating, hands in pockets, eyeing Heather's ex with suspicion. He held out his hand. 'I'm Ewan.'

'Paul.'

Ewan looked at Heather for an explanation.

'Paul helped us get the campervan to the garage,' she said.

Ava noted that she didn't mention Paul was her ex-husband.

'OK,' Ewan said. He looked at the others. 'Where's—?'

Heather butted in. 'The guys at the garage reckon it's the coolant system.'

The sound of ringing, then Paul pulled his phone out.

'Speaking of which,' he said, answering.

His face fell while the garage guy spoke. 'When?'

'What is it?' Heather said, touching his arm.

Paul was still listening on the phone. 'Shit. We'll be right there.'

'What the fuck, Paul?' Heather said.

Paul ended the call and looked around the table.

'The campervan is gone.'

33
LENNOX

He was running along the road before he'd had a chance to think. The rest of them were just getting out of their seats as he passed a row of small white houses. He sprinted past two hikers in yellow, round the corner and onto the main Drumnadrochit road, past bigger houses and gardens then he was at the garage. It had been so fucking stupid leaving Sandy in the campervan.

Paul's mechanic mate Ian stood outside the building, hands out in apology.

'What the fuck?' Lennox said. He leaned forward, hands on knees, gasping in air.

Ian shook his head like he couldn't believe it himself. 'There was nothing I could do. They just came and towed it away. Held me through the back while they rigged it up so I couldn't even call you.'

'Who?' This was Ewan arriving.

Lennox saw the rest of them behind, Ava at the back.

'The police,' Ian said.

Ewan held out his phone. 'These guys?'

Ian looked at the screen. Lennox saw a picture of a guy in a suit, several bouncer types with him. It was a little blurry but Lennox didn't recognise them.

Ian shook his head. 'No, uniform cops, local guys. They were asking questions.'

Everyone was here now, Ava leaning against a beaten-up Škoda.

'What sort of questions?' Paul said.

'Who brought it in, how long I'd had it. Said they'd had an alert about it on the system from the force in Edinburgh, had orders to impound it and find the owners. I said we'd had it since yesterday, gave them a fake name and address over in Applecross. It'll take them hours to chase that. I said the owners were picking it up tomorrow.'

Paul turned to Heather, relief on his face. 'It could've been worse, right? I mean, you've got your stuff, it's just the van that's gone.'

Heather's face whitened.

Ewan looked at Heather then turned to Lennox. 'Wait, was...?'

Lennox stuck his lip out and nodded.

Paul looked around, trying to get a handle on this. Drilling noises came from the back of the garage, an engine spluttering.

'What did I miss?' he said.

'Nothing,' Heather said.

Lennox glanced at Ava, she looked like she might throw up.

He stepped into the road, looked up and down. No traffic, just straight tarmac in both directions, trees everywhere, wind rustling the leaves. He moved further away and placed his fingers to his ears, closed his eyes and tried to concentrate.

<Sandy?>

Birds chirped in the trees above, calling to each other.

<Sandy, can you hear me?>

He knew nothing about this shit, what was the range? Why weren't they answering? He thought about being inside their body, slipping through the water of Loch Ness as if it was the most natural thing in the world.

<Sandy, please talk to me.>

A delivery truck went past on the road and he stuck his fingers deeper into his ears and screwed up his eyes.

<New partial Sandy-Lennox?> Sandy's voice.

He felt his heart in his chest like a cannon.

<New partial Sandy-Lennox?>

<Sandy, fuck, are you OK?>

Their voice was faint, a long way down a line. <New partial Sandy-Lennox is stretched thin.>

He guessed they meant they were being separated and his heart fluttered. <Are you OK?>

<We are in travel device. But without partial Sandy-Lennox, partial Sandy-Heather, partial Sandy-Ava.>

He'd never heard them mention the women before, what did that mean? <The cops took the van, yes.>

Silence for a few moments. <Colloquial term for law enforcers. Not clear.>

<What do you mean?>

<We don't understand enforcement.>

This wasn't the time to get into this shit but Lennox couldn't help himself. <What if someone breaks the law?>

<We don't understand law.>

He chewed his lip and tried to think. <Just stay safe in the van, we'll come and get you.>

<Do you want us to contact law enforcers?>

<Fuck no. Just stay hidden, OK? I'll be in touch soon.>

He walked back across the road and took Heather's arm, led her away. 'Sandy's safe for now, but we need to get them back.'

Heather had a worried look on her face. 'There's something else I never told you. There are others trying to find us.'

'More cops?'

'I don't know,' Heather said. 'Ewan met them in Edinburgh. He thinks they're security forces or some weird government department.'

'The guys in the picture on his phone?'

'Yeah.'

'But they'll be in contact with police forces across the country, right?'

'I'm not sure. It sounds like the Highland police will be looking in Applecross for the next few hours.'

Heather turned to Ian. 'Where would they take the van?'

'The only vehicle impound in the Highlands is in Inverness.'

Heather looked at Paul and he said it before anyone else had the chance to.

'We need to go to Inverness.'

34
AVA

She leaned on the Škoda and felt like she was a million miles away. She was queasy and worried about vomiting up her fresh orange and lemonade, imagined it skittering across the car bonnet onto the concrete. Raging heartburn spread from her gut to her gullet, and she burped several times. Shouldn't have had a fizzy drink and definitely shouldn't have run along the road. She couldn't hear what anyone was saying. Lennox had obviously been trying to contact Sandy, then came back to chat to Heather. She felt a twinge of jealousy, the three of them were in this together, weren't they? But then she couldn't even stand up at the moment. Her heart thumped in her chest and echoed in a throbbing headache at the base of her skull. She remembered her stroke, like a jackhammer on her brain. What if it was happening again?

She splayed her fingers against the car to steady herself. The light in the glen was fading and a chill hung in the air. Her heartburn got worse then she was sick down her front. Her head spun and tears came to her eyes, blurring her vision. Her hand went from the car to her stomach and she pressed her flesh, desperate to feel a kick to let her know she wasn't alone in the world, she was going to be OK, she was a good mother. But she didn't feel anything and panicked. She pressed deeper, imagined breaking through the skin and muscles and pulling her daughter out, holding her to her face and nuzzling, smearing blood over the two of them like a primal ritual.

Her other hand slipped from the car and she collapsed, knees buckling, in slow motion but unstoppable. Her head thunked off the concrete and she pictured slow ripples from the impact passing through her body to her uterus, her placenta doing its best to shield the little one. Her bladder released and warm piss flowed down her legs. She saw the shapes of people a few yards away, like ghosts drifting towards her.

She closed her eyes and pictured being underwater with Sandy, her stomach flat, the baby swimming alongside, the umbilical cord still connecting them, trailing thin ribbons of blood in the water. Sandy was showing them the way, giant ice floes overhead scattering blue and green light, a throbbing red glow below in the depths. She reached over and held her baby, began sinking, the cord hanging loose between them like a skipping rope. Some force pulled them down towards the bottom of the ocean, Sandy fussing and tugging at Ava and the baby to no avail. Her feet began to burn in the hot water as she hugged her girl to her chest and sank further. They were going to die in a fiery underwater volcano.

'Ava? Christ.' Heather's voice.

Ava opened her eyes.

Someone's jacket was under her head as a pillow. Cars were still being worked on, the noise of a drill somewhere. A spread of worried faces over her, Heather kneeling. It looked uncomfortable, kneeling on the bare ground. Ava remembered her dream and touched her stomach, the stretched skin. She felt the baby's feet kick beneath her fingers and smiled. Still safe.

'We need to get her to a hospital.' This was Paul.

If she went to a hospital the police would know, Fellowes would know, Michael would know.

'No hospital.' She took Heather's hand to help her sit up and leaned against the grill of the Škoda. She smelled sick and piss, saw the dark patch on the concrete between her legs.

Heather followed her gaze. 'That's not...'

She shook her head. 'Just pee.'

Paul looked confused. 'There might be something wrong with the pregnancy.'

'I'm fine.' Ava went to stand, felt weak knees, slid back and plonked her bum on the ground.

Paul spoke to Heather. 'I understand you're in a situation but she needs to see a doctor.'

Ava gritted her teeth and shook her head.

Heather stared at her for a long time then nodded. 'If you're sure.'

'I just need rest.' Ava pictured a king-size bed covered in plump pillows.

Paul shook his head. 'Well, you can rest up at Toll Sionnach. The place I have with Iona. It's a few miles up the road, in the hills.'

Heather stared at him. 'Who's Iona?'

Paul looked sheepish. 'My wife.'

35
HEATHER

She sat in the passenger seat of Paul's pickup and stared out of the window as they drove north along Loch Ness. The hills across the water had been replaced by a low, forested expanse. She glanced at Paul. He was within his rights to remarry, of course. They were over, they had separate lives. But still. Fuck's sake.

Ewan and Lennox were in the back of the pickup, watching over Ava laid out on a mattress and blankets. Paul was obviously used to carrying people around in his truck. She wondered if he'd ever fucked Iona on that mattress, sat naked with her at night, sharing a joint and staring at the stars.

Fuck, she had to get her shit together.

Heather saw a hairpin left turn. Paul swung the truck round in a turning place then drove up a steep slope. The road was a narrow switchback with passing places, zigzagging up the hill. On one bend they met a coal truck and Paul expertly reversed round a corner to the nearest passing place. Heather gripped the dashboard, stared at the long drop out of her window.

Eventually they levelled out on a flat, high moorland, burns and lochans hiding amongst heather. There was an occasional house set back from the road, tiny specks in the wilderness. Small patches of forest here and there, some boggy marsh. They drove past a *Passing Place* sign with bullet holes in it. The views were astounding in every direction, distant hills like a ruffled duvet.

They turned off the road down a long dirt track, through some tree cover, then she saw a white cottage with some outhouses and a woodshed. The track continued round the side of the cottage towards a back road out of the glen. It wasn't exactly hidden but you could see anyone coming from miles.

They parked outside. Heather saw a hand-carved driftwood sign at the door that read *Toll Sionnach*.

'It means foxhole.' Paul gave her a look and she flashed back to being with him and Rosie in their Dirleton garden.

'Appropriate.'

She got out and went to the back of the truck where the guys were helping Ava out. Her face was a better colour and she grabbed Heather in a hug. Heather felt Ava's bump press against her.

'I'm fine,' Ava said. 'Go get Sandy.'

They'd discussed this briefly back at the garage. Lennox was keenest to get to Inverness, Ewan took a backseat in the conversation. Heather wanted Ava to rest up and thought they could all do with a few moments to regroup. She figured the local police would still be on the wild-goose chase to Applecross Ian had sent them on, and hoped Fellowes wouldn't yet know about the van, since the alert was from the Edinburgh police. It was a gamble, but Heather was starting to think that if they lost Sandy it might not be the worst thing. Let someone else care. Maybe Heather and the rest could live out their lives in this foxhole, checking every vehicle that came down the track to the house.

'Hi.'

Heather turned to see Iona nervously wiping her hands on her jeans. She was tall, slim, pretty enough to carry off an auburn pixie cut, in a maroon sweatshirt with a twisted Celtic band around the chest. She had bright eyes and an uncertain smile. She was about forty, maybe, so ten years younger than Paul. And Heather. A decent upgrade.

'I'm Heather.'

Neither woman went to shake hands.

Iona looked at Ava. 'Paul said what happened, come and lie down and I'll get you a change of clothes.'

She put an arm around Ava's shoulder and guided her through the front door. They all walked through a homely kitchen to a large dining area, Heather watching Iona with a knot in her stomach.

'Sit,' Paul said, pointing at the dining table. The windows looked over the glen and beyond, miles of rolling hills, grass and trees, spotted with farm buildings. The view was crazy beautiful, Heather could see why he lived here.

Ewan and Lennox took chairs. Heather hesitated then sat. Paul left to put the kettle on, the sound of it rushing from the other room.

'We need to get Sandy,' Lennox said under his breath.

Heather felt suddenly exhausted. Part of her just wanted to give up, let the chips fall where they may.

'Now,' Lennox said.

'We don't know they're in trouble,' Ewan said.

Heather felt sorry for him. He had no skin in this game that she could see. He wasn't connected to Sandy, maybe he was just after a story. There had maybe been a hint of something between her and him at the start of all this in The Open Arms. But seeing Paul with Iona had made that part of her shrivel and die.

'Sandy's in danger,' Lennox said, scratching at the table with a fingernail. 'I know it.'

'Let's just take a minute.' Heather spread her hands on the table. 'We don't know whether information has made it from the local police to whoever is after us. I get the feeling things move a little slower around here. And Paul's mate at the garage has done us a favour sending them somewhere else looking for us.'

'Maybe I can find out more,' Ewan said. 'From my contact.'

Lennox shook his head but didn't speak.

Heather wrinkled her nose. 'They'll track the call.'

Ewan shrugged. 'I trust her, I don't think she's a fan of this other lot. She wouldn't run to Fellowes with information.'

'I don't know,' Heather said.

'Either way, we need to get to Inverness,' Lennox said.

'The camper?' Paul said, coming back in with a tray of tea.

'We need to get something out of it,' Heather said. 'Something valuable.'

'What?' His look round the room made everyone squirm. He held up a hand. 'It's better if I don't know. Deniability.'

'So you'll take us to Inverness?' Lennox said. 'Do you know where the van is?'

Paul nodded and poured tea. 'The police use Carter's Recovery on Longman Drive in Inverness, it's the only impound lot in the Highlands.' He looked at his watch. 'But it'll be closed.'

'We need to go now,' Lennox said. 'Before the Edinburgh cops get there.'

'Like, break in?' Paul looked at Heather.

She nodded and her cheeks flushed.

Paul stood over them for a long time and Heather watched steam rise from the mugs. 'I can drive you but I'm not getting involved in any of that.'

'That's OK,' Lennox said. 'I'll do the rest.'

'I'll come too,' Ewan said.

Lennox shrugged. He wouldn't admit to needing help but Heather was glad Ewan was going along.

'Maybe I'll stay here, keep an eye on Ava.' She said this looking at Paul. She didn't mean it to sound as if she didn't trust Iona but that's how it came out.

Ewan's phone rang and they all jumped.

'It's Nina,' he said. 'Should I answer?'

Heather didn't know what to say. She just needed not to make a decision for a few minutes. She didn't know the right thing to do and sometimes that's OK.

'I'll take it outside,' Ewan said, heading for the door.

36
EWAN

He pressed reply then it immediately beeped and cut out. He checked the bars on his phone, one flickering to zero. He was walking back into the kitchen when he met Paul.

Paul pointed over Ewan's shoulder. 'Try up the hill.'

He jogged through the trees up the track waving his phone in the air trying to pick up a signal. The sun had set but the sky was still light, blue fading to orange in the west. He imagined meteors blazing through the sky all around, smashing into trees, farms and fields, the same down at the loch, pummelling into the water with giant splashes.

His phone rang. He kept walking up the slope, panting with the effort.

'Hey,' he said.

'Did you just hang up on me?' Nina said.

'No reception here.'

'Where?'

'Come on.'

'You know I can trace this call.'

Ewan thought about that. They needed triangulation with phone masts. He looked around the spread of hills, couldn't see any. So if the nearest mast was miles away, did that mean it was less accurate?

'What can I do for you, Nina?'

She was sipping coffee by the sound of it. He pictured her in her Edinburgh office, it felt like a different planet. Crows blustered from a nearby tree, cawing and clacking. He spotted a buzzard circling high up through wisps of cloud.

'What's in Applecross?'

'What?'

'You know these people,' Nina said. 'What are they doing in Applecross?'

She was lagging behind the action just enough that he wanted to laugh. *These people.* She didn't realise he was one of these people, he was all in. He was running with fugitives and working out how to break into an impound lot in the middle of the night to rescue a telepathic octopus. He tried to get the smile off his face, in case she could hear it in his voice.

'I don't really know them.'

'You know more than we do, you've met them for a start.'

'I'm just following the story,' he deadpanned.

'How long are you going to keep this up?' Nina said, sighing. 'It feels personal. What's going on with you?'

'Nothing.'

'So tell me about Applecross.'

He thought about it. It suited them if the police thought they were in Applecross for as long as possible. Ewan guessed that Applecross wasn't exactly a metropolis, it wouldn't take long to go door to door. He wanted to throw them a false lead but couldn't think what. Anything about Ava they would check with her husband. Lennox had never been outside Edinburgh. And if he mentioned Heather they would find the ex-husband, leading them here.

'I honestly don't know,' he said weakly.

Nina sipped and sighed. 'I've just about had enough. You're dicking me around so much.'

'So why call?'

A long pause. 'Let's just say I'm not enamoured with our visitors from down south.'

'Fellowes?'

'I think it would be best if we find these people first. Fellowes doesn't intend to bring them in for gentle questioning. You saw the guys he was with.'

'Where is he?'

Nina laughed. 'Come on. You don't tell *me* anything, then expect me to give up info just like that?'

'Have you told him about Applecross?'

Silence down the line. 'Not yet.'

Ewan heard a noise and turned to the trees. The crows had settled back in the branches but were calling to each other, the buzzard still overhead. The crows had strength in numbers, were looking out for each other. Sometimes you can survive even if you're not top of the food chain.

'Ewan, you do realise that Scotland runs out eventually? Edinburgh to Ratagan, the campervan in Drumnadrochit, now they're in Applecross. The Highlands are big but they don't go on forever. Eventually there's no place left to run except the Atlantic.'

Ewan thought about Sandy. Maybe that's where they were heading, back to the water.

'Campervan?' He'd waited until she mentioned it so as not to make her suspicious. He was glad this wasn't a video call, his face would've given him away.

'Come off it, Mr Ahead-of-the-Game. You already know the Highland police have the van.'

'News to me.'

He wanted to ask if they'd searched it, had forensics in, if Sandy was captured or dead or in some weird lab. But the fact she mentioned the van matter-of-fact was good. It meant the local cops hadn't searched it yet and Fellowes didn't know.

'Found it in a random spot check being repaired in a garage by Loch Ness.'

She was fishing but he didn't bite.

The sky had darkened but there was still enough light to see. The crows took off again, a fluster of wings as they swirled in a chaotic pattern. The buzzard swooped towards them, aiming for the heart of the birds. Instead of scattering, the crows rose to meet it, shrieking and flapping, a maelstrom of noise. The buzzard turned away to find easier prey. The crows settled back into the tree.

'So what now?' Ewan said, then realised his phone had gone dead. At first he thought Nina had just had enough, but his phone had no bars. He wondered how long he'd been listening to a dead line.

He walked back to the house. As he came out of the trees, he saw Heather standing outside the front door, hugging her mug of tea.

'Hey,' she said, then, nodding towards the house, 'I just needed some air.'

Ewan thought about that. She was a beautiful woman, same age as him, and they had flirted on the phone the other day.

'You never said if anyone would miss *you* back home,' Heather said.

'What?'

'On the phone yesterday. When you were fishing about my romantic life.'

'Jesus, Heather, I wasn't—'

'It's OK.' She pointed her mug at the front door. 'Now you know, an ex-husband who's moved on to a younger model.'

There was something more than that, a sorrow that hung over her that he couldn't place.

'I'm not doing any better,' he said. 'My ex-wife Diana and our two daughters live in Christchurch, New Zealand. With Greg, a property developer they now call Daddy.'

'I'm sorry.'

He shrugged. 'It is what it is. You got kids?'

He realised from her face it was a mistake. Sometimes, he just couldn't shut up, always had to know more.

She recovered and thought for a moment, glanced at him then away.

'We had a daughter, Rosie.' She let that 'had' hang between them for what seemed like a lifetime. 'Leukaemia.'

'Christ, I'm so sorry,' Ewan said, mortified. 'I shouldn't have asked, I'm a fucking idiot.'

She waved that away. 'It's OK. It's part of who I am now. There's no word for a parent grieving their child, isn't that insane?'

Ewan wanted to hug her, but knew enough not to. When this was all over, he would get to know her, really get to know her. When this was all over.

37
LENNOX

He looked past Ewan and Paul in the truck to the darkness outside. On the other side of the loch occasional lights glimmered in the distance. He remembered being in that water with Sandy, surrounded by their body, gliding with such power.

He scrunched his eyes shut and touched his temples, paused the Paramore track playing on his headphones. He didn't think it made a difference but he'd seen it in enough movies to try. He concentrated on Sandy, touched his earlobe and tugged, hoped to hear their voice ring.

Nothing.

Maybe they were sleeping or out of range. Or dead.

He resumed playing the track as they left the loch behind, the land flattening to a floodplain of trees, fields and sheep, just visible in the night. It was a shadow world, darkness except for their headlights. He never saw proper darkness back in Edinburgh, there was always ambient light in a city. He looked up and saw stars, more than ever before, strings and patterns instead of the occasional flicker back home. He wondered about Saturn, Enceladus. He imagined what it would be like to have a giant ringed planet taking up half the sky, looming over everything.

The van was tense. He didn't know what was happening with Ewan and Paul, but it had to do with Heather. Lennox tried to disappear into the melodies and groove in his ears. He closed his eyes, imagined hearing Sandy step into the track, start singing over it in their weird head voice. He wondered for the millionth time what his birth mother was like – tall or short, fat or thin, black or white. He'd created countless scenarios to explain why she might've given him up or why he was taken from her. She was an international spy or a promising Olympic gymnast, focusing on her career. Ridiculous pipe dreams. Most likely she was an addict or in an abusive relationship, mental-health problems, unable to look after herself, let alone another human.

He thought about Geoff back at the children's home, the nearest he had to a father figure in the last few years. He was just a balding middle-aged manager, struggling to cope like everyone else. The one thing Geoff had taught him was to be kind, think of the feelings of others. And Lennox had repaid him by stealing his car. Thinking of the children's home made him remember Estelle, the twelve-year-old who obviously had a crush on him, followed him around both at home and at school, stared at him across the playground. It was annoying but, like everyone at the home, she had abandonment issues and he couldn't hold it against her. He wondered how she would get on without him. He'd jumped in to protect her a couple of times at school from dickhead bullies. Without him there, she might get picked on more, and he felt bad about that. She would be sad but soon her affections would find some other target. We all need someone to hold on to, to keep us going, even if we don't know why.

The flow of the groove in his ears had a soothing effect, and he almost forgot where he was and what he was about to do. Eventually he opened his eyes and could see Paul was talking. He sighed and stopped the track.

'I don't want to know what you're doing tonight but can you at least tell me what happened down south?'

Ewan was in the middle seat. He made an exaggerated turn to Lennox, to hand the explanation over to him. Lennox just stared him out. Ewan straightened his shoulders and turned back.

'What do you mean?'

Paul slowed as they came up behind an Asda lorry. They drove past a golf course, over a bridge, through a roundabout and into a more built-up area. This was the start of Inverness.

'Come on,' Paul said. 'The news said you went missing after two violent incidents in East Lothian. That you shouldn't be approached.' He glanced at Lennox. 'You don't seem like violent criminals.'

Lennox shrugged.

'I was married to Heather for sixteen years, I know her. She's the most caring woman I've ever met. She wouldn't be involved without good reason.'

'You should take this up with her,' Ewan said.

The streets were lined with buildings now, but it still had the feel of a dinky city, light traffic, small houses, a sense of space.

'I'm asking you,' Paul said.

Lennox didn't want to be a part of this. These two were sparring over Heather, the same macho bullshit he saw everywhere. He hated alpha males, whether they were old journalists, divorced truck drivers, school bullies or random cops.

'It's a misunderstanding,' Ewan said.

'Whatever you've got Heather mixed up in, she doesn't deserve it. She could do with a fucking break, understand?'

'If she's so amazing how come you're divorced?'

The air chilled in the cab. They drove over a wide river and Lennox saw church spires, lots of grass.

'We went through some stuff,' Paul said. 'You don't want to know.'

'Try me,' Ewan said.

Paul went over a roundabout too fast, then a couple more turns. The shops and houses were replaced by offices and factories, corrugated iron walls and plastic signage. Fences around the buildings, CCTV up high.

'Our daughter died of leukaemia,' Paul said. 'We never came back from that.'

Lennox thought about Heather. Stones in her pockets, saved by Sandy. He squeezed his eyes shut and tried again.

<Sandy? Are you there?>

It was like Paul had sucked the air out of the truck. Lennox felt embarrassed for Ewan, a hapless guy stumbling through, just like everyone else. He thought he knew something, but he didn't. That's what Lennox was coming to understand from Sandy, none of them had a clue about life, the way the universe worked. There was so much mysterious, incomprehensible shit out there making a mockery of their pathetic concerns, their wee lives.

'Anyway,' Paul said to Ewan. 'What's your interest in this? You weren't mentioned in the news. How come you're involved?'

Ewan shook his head.

'I was given a story,' he said under his breath. 'Told to follow up, but it didn't make sense. So I kept asking questions and it led me here.'

The truck slowed in an industrial estate. They went past a kitchen showroom, Scottish Water offices. Paul peered at the signs in the streetlight. Lennox noticed that the lights were far apart, gloomy areas between. They turned past an Asian food wholesaler and a Volvo garage.

Lennox concentrated again, clenched his fists. <Sandy?>

Paul turned to Ewan and Lennox. 'Just don't fuck with Heather. If you fuck with her, you fuck with me. Understand?'

Paul pulled in between overhead lights. He put on the handbrake and nodded across the road.

'We're here.'

There was a large hangar with *Carter's Recovery* over the door, a giant carwash for articulated lorries and a concrete lot full of cars and vans, all enclosed by a high fence topped with barbed wire. The gate was locked with spikes on top but it looked easy to climb.

<Partial Sandy-Lennox!>

Lennox jumped so hard he thumped his fist on the roof of the truck.

<Partial Sandy-Lennox, we are together again.>

The joy in Sandy's voice was unmistakable and it ran through Lennox's body like an electric shock.

38
HEATHER

The blanket of stars above her was astounding. She'd never seen so many shimmering lights across the sky. The moon cast a ghostly glow over the fields next to the house, light spilling from the kitchen in two thin beams.

She was on a bench in the back garden, although there was no separation between the garden and the miles of grass in every direction. She could see two houses across the glen, beacons in the darkness, and thought about the Fidra lighthouse and Yellowcraigs. She looked up again, picking out shapes and patterns, lines of stars that meant something to the ancient Greeks, gods fighting or hunting or cavorting. So much life up there.

She thought about Sandy, their communication with Lennox was so opaque. But then she wondered what it would be like if they developed the ability to talk to all animals. You might literally understand what a monkey, eagle or octopus was saying, but would it actually make sense? Their worldviews were so completely alien. How can we ever hope to bridge that divide between utterly different minds? Sandy didn't even have a single mind. Lennox talked about octopuses having a collection of mini-brains around their bodies making autonomous decisions. That's why Sandy was plural, a collective of consciousnesses like a hive mind. Working together but separate. A bit like her, Ava, Lennox and Ewan.

Light spilled from the back door and Iona appeared, silhouetted against the doorway. 'Mind if I join you?'

Heather gritted her teeth. 'Sure.'

Iona sat on the bench, moving with careful grace. She looked up. 'Beautiful, isn't it?'

'Stunning.'

'It's so peaceful.'

'I can see why you and Paul live here.'

'It's good for us.'

Heather glanced at Iona as she looked at the sky. Long, slender neck, beautiful skin, kind eyes.

'I was just thinking,' Heather said. 'The menfolk are off gallivanting while we womenfolk sit at home and twiddle our thumbs.'

'Like something out of *The Odyssey*,' Iona said.

'Such a misogynist cliché.'

Iona shook her head. 'But neither of us is that kind of woman, are we?'

'And they're not alpha males either.'

'I hate all that shit.'

'Same.'

'Yet, here we are, staring at the stars.'

Heather laughed. She wondered about Iona's life, what had led her here to Heather's grieving ex-husband.

'I know this is hard for you,' Iona said eventually. 'Being here, seeing Paul.'

Heather nodded. A dull throb at the base of her skull made her raise a hand to her neck. She thought about her brain slowly killing her.

'You were a surprise,' she said. 'He never mentioned you.'

'But you weren't in touch, right?'

The tone of Iona's voice made Heather realise she was nervous. She tried to see it from Iona's side, an ex-wife with a whole bunch of history turns up and asks for help.

'No, we didn't stay in touch.'

'He never really mentioned you,' Iona said. 'To be brutally

honest, I was glad. But I realise it runs deep. He talks about Rosie sometimes but then gets this look in his eye and clams up. It must be so hard.'

Heather reached into her pocket and touched the photo of Rosie. Thought about taking it out but didn't. 'It is.'

Iona leaned back a little. 'All that has come up again recently.' She looked at Heather. 'I wasn't sure if I should tell you but fuck it. I'm pregnant.'

Heather felt like she'd been cut adrift in the sea of stars, dizzying specs of light making her head pound. 'OK.'

'It wasn't planned,' Iona said. 'But I'm happy. We're happy.'

Heather swallowed, felt like she was drowning. She breathed in then her body shivered as she exhaled.

'Of course,' she said. 'You should be.'

'I shouldn't have said anything.'

'No.' Heather put a hand into the air between them. 'I'm glad you did. I'm happy for you. And Paul. He deserves to be happy.'

Iona shocked her by taking her hand. Heather almost jerked hers away. Iona's skin was soft and Heather caught a scent from her, hippyish but fresh.

'We all deserve happiness,' Iona said.

'You think?'

'Of course. But it's not easy to find. You have to grab it where you can.'

Heather removed her hand from Iona's as smoothly as she could, hoping it didn't seem weird. 'You and Paul are happy?'

'Yes. It took me a long time to realise that I deserved to be happy.'

Heather gave her a look.

Iona shrugged. 'I didn't have an idyllic childhood, let's put it that way.'

Another silence. Heather had no right to resent Paul or Iona and she tried hard to find the truth in that. But she was human and it stung that her ex-husband had another life, another child. After what happened. Iona was right, they all deserved happiness. The trick was how to find it.

Iona cleared her throat. 'Do you think the *menfolk* will be all right in Inverness?'

Heather thought about what she'd seen Sandy do. 'They'll be fine.'

'What's so important in that van anyway?'

Heather felt a familiar sweep of pain flooding in from her neck up the back of her skull, another tumour headache sent to destroy her. She swallowed hard, her mouth filling with saliva, and clutched at the bench underneath her. The stars spun overhead.

'Are you OK?' Iona said.

Heather leaned away from her, shaking her head, carried away by the pain pulsing behind her eyes, then her stomach heaved and she puked watery bile on the ground. When had she last eaten?

'Oh my God,' Iona said. Her voice sounded a million miles away.

Heather convulsed three more times, each one with less force, her stomach empty. The pain receded as quickly as it came, leaving her washed out in its wake. She was still gripping the bench as she spat and righted herself.

'You're not well,' Iona said.

Heather widened her eyes.

'How bad is it?'

Heather tried a nonchalant shrug, a shivering aftershock through her body. 'Not good.'

'Does Paul know?'

Heather breathed deeply, tried to come back to the world. 'You can't tell him.'

She looked at Iona, who held her gaze. Somehow she understood and nodded.

'Heather.' Ava's voice made Heather turn. She stood in the

doorway in the sweatshirt and joggers she'd borrowed from Iona, one hand resting on the frame, the other at her crotch. She stepped into the garden and Heather saw the material of the joggers was dark under her hand.

'I'm bleeding,' Ava said.

39
EWAN

Ewan couldn't let the kid go alone and Paul had made it clear he was only the driver, so he turned to Lennox. 'So, what's the plan?'

Lennox leaned in and spoke under his breath. 'They're here. Inside.'

'How do you know?'

Lennox tapped his ear. 'They talk to me.'

'Christ.'

Paul cranked the window and lit a cigarette, blew smoke out.

Lennox nodded across the road. 'The gate doesn't look too bad. There's bars across the middle I can use as footholds.'

'And big metal spikes on the top,' Ewan said.

'Hang on,' Paul said. The cigarette hung from his lip as he reached behind the seats. He opened a toolbox and rummaged. Ewan watched him and thought about how he didn't own a toolbox. Some guys were toolbox guys, and he wasn't one of them. He wondered if he would ever see his home back in Edinburgh again. It seemed an impossible dream.

Paul held up a pair of heavy bolt cutters. 'These will work on the fence.'

Lennox reached across and took them, then he was out of the truck, Ewan scrambling behind. They crossed the road, Lennox with his hood up, head down, bolt cutters hidden up his hoodie. He had an empty backpack on his shoulder that had been stuffed in the footwell for the journey.

'Hey,' Paul said from the cab.

They turned.

Paul nodded at the fence. 'Between the lights.' Then he looked at a CCTV camera on a pole. 'And away from the camera.'

'Thanks,' Ewan said and it sounded pathetic. He turned up the collar of his jacket but he was still obviously recognisable.

They reached the fence, knelt down in the weeds by the verge. Litter was caught in the scrub grass and fence links. Lennox pulled out the cutters and began snipping sections in a vertical line from the base up. When he'd done enough he bent one side away. Ewan bent the other and they stepped through.

There was enough light overspill to see around. The lot was flanked on the left by a cement works full of angular machinery and connecting funnels. Over the back were what looked like huge grain silos. It felt like they were being watched over by ancient gods. Dozens of cars and vans were parked up, squeezed into the space. Lennox walked along the first row, looking for any vehicle that was the right make and age. He had his finger to his ear like a bodyguard.

They moved to the next row. They found one camper but it was the wrong colour, much newer, bonnet caved in from an accident. Lennox jumped to the third row, ran up to each vehicle in the gloom, then away. Ewan moved to the fourth row, thinking about cameras. Maybe they weren't on CCTV when they cut the fence, but surely there was coverage here. But what else could they do? He tugged at his collar again, kept his head down, checked the vehicles he came across. When he got to the end of the row, Lennox was there.

'It's not here,' Lennox said.

Ewan looked around. Two articulated trucks were parked to the side of the lock-up garage, but there were no other vehicles.

'It must be in the garage.'

Lennox was already on his way, bolt cutters ready. The large, corrugated-iron door was padlocked at the bottom and he cut through the bolt easily. He pulled the door up, the crank and rattle was almost deafening.

'Jesus,' Ewan said.

Lennox lifted the door a couple of feet off the ground then rolled under like Indiana Jones. Ewan followed. Inside was darker so he switched on his phone torch, swept it around. There were a dozen vehicles in here, some on risers for mechanics to work underneath. Lennox disappeared into the gloom at the back and Ewan searched in the other direction. He found the campervan against the wall and felt a thrill run through him.

'Here.'

Lennox jogged over as Ewan got the spare keys out and opened the side door.

As soon as he did, he saw a shimmering light show, sinuous blues and greens pulsing into yellows and oranges, spotted patterns expanding and contracting, ripples over Sandy's body as they launched themself into Lennox's arms, tentacles swimming around him, touching his face, wrapping him in a hug, pulling him close. Lennox's face was lit up and grinning.

'Hello?'

This was from outside the lock-up, followed by the grind of the door opening further. A torch beam played over the vehicles.

'Shit, get down,' Ewan said, crouching behind a Nissan and yanking Lennox's sleeve.

Lennox dropped with Sandy still in his arms. He stared at them and the light show faded to muted greys then disappeared.

'Is someone in here?'

Inverness accent, rough and gravelly.

Ewan sneaked a look around the Nissan, saw a security uniform. The torch beam swept towards the car and he ducked back.

'Get them in there,' Ewan whispered, pointing at the backpack.

Lennox opened it and Sandy slid inside, shrinking their body and settling in, pulling tentacles inside.

Lennox zipped it closed. The noise of the zip was louder than Ewan expected.

'Hey,' the security guard said, torch sweeping in their direction. 'The police are on their way. You're in a lot of trouble.'

Ewan edged his head around the bumper, ducked back as the light swept past again. The guard was walking in their direction. The beam swept towards the back of the building and Ewan spotted their chance.

'Go.'

He shoved Lennox who bolted off, bag on his back, bolt cutters in hand. He was fast. Jesus, to be a teenager again. Ewan scurried towards the open door, looking in the direction of the guard. He didn't notice the oil canister until he tripped over it, heavy clang as oil sprayed over the ground and Ewan's legs, making him slip and fall.

'Hey.'

The torch beam lit him up and he could see the way to the door, where Lennox was already ducking under and away. He picked himself up and sprinted as fast as he could manage, slipping on the oil but righting himself.

'Come back,' the guard said, but Ewan didn't turn. He slid to the ground and rolled under the door, his knees grazing the tarmac. He stood and ran for the fence where he could see Lennox crouching to get through.

Beyond the fence, Paul had the engine running.

'We've got you on camera,' the guard shouted behind him. 'The police will get you.'

Ewan reached the fence and climbed through, heart pounding, knees aching, legs weak, but feeling more alive than he had in years. He heard a laugh and was surprised to realise it came from his own mouth.

40
AVA

She gripped the back of the chair and stared at her knuckles. She'd tried sitting down, lying flat, on all fours, but she couldn't get comfortable. So she stood in the kitchen and leaned on the chair. She felt the cramp in her uterus spread outward, grimaced at the tension in her body, watched her knuckles whiten.

It passed. But they weren't contractions, she was sure of it. Braxton Hicks, definitely. And there had been no more bleeding. She'd Googled it obviously. It was possibly still spotting in late pregnancy, maybe the cervix getting ready, or more worryingly there was some chat about the placenta detaching from the uterus.

They could easily do heart transplants these days, yet childbirth still felt like a black art, some form of ancient witchcraft. If men gave birth you could bet they would've worked out a trouble-free, painless way to do it. This felt like she was channelling the stress of a million years of womanhood. She felt sure it wasn't labour, but truly she had no fucking idea. She hated all that instinct stuff that went on around pregnancy, women telling her that she would just know how to be a good mother. What if her instincts were shit? What if she strangled the baby with her umbilical cord, what if her breasts didn't work, what if she couldn't look after her daughter?

She tried to breathe. In, out, in, out.

Iona came in with a woman younger than Ava. Blonde hair in a pony and fringe, big round glasses, chunky cardigan and high-waisted jeans. She looked like a teen influencer and Ava felt old.

'This is Doctor Millar,' Iona said.

'Katy,' the woman said. She held out her hand then dropped it after a few seconds of Ava staring at it.

Iona walked round the room. 'I work with her at Raigmore. She lives over the other side of the glen.'

Heather lurked in the doorway looking uncomfortable. Ava wanted to hug her.

Katy put an arm on Ava's back. 'Let's get you comfortable.'

Ava felt another cramp through her body and held her belly. She hadn't felt the baby move recently and that terrified her. What if something was wrong with her? Ava would rather die than fuck this up. The cramp got worse and her mind went hazy dealing with the pain. She let herself be led to the next room. She lay down on the sofa and waved OK when the doctor asked to examine her. Joggers and pants off in front of strangers and she couldn't think straight. She stared at cracks in the ceiling as she felt the doctor's gentle touch. The pain ebbed for a moment.

Katy didn't speak, just helped her pull her clothes back up. Then she sanitised her hands and took Ava's pulse and blood pressure. Checked her eyes with a torch, made her look in different directions.

She quizzed her about the blood and pain in a calm voice which started to work on Ava despite herself. She felt the anxiety in her chest gradually fading. It helped that the doctor was a woman. Ava had been controlled by men for too long.

She wondered where Michael was right now. Ewan had said he thought he was at Mum's house. That made Ava picture her mum going through all this shit when she had Ava. Being pregnant made you realise what a selfish brat you'd been your whole life.

But Michael had turned her mum against her in recent years, that's how it felt. It wasn't Mum's fault though, Michael had driven a wedge between them. Ava had fallen for his charm, so she couldn't blame Mum for the same thing.

'There's heavy spotting,' Katy said. 'That can sometimes happen even this late in pregnancy. It doesn't appear that labour has started, but these things are never a hundred percent. I think the cramps are Braxton Hicks. However your blood pressure is high. I'd recommend going to Raigmore for tests and an ultrasound.'

Ava shook her head and stared at a picture on the wall. It was a framed painting of Loch Ness, dark and brooding. She thought about Sandy and Lennox under the surface.

'I need to speak to Heather alone,' she said.

Katy and Iona stared at each other but went to the kitchen without speaking.

Ava caught Heather's look. She thought about what Heather went through, seeing her teenage daughter die, and felt sick.

'I can't go to hospital,' she said.

Heather took her hand. 'You have to do what's best for you and the baby.'

'It's Braxton Hicks and the bleeding stopped. This is overkill.'

'But your blood pressure.'

'What about Michael?' Ava said, touching her neck. 'He'll find me.'

'How?'

'He just will, he has ways. He's probably got nurses in every hospital on the lookout. To give a worried husband the nod, let him know I'm safe.'

Heather shook her head. 'They wouldn't do that.'

'You don't know him, what he's capable of. He's friends with the police. If they find us, that's it. It'll be the same for hospitals.'

'You could use a fake name.'

'The police know we're in this area, it's too risky.'

Heather stroked the back of Ava's hand. 'I think you're wrong but it's your decision. No one else can make it.'

Ava felt tears at those words. She could make her own decisions, she had agency. How long had it been since that was true? 'No hospital.'

She felt something in her stomach and grinned. The baby, flipping and squirming, pushing against her bladder, letting her know she'd made the right decision.

41
LENNOX

Paul gunned the engine. 'Fuck's sake.'

Lennox looked at the impound lot and saw the bobbing torch of the guard on the other side of the fence. Paul swerved the truck round the corner, engine growling as they raced through the industrial estate and onto Longman Road.

'I saw him coming to check the place,' Paul said eventually. 'But there was no way to let you know.'

Ewan was pale in the middle seat, sweat on his brow.

Lennox clutched the backpack on his lap, felt Sandy wriggle inside.

Paul glanced at him, then the bag.

Lennox stared at the bag. <Stay still.>

<Reason?>

<Just do it. Quiet.>

It was so good to hear that voice again. He'd felt like part of him was missing when Sandy was out of range. He'd always felt alone, an outsider at school. He felt it was him against the world and nobody could possibly understand. But Sandy understood. He imagined telling that to someone back home, then realised he didn't really have a home anymore. It had never felt like home to be honest. But here, in a van in the Highlands, with Sandy on his lap, he felt at home.

Ewan laughed. 'Fuck, that was something.'

Lennox had felt the buzz too but he'd been more concerned about Sandy. Now they were on the A82 leaving Inverness behind, he felt a wave of relief. He didn't know what he would do without

Sandy. Then he thought about the guys Ewan talked about, government goons or whatever.

'Whatever you got in there, I hope it's worth it,' Paul said as he turned off the main road into the hills.

Lennox and Ewan shared a look and Ewan smiled. Part of Lennox wanted to tell Paul, let the world know about this incredible creature who'd travelled millions of miles to become part of Lennox's life. He stayed quiet and made sure the zip on the bag was closed.

<Partial Sandy-Lennox happy.>

Lennox smiled. He wasn't sure if it was a question or statement. <Partial Sandy-Lennox happy.>

The road levelled out and he saw a glimmer of moonlight off a distant lochan like a shooting star. He remembered that first time he'd seen Sandy's light, come all the way from Enceladus to flood his brain with energy. And seeing Sandy's body on the shore next day.

<Sandy, when we first met, were you not well?>

A pause. <Long journey, loss of energy. Also, your gravity is strong, it took time to adapt our body. Tiring.>

<Why are you here? Why come all this way?>

Another pause. He wondered if they were consulting the internet, trying to assimilate their experience into something that could make sense to him.

<We ... don't know.>

That's the first time he'd heard hesitation from them.

<How can you not know?>

He spotted something through the fabric of the backpack, a bright pink pattern of glowing and throbbing. He shuffled the bag to the truck door and shielded it with his body.

Paul glanced over then his eyes went back to the road.

<Sandy partial not fully understand. Better understand Sandy-Other Sandy complete.>

Lennox frowned at the bag. <Other Sandy? Complete?>

He saw Paul's house to the left, they were nearly there.

<We have found Other Sandy, while Sandy-Lennox partial stretched.>

'What?' Lennox said out loud.

Paul and Ewan turned to him, Ewan glaring, Paul confused.

Lennox swallowed. <Do you mean there are others like you?>

<Others *are* us. Sandy-Other Sandy complete.>

Were they part of the same entity? <Here on earth?>

<Near.>

<Where?>

The zip of the bag opened an inch and the end of a tentacle darted out and touched his hand, suckers gripping tight. He lost all balance and shot through the roof of the truck, flew through the night sky, high enough to see Loch Ness to his left like a tiny puddle. He was wrapped in Sandy's body again, this time racing through the night, tumbling and spinning. He felt calm, heartbeat slow and regular, warm and safe in Sandy's embrace, tentacles holding his back. The stars were brilliant, more brilliant than he'd ever seen, and he wondered if he was seeing things the way Sandy was. Animals on earth had different perceptions, so maybe this was what the world looked like to Sandy.

He tried to speak but his mouth didn't work. He tried to think a message but his brain wouldn't let him. He had more composure than last time Sandy showed him something, realised it was some kind of freaky mind projection.

He looked down at the shape of Scotland. He could see the lights of towns further south, but directly below was darkness, just rippled moonlight on lochs, mountains and forests. He felt like a baby in a womb, pushed Sandy's body to test it, felt it spring back.

They descended over knuckled mountains and swooped along a large sea loch. Lennox remembered the fighter jets at Ratagan, the noise and arrogance of them. He and Sandy were silent as they flew low then went under the loch's surface with a tiny splash. They sped up then leaped out again and Lennox saw a small town at the head of the loch, a spray of white houses along the shore, a cumbersome ferry anchored at a jetty, lights on and engine running.

Sandy went straight up for a few moments then spun and dived under the water right next to the ferry. Lennox saw something in the distance, glowing lights getting larger, millions of sweeping patterns and shapes in every colour imaginable, some he couldn't put words to. He sensed intense happiness, a feeling of homecoming from Sandy that overwhelmed him as the lights got closer and he started to make out shapes in the gloom.

'We're here.'

Paul's voice pulled him back to the truck and his head thumped against the headrest as he opened his eyes. His mouth was dry and he saw they were at the house. He glanced at the bag but the zip was closed. He touched it and felt movement, relief flooding his body.

Sandy's voice clear in his mind. <You call it Ullapool.>

42
HEATHER

She liked being awake when everyone else in the house was asleep. She remembered weekend mornings in Dirleton with Paul and Rosie when they were her world. She would get up at sunrise without an alarm. The baby years with Rosie had destroyed her ability to sleep in. Kids ruined you in so many ways but they amplified your life a millionfold too. She used to sit on the patio and look over the garden, steam from her coffee disappearing into the air like a vanishing spirit.

Now she sat on the bench outside Paul and Iona's house and watched the vapour from her coffee curl and become invisible. She looked at the patch of ground where she'd vomited last night, but Iona must've cleaned it up.

She looked around and tried to imagine she was back home. Except she didn't have a home anymore and this was her ex-husband's place. New wife, new baby, new life.

She read the sign by the door, *Toll Sionnach*. The Foxhole. That meant a hiding place for snipers, not exactly a safe refuge, although safer than being out in the open.

Sparrows flitted in the trees, a thin burn rippled over stones. She looked up the lane, no movement except for a buzzard high overhead in the pale sky.

She remembered late last night, when the others got back from rescuing Sandy. Lennox had taken her and Ewan into a bedroom down the hall and laid out everything he knew for them. Heather had presumed Sandy was alien, but had never discussed it explicitly. Sandy was from Enceladus, one of Saturn's moons.

Lennox talked about a moon-wide ocean under a crust of ice. Saturn looming in the sky, Enceladus racing through its dusty rings as it orbited. The sun a tiny dot. Heather wondered what the night sky looked like from Enceladus.

Lennox also told them that he could communicate with Sandy at a distance because they put a part of their tentacle in his ear, like a radio receiver. There were others like Sandy, other Enceladons, and they needed to be reunited. Somewhere near Ullapool. This was insane. A creature from another planet here in Scotland. Ava and Heather absorbed it quietly. Ewan had seen Sandy attack Michael, so he knew they were exceptional. He was still shocked, but as a journalist he kept asking questions. How? Why? Why them? Why now? Lennox couldn't answer.

The sound of the kitchen door made Heather turn and there was Paul, coffee in hand, bed hair, rubbing his jaw.

'Mind if I join you?'

She waved at the space on the bench. She was reminded of last night, Iona revealing she was pregnant. Paul sat down and she imagined the two of them were back home, Rosie still sleeping inside, exhausted from the chemo. Back when worrying about her was all Heather had to do. Now she was worried for the others. Lennox roughly the same age as Rosie, Ava about to give birth, Sandy. Iona in her first trimester.

She sipped her coffee and Paul did the same.

'I spoke to Iona last night,' she said.

Paul nodded, blew on his coffee mug.

Heather swallowed. 'She seems nice.'

Paul sucked his teeth. 'I should've told you about her before now.'

Heather looked at him and he held her gaze. 'Yes, you should've.'

'But I didn't want you to think...'

'That you moved on? I'm glad you did.'

Paul shook his head. 'It's not about moving on, you know that. We can't leave the past behind, we carry it with us. But at some point we have to forgive ourselves and start living again. It's what Rosie would've wanted.'

'It's not that simple.' Heather blew a laugh out her nose and took the picture of Rosie from her pocket, unfolded it, showed Paul.

He swallowed. 'Wow.'

Heather nodded. 'I brought it from the house. I'm not sure if I'll ever be back there.'

Paul touched the picture, traced a finger along Rosie's hair, down her shoulder. 'She was so...'

Heather felt herself well up. Paul was right, it wasn't about moving on, it was about carrying on with the weight of it all on your shoulders.

She thought about stones in her pockets, cancer in her brain. The hole in her heart filled by all the noise and bluster of the last week. She'd been too busy surviving and protecting others to think about herself. She felt like a mother again.

'She told me,' Heather said. She looked at the photo for a few more moments, then put it away.

Paul glanced at her then looked down. He knew what she meant. She remembered reading somewhere that only seven percent of communication was verbal, the rest was body language. She knew Paul's thoughts from his face, his gestures. She wondered about other forms of communication, the buzzard above, sparrows in the trees, worms in the earth. Sandy. How can we ever really understand?

'I'm sorry,' Paul said.

'Don't be.'

'We didn't mean for Iona to get pregnant.' He threw a smile her way. 'But these things happen.'

'It's good.' Heather sipped her coffee to hide the waver in her voice. 'Life goes on.'

'Heather, please.'

Heather shook her head.

The sound of the latch on the kitchen door made them turn. Heather expected Iona and felt guilty about sitting here with Paul. But the door opened and it was Sandy, vivid in the morning sunlight, body throbbing peaceful green and orange, two tentacles gripping the edge of the door as they glided into the space outside the house, the other three tentacles like legs propelling them.

The sparrows fell silent and Paul dropped his mug on the paving stones. The mug cracked and coffee splattered, darkening the ground as Paul scrambled behind the bench.

'What the fuck?'

Sandy looked around, eyes wide, black orbs surrounded by gold, spots on their tentacles as they held three aloft, tasting the air. Heather was already used to their behaviour, knew they were exploring the environment. They shuffled closer and Paul froze. He glanced at Heather. She raised her mug and sipped her coffee as Sandy scuttled past them, lowering their body gracefully to the ground then sliding into the thin rivulets of the burn, nestling in the clear water, splashing their tentacles.

Paul stared.

Heather wondered if she should speak but couldn't think what to say.

Sandy sank their body deeper into the water with a crunch of pebbles, flattened into the landscape. Their body took on the colours of the water and the bank, green and brown, grey and blue-black. They splashed water over their head, clearly having fun.

Paul turned to Heather. 'This is what they were getting from the van last night.'

Heather nodded. 'Their name is Sandy.'

'What the fuck is going on?'

'It's hard to explain.'

His knuckles tensed as he gripped the bench. 'Try me.'

She sipped coffee.

'Heather, I risked my neck rescuing a fucking octopus?'

'They're not an octopus.'

'What?'

Heather pointed. 'Only five tentacles.'

'Heather, fuck's sake. What is this about?'

Heather thought about the weird comet, her life saved, the stroke, the recovery, being drawn to Sandy. The drive through the Highlands. Enceladus, just the idea of that. They were all in so deep. She was in deeper than she could ever explain. She didn't have the words.

Paul couldn't take his eyes off Sandy in the burn. Heather was the same, watching them splash in the trickle of cold water.

'Everything is about Sandy,' she said.

43
AVA

She'd slept soundly and that worried her. Normally she was kept awake by the need to pee, the baby shuffling around, heartburn, sore ankles and back, sore everything. And it was strange that worry hadn't kept her awake. The doctor said things were OK but wanted Ava to go to hospital. She thought about how easy she would be to find in a hospital.

She eased out of bed, pulled on a dressing gown Iona had given her and opened the curtains. The sloping fields led her eye across the glen. The mountains on the other side gave her a sense of perspective. How long would it take to get over there? Was there a mirror Toll Sionnach on that side with an oddball cast of misfits protecting an alien?

She breathed, rubbed her stomach. No movement. She wanted nothing more than to have her daughter out of there, hold her. But she also wanted her to stay put forever.

She left the room and walked to the kitchen where Lennox sat at the table with his headphones on, a big pile of toast in front of him.

Ava walked to the kettle. 'Hey.'

'Hey.' He demolished another slice.

She switched the kettle on and stared out of the window, saw Heather and Paul in a heated discussion. 'What's that about?' She had to speak over the sound of the kettle.

Lennox glanced up. 'Paul met Sandy earlier.'

'Shit.'

'Yep.'

'And?'

Lennox shrugged and chewed. 'I think she's talking him down from the edge.'

'He's not going to give us up, is he?'

Lennox looked at her. 'I don't think so, he seems cool. Are you OK, you look tired.'

'Fine.' She made a mug of tea, watched the two outside. Lots of hand waving, head shaking. But the body language was friendly, comfortable.

She turned to Lennox. 'Where's Sandy now?'

'Downstairs bathroom.' He nodded back the way she'd come. 'They like the water. Iona is upstairs, she doesn't know yet. We can't stay long.'

Ava sighed. 'It doesn't feel like we can ever stay in one place for long.'

Lennox lifted his shoulders noncommittally. 'Maybe in Ullapool.'

Ava had her mug at her lips and paused. 'What?'

'It's a town on the coast, northwest of here.'

'I know where it is,' Ava said. 'Why Ullapool?'

'Sandy wants to go there.'

'They told you that?'

He nodded and finished his last piece of toast.

Ava sipped tea. 'Why?'

'I think there are others there.'

'Like Sandy? How many?'

Another shrug. Ava didn't know what to think. It was the right thing to get Sandy back to their tribe or species or whatever. But what did that mean for the rest of them? What did it mean for humanity? What did it mean for her and the baby?

Lennox was on his phone, the conversation done.

Ava walked down the hall and paused outside the bathroom. She heard light splashing. Footsteps down the stairs, then Iona appeared.

'Hi,' Ava said, her face reddening.

'You OK?'

'Cool.'

It looked like Iona would stop to talk but Ava's body language must've told her otherwise and she moved on to the kitchen.

Ava waited then turned the door handle, went inside.

Sandy was in a large, roll-top bath, chipped and scuffed. They were glowing pastel colours, yellow to lilac through green. Slow pulses along their tentacles, body getting brighter and darker, a slow throb. Three tentacles were draped over the side of the bath, moving around the rim.

Ava approached and Sandy seemed to notice, their body enlarging, shapes moving over the surface. Their head turned so that Ava could see their eyes, black and gold, bigger than she'd seen before. She stared into those eyes for a long time, tried to tell something from them. The windows to the soul, apparently.

'I need your help,' Ava said, putting her tea down on the side of the sink and stepping closer.

Sandy's head flashed blue-green, the same colour Ava saw overhead in the car all those days ago.

Ava was at the side of the bath. It felt normal, talking to an octopus in a bath in the Highlands. This was her life now. It was amazing how quick you could get used to something once your eyes were opened.

'You seem to ... know things,' she said. 'You can sense things inside us that we don't know for ourselves.'

She took her dressing gown off so she was just in a borrowed T-shirt and pants. She stepped into the bath and Sandy made space for her, moved to the other end. The water was cold, goose-pimpling her skin, legs reddening as she slid into the water and caught her breath. The T-shirt soaked through and stuck to her body. She felt the brush of tentacles against her legs, inquisitive and precise. Sandy faced her, the water between them a nest of tentacles squirming around.

'I need to know if my baby is OK,' Ava said, breath shallow from the cold. 'Can you speak to her?'

Sandy's colouring darkened to purple and maroon, dull pulses of light in their tentacles. They offered a tentacle to Ava's hand and another hovered by the side of her face. Ava took them, felt a jolt of energy through her.

<Do we have your permission?>

She gasped. The water seemed warmer now. Maybe she was just used to it or maybe she'd pissed herself again.

'You have permission.'

The suckers of one of Sandy's tentacles attached to her wrist while another tentacle snaked upwards, its tip entering her ear. She felt dizzy and overwhelmed, closed her eyes as the world spun, flashes under her eyelids as she felt Sandy's presence sweep through her. How was this possible? She felt like they were the same being, somehow separate and distinguishable but parts of the same thing. Warmth flooded her chest and stomach, made her groin and legs tingle. She felt the baby respond, a moment of stillness followed by enthusiastic movement, full of energy.

<Welcome new Sandy-Ava-Ava-offspring partial.>

Ava tried to speak but her mouth didn't work. She held her breath and sank her head under the water, tried to feel what it was like to be a sea creature.

<How is this possible?> She was shocked that the question formed in her head, crystalline and clear.

<New partial is good knowledge. Welcome new partials for all positive entities. New entities share love.>

She felt a swell at the word 'love'. She still had her head underwater. <Ava offspring. How is she?> She sensed a moment of puzzlement as more suckers attached to her arm.

<Ava-Ava-offspring share body. Not mind?>

How could they share a mind? They were two different people. <No. Humans can't do that.>

The tentacle in her ear shivered.

<Unusual.>

Her lungs began to burn a little. She almost raised her head to take a breath but something stopped her. She felt the baby kick. <Please.>

The pattern changed on Sandy's tentacles, like arrows pointing away from their body. Two tentacles rested on Ava's stomach, moving slowly.

<Ava offspring is happy entity. Mind and body. Excited to meet Ava. Excited to meet Sandy-Ava partial.>

Ava was running out of breath now, but worried that if she broke the surface of the bathwater she would break the spell. She felt tears leave her eyes and drift away in the bath. <I love her so much.>

A flash of bright green ran up Sandy's body. <Ava offspring is love. Sandy-Ava-Ava-offspring partial is love.>

Ava sat up and gulped in air, water splashing on the floor, Sandy's tentacles retracting from her ear and arm. The baby kicked again, keen to get out and meet her, alive and healthy and happy and full of love. Ava wiped tears from her eyes and smiled as widely as she could ever remember.

44
LENNOX

He breathed in sharp air and stared at miles of sky. Candy-floss clouds flitted across the blue, crows like smudged thumbprints. He'd been tramping over the moors around Toll Sionnach, feeling his trainers squelch through the moss, spotting rabbits and foxes in the heather. Wet Leg whooped and clattered in his headphones, a weird juxtaposition to the serenity around him, but he liked that.

He felt like there was no one else on earth just now. He imagined never going back to the house, just traipsing across these never-ending mountains. But the land ended, eventually he would reach the sea. And that made him think of Sandy.

He'd come away from the house to get a better reception on his phone. He'd Googled their story but the news sites hadn't updated recently. He'd also searched for Oscar Fellowes, along with government, police, even special forces. He found a mention on a government website but no details, just a faceless civil servant, apparently.

He'd also looked up Ullapool. A pretty town on Loch Broom, the place to catch a ferry to the Hebrides. Whitewashed cottages on the shore, a chippy and two bookshops. Loch Broom was the key, not the town. He had to see the world like Sandy. Seventy percent of the earth's surface was water, it was wrong to think of the planet as land-based. Anyone coming from space would assume that life was marine.

He'd tramped in a large loop from the house, far enough that it was a bump on the horizon now. He walked through trees then out the other side and stopped. A hundred yards away was a small loch, rotting tree stumps jutting from the edge. Amongst the stumps were five deer chewing on moss, their hides glossy in the sunshine, woody antlers like furniture. One of the deer wasn't red like the rest but a dirty white, pale eyes, stark against the land.

Lennox pressed pause on his music and watched the deer for a long time, listening to his own breath, determined not to distract them. They moved along the edge of the loch, occasionally looking up. Lennox crouched to make himself smaller. He heard his heartbeat in his ears and wondered about Sandy. There were millions of different animals on Earth, wouldn't there also be countless species on Enceladus?

He tried to imagine why they were here. Introducing a species from one planet to another was unfathomable. Humans had spent hundreds of years categorising and killing animals on earth, a colossal genocide. What would we do to a whole moon full of other species, potentially billions of beings? It would take a hundred lifetimes to understand them and that's if humans considered them benign. If they *were* benign.

He felt dizzy at the scale of it, too much to think about. How an individual from an ecosystem a billion kilometres away had come into their lives just like that. What it could lead to.

And he wondered how the fuck they had got here. He liked studying engineering, had always been interested in how things worked, and he knew enough that a journey across a billion kilometres of frozen, empty space was a logistical nightmare. Sandy was so different from humans, didn't appear to have a spacecraft or vessel of any kind. But that was only one of a million questions he had – how did the telepathy work, how many others were there, were they all the same species or a variety, if there were others, where were they now, had Sandy and any others been spotted by telescopes, the military? And what about the strokes, and their seemingly random recovery?

But whenever he was with Sandy, talking to them, those

questions seemed to melt away as the space between them closed, and all he cared about was helping them.

The deer raised their heads and looked left in unison, ears pricked up. He followed their gaze and saw the roof of a police car flickering behind a hedge, heading for the house.

The deer bounded in the other direction into a gully and out of sight. Lennox ran towards the house, keeping his eye on the car. He squelched and fumbled through the moor, saw the car turn into the drive for Toll Sionnach. He kept running, regulating his breath, approaching through the trees at the front of the house. He slowed to walking, got his breath back, quietened his body, touched the beech trees as he passed, feeling moss under his fingers.

He heard voices and crept the last few yards to the edge of the trees. He saw two cops, a man and a woman, standing in protective vests, thumbs in their belts, talking to Paul outside the house.

He inched forward to listen.

'Come on, Paul, just let Jenna and me have a wee look round then we'll be on our way.'

Paul was deadpan. 'I don't think so, Fergus.'

Fergus straightened his shoulders. 'How long have we known each other?'

'I can't do it.'

Jenna raised her chin. 'Why not?'

'Not unless you have a warrant.'

Fergus shook his head. 'You know we don't have one yet. We've only just got the info from CCTV.'

Jenna stepped to Paul's truck. 'Would you care to tell us what your vehicle was doing outside Carter's in the middle of the night?'

'Out for a drive.'

Fergus frowned. 'In an industrial estate in Inverness.'

'I have trouble sleeping.'

'Was anyone with you who can confirm your story?' Jenna said.

Paul sucked his teeth. 'No.'

Jenna looked at the truck, checking from all angles, then she crouched and looked underneath. Lennox froze. If she turned round now she would see him.

Fergus shook his head. 'There was a break-in at Carter's. It looks very much as if you were involved.'

'Ridiculous,' Paul said.

Jenna peeked inside the truck, driver's side then passenger. Again, if she just changed her focus she would spot Lennox's hair amongst the foliage.

She turned back to Paul. 'You were seen yesterday in Drumnadrochit with the owners of a campervan.'

'OK.'

'The same van that the police recovered and placed in Carter's for safekeeping.'

Paul shrugged.

Fergus sighed. 'We're very interested in finding the owners.'

He stepped closer and lowered his voice, and Lennox strained to hear.

'I'm getting heat from high up on this, Paul. I can't let this one go.'

Paul held up his hands. 'And I can't let you in the house.'

Jenna stepped up to Paul. 'Then you'll need to come to the station and answer a few questions.'

Fergus shook his head. 'I'm sorry, mate.'

Paul smiled. 'It's fine, let's go.'

He walked to the police car, Fergus behind. Jenna stared at the house then looked around. Lennox ducked into the trees and held his breath, pressed his back against a trunk, smelled resin and moss.

He heard the car doors open and close and the engine start. He waited until the sound of tyres on gravel had faded then he emerged and stared at the police car vanishing in the distance.

45
AVA

Sitting down made her back hurt, but standing made her ankles sore. If motherhood was supposed to be so natural, why did it hurt so much? She leaned her hip against the kitchen worktop. She felt like an observer at a summit, Iona and Heather either side of the kitchen table like some Cold War standoff. Lennox and Ewan skulked at the edge of the room. She threw Lennox a glance which he caught and returned so deadpan that she almost laughed.

'He's in jail because of you,' Iona said, hands agitated on the tabletop.

Heather had her fingers splayed, trying to prevent an approaching tidal wave. 'He's not in jail, they just took him in for questioning.'

'About a break-in you got him involved in.'

Ewan swallowed and took a seat between the two women. 'We didn't make him do anything, he volunteered.'

Iona turned to him, cheeks flushed. 'I knew you were trouble. We never should've helped. You're wanted by the police, for fuck's sake.'

'Iona,' Heather said.

She swung back to face Heather. 'My heart sank when you called him, you know that? We'd both seen the news but I could tell from the look on his face. He's a good man and you used that.'

Heather shook her head. 'We didn't have anyone else to turn to.'

Iona slammed the table and Ava jumped, banging her hip against the worktop.

'What the hell is this about, anyway?' Iona said, shaking. 'I mean, look at you all.'

She waved around the room. She was right, they were ridiculous, the weirdest four musketeers you could imagine.

'Paul didn't ask why you were running or why they're after you because he's too nice. I'm not. I want to know what this is about right now.'

Ava caught Lennox's eye. How to explain? She remembered sitting in the bath two hours ago with Sandy talking to her unborn baby. They couldn't tell Iona the truth, she would throw them out. She might anyway.

Ewan lifted his head. 'It's complicated.'

Iona gritted her teeth. 'You're the journalist, tell me this story, nice and simple.'

Heather reached towards Iona, who recoiled from her.

'I'm so sorry for getting you involved,' Heather said.

'Not good enough.' Iona seemed to lose her nerve and anger. 'What if they arrest him? We don't have a lawyer, I have no idea what I'll do if...'

She lowered her head, keeping in tears. Ava wanted to hug her but she would probably get a fist in the face.

Heather shook her head. 'He won't get arrested, he's done nothing wrong.'

'Since when did that matter?'

Heather's face was calm. 'He'll be home soon and we'll be gone, out of your life forever. I promise.'

Iona looked up. 'Promise?'

Heather was about to speak when a phone rang. The handset was mounted on the wall at the kitchen doorway. All five of them stared at it. Each ring made Ava tense up.

Iona scraped her chair back against the stone floor. 'Maybe that's him from the station.' She went to the doorway and picked up the phone. 'Hello?'

They all watched. The interruption gave the room a deflated feel.

Iona listened on the phone and looked round the room. Her eyes widened at Ava.

'Just a minute.' She covered the mouthpiece and held the handset out to Ava. 'It's for you.'

Ewan stood up. 'Who is it?'

'He wouldn't say.'

'No one knows we're here.'

The volume seemed to turn down in the room as Ava blinked heavily and felt a tremor up her legs. It could only be one person. Of course he would find her, what was she thinking?

'It's Michael,' she said.

Ewan shook his head.

'Hang up,' Heather said.

Ava bumped her hips off the worktop. 'No. I'll speak to him.'

Heather put a hand out. 'That's not a good idea.'

Ava waved it away. 'I might learn something.'

She crossed the room and reached for the phone. Iona hesitated then handed it over. Ava walked to the other room, stretching the coiled cord. She couldn't stand an audience for this. She looked at the rolling hills out of the window and composed herself. Clouds high in the sky. She put the phone to her ear, listened to the crackle. She could hear him breathing, recognised it somehow.

'Michael.' She imagined him tensing, trying to disguise his fury.

'Ava.' Calm, in charge. Michael knows best. 'Are you OK?'

She bridled at that, asking after her as if he cared. 'I'm fine.'

'And the baby?'

'What do you want?'

'Honey, please, I'm just worried about you. You're off with a bunch of strangers, in your condition, just out of hospital.'

'Tell me what you want.'

'I want us to be a family again,' he said softly. 'I want things back the way they were.'

Ava swallowed. 'You bullied and abused me for years. You controlled everything I did, made me a slave. You want that back?'

Silence, then he came back sounding hurt. 'I'm sorry if that's what you think, Ava, really. I just want what's best for us. I miss you so much.'

His voice cracked and she was amazed to hear him sobbing down the line. The brass neck of it. Shedding tears over not being able to rape his wife-slave.

'Shut up,' Ava said. 'You don't get to cry about me. You never gave a shit about me or the baby, this is all about control.'

She felt sick. Heartburn leapt up her throat and she swallowed it down.

'Please, Ava, come back.'

Ava stared out of the window. 'Go fuck yourself, Michael.'

'No.' His voice switched in an instant. 'You don't speak to me like that. I'm your husband.'

'You're nothing to me anymore.'

'You're my wife, Ava, and you're carrying my baby. I'm coming for you both. Either you come home or I keep the baby myself. You think they'll let you keep it after this? Losing your mind and running off with a teenage boy? You'll never see it again unless you stay with me. I'll have you committed, you know I can. You'll be in a mental hospital the rest of your life.'

'You're delusional,' Ava said, but the mention of the baby had got to her, just like he meant it to. 'You're never going to see me again.'

She walked back to the doorway. 'Fuck you, Michael.'

She slammed the handset down. Her body shook with adrenaline and only then did she realise she'd never asked how he got this number.

46
EWAN

'We have to leave.'

Ewan broke the silence that had fallen over them when Ava slammed the phone down. She trembled as she leaned her forehead against the wall. Ewan stood up and went to her, hovered a metre away. He wanted to hug her but the last thing she needed was a middle-aged deadbeat putting his hands on her. So he was surprised when she leaned into him and held on, crying into his shoulder. He felt like a dad again, able to be here and support. He thought of his family on the other side of the world and wondered how he could ever explain any of this to them. Then whether he would ever see them again.

Eventually Ava loosened her grip and stepped back, wiping her tears with the backs of her hands, fanning her face.

'Shit, that man gets to me.'

There was silence for a moment then Heather spoke. 'Ewan's right. If Michael knows we're here, so do others.'

Iona looked bamboozled. 'Who was that?'

'My husband,' Ava said. 'He wants me back to control me and take the baby.'

'How *does* he know you're here?' Iona said.

Ewan shook his head. 'Must be through the police. He knows people in the force. But he must be hammering his contacts to turn this up so quick. Inverness police found the camper, now they're talking to Paul. It doesn't take a leap to place us here.'

Lennox stepped out of the corner. 'The cops will come back with a warrant.'

Ewan nodded. 'And Michael will be on his way.' He turned to Ava. 'Was he on his mobile?'

'Sounded like it.'

'Then he could be just up the road.'

He looked out of the window. You could see the road for a few miles, no cars, no flashing lights.

Iona held her hands up. 'Don't tell me where you're going, I don't want to know. But does Paul know?'

Heather shook her head. 'He won't tell the police.'

'Why should he protect you?'

'They wouldn't believe him.'

'Why not?'

'It's unbelievable.'

Ewan spotted something out of the corner of his eye. He stared out of the window, thought he saw movement, maybe just trees in the wind. He watched the road in the distance, which dipped in and out of view. Then he saw something, a flash of black metal heading their way. He stepped to the window and gripped the sink. They reappeared, rising like whales breeching the ocean, two black SUVs, the same ones he'd seen in Edinburgh.

'Fuck, they're here.'

Ava joined him at the window. 'Michael?'

'Fellowes. Maybe Michael is with him.'

'Who's Fellowes?' Iona said getting up.

Heather stood up too. 'Bad news. We need to go.'

Lennox had already bolted out of the room to get Sandy.

Ewan kept his eye on the cars. They were a few minutes away. 'Shit.'

Heather looked at Iona. 'I know you don't know us and we've got you into this shit, but we need the truck.'

Iona didn't reply. She stared at Heather long and hard. Eventually she went to the basket by the kitchen door, picked up the keys and tossed them over.

Ewan turned back and the SUVs were closer. He was starting to think of a plan.

Lennox returned with the backpack and went straight out the door. Ewan ushered Heather and Ava out and followed, Iona bringing up the rear. They hustled into the truck, Lennox and Ava in the passenger seats, Heather behind the wheel. Ewan went to her open door.

'Go, I'll stall them.'

Heather shook her head. 'No, we all go together.'

Ewan waved down the road. 'They'll catch us in minutes. We can't outrun them. You need time to get away.'

Heather glanced over his shoulder. 'Iona can do it.'

'She's not part of this.'

'What about you?'

'I know what I'm dealing with.' He shut the driver's door and banged on the side. 'Go.'

Heather hesitated then started the engine and gunned it along the track round the side of the house, heading away towards the back road down the hill. Ewan watched until they were out of sight then turned. The SUVs weren't at him yet so hopefully they hadn't seen the others escape.

He turned to Iona, who was standing in the doorway with a baseball bat. 'Give me that and get in the house.'

He took the bat, turned and ran up the front path. He reached the top and saw them coming over a low hill, the grill of the front SUV like a grimacing comic-book villain. They were at him in no time and skidded to a halt. He stood in the middle of the road with the bat raised. The cars stayed like that for a few seconds and he resisted the urge to look back at the house. Even this little pause was enough to get them further away. He hadn't thought about what would happen to him and in the silence now he wondered if he was going to survive this.

The passenger door of the first car opened and Fellowes got out, two suited thugs climbing out of the other SUV. Fellowes removed his shades and stepped closer, the others behind.

'On the one hand, I'm surprised to see you here.' That cut-glass accent grated, hundreds of years of privilege, and here he was driving around the Highlands doing whatever he wanted. 'On the other, I suppose it was inevitable. We've come a long way from Edinburgh.'

Fellowes waved his finger and the thugs strode past him and pulled out guns. Ewan swung the baseball bat, but it was pathetic. He narrowly missed one guy but as he was swinging, the other guy reached him and rammed the butt of his gun into Ewan's head. He staggered back, the bat wavering. The first thug aimed carefully and shot Ewan in the left foot. Burning pain shot up his leg, through his body to his brain as he shifted his weight to the other leg. Tears came to his eyes as he leaned on the bat. The second guy took two steps and pistol-whipped him again and he fell to his knees, the gravel rough, the pain in his foot throbbing like a bastard. He slumped to the ground, closed his eyes and drifted away.

47
HEATHER

She looked in the mirror then turned back to the road in front and swerved around a narrow bend squeezed between hedges. They'd been driving for half an hour and there was no sign of being followed. The roads were single lane to start with and she drove too fast around turns and over humps, waiting for a bus or lorry to smash into them. Her hands were sweaty and her throat dry as she tried to remember to breathe.

She thought about Ewan. Given what he'd told her about this guy and his armed goons, maybe they'd killed him. She felt sick and guilty that he'd sacrificed himself to give them time. And she was angry that he'd pulled that on her last minute, didn't give her a chance to argue. It should've been her. And she thought about Paul at the station, Iona in the house. This was such a mess and she was responsible. She'd brought this to Paul's door.

Every few minutes they hit a junction and took the road that looked less well travelled. Narrow single lanes, high hedges, less chance of being found. At one point they crossed an A road but didn't take it. But eventually they had to use a proper road. Lennox pulled up the map on his phone. Between them and the coast was a large spread of hills, no through roads, only farm tracks and dead ends. They had to go round, so they joined the road northwest. The traffic was light and Heather went back to checking the mirror. No sign of an SUV, only delivery vans and cars.

The countryside opened out as they gained altitude, lochs here and there, rolling grassland giving way to bleaker moors. There was a sense this was the real Highlands, waiting for millions of years for something to happen. They did a long stretch alongside an open loch, dammed at the end. The brown bracken and heather was like a quilt over the surrounding hills. The sense of space was immense, like they were driving into the heavens.

Their truck was stuck behind a car with Dutch plates pulling a caravan. Heather remembered holidays in the Highlands in the campervan with Paul before Rosie was born. They'd been to Ullapool once. They'd driven round the north coast before it was marketed as the North Coast 500, bringing too many tourists. Nothing ever stayed the same but that didn't mean things got better. She had the feeling now this wouldn't end well. She tried to picture a happy ending and couldn't see it. She remembered she was dying. In all this shit she'd forgotten. So that was her ending, whatever happened to the rest.

Ava shifted in her seat.

Heather glanced over. 'Are you OK?'

Ava gave an eye roll and a sigh. 'Bursting for a pee.'

Heather looked around. Not a tree in sight, just open land. 'How bursting?'

'Very.'

She signalled and pulled onto the verge. There was a shallow ditch alongside, enough to crouch in. Heather waited for a car to pass then got out, as Lennox let Ava out then climbed back in.

'Don't look,' Ava said to him.

Heather helped her into the ditch and handed her a wet wipe from her bag.

Ava pulled down her trousers and Heather turned to check for cars.

'Sorry,' Ava said.

Heather heard the pee patter on the gravelly soil. 'Don't be. You're listening to your body.'

She heard an engine then saw a big black car appear round the bend. Her chest tightened but as it got closer she saw it wasn't Fellowes, just a rich mum heading somewhere.

'OK,' Ava said when the car had passed. 'That's better.'

She tapped on the truck door and Lennox let her in. Heather got in and they drove in silence for a while.

'What are we going to do?' Ava said eventually. She turned her head to each of them in turn.

'Just get to Ullapool,' Lennox said.

'Then what?' Ava said.

He shrugged and touched the backpack. Heather saw a tentacle emerge from the small opening at the top, flashing orange. This was so insane she couldn't handle it. And yet here she was, handling the shit out of it.

Lennox touched the tentacle and his eyes glassed over then he was back. 'Get them back to their family.'

Heather frowned. 'Did Sandy tell you that?'

'Not exactly but that's what it feels like.'

'And then?' Ava said, rubbing her eyes.

Heather knew what she meant. If they returned Sandy to the sea, what was left for them? Heather was dying, Lennox had formed an attachment, and Ava would have her baby soon. And there was Michael, Fellowes, the police, the dead body in East Lothian to account for. And Ewan, Paul and Iona, the whole fucking mess.

'Dunno,' Lennox said with a shrug.

Heather laughed. 'Fucking hell.'

Ava shook her head.

They reached the head of another loch which widened into an estuary.

'Loch Broom,' Lennox said, consulting his phone.

They drove along the loch side for a few miles, Heather checking the mirror and thinking about Ewan, hoping. She glanced over and saw the backpack moving, Lennox with his hand in as if to stroke a puppy.

She looked back at the road as they reached a bend. They were high up and beginning to descend towards the mouth of the loch. Ahead was a thin strip of white houses jutting into the middle of the water on a low headland. She recognised Ullapool from years ago, in a different vehicle, a different world, a different life.

'We're here,' she said.

48
EWAN

He was sitting on the deck of a yacht, dangling his foot over the side. Except instead of cool blue waters the sea was boiling lava, red and black, burning his foot. He saw the skin shrivel, flesh melting away, sinews snap. The bones dissolved into the molten sea, leaving just a stump at the end of his leg.

'Wake him up.'

The voice pulled him out of the nightmare but the burning in his foot persisted, intense fire running through every nerve, his body incandescent with pain. He kept his eyes shut, maybe the lava sea was real, then he didn't have to face what was coming.

His face jolted from a heavy slap. He flushed and bile rose in his throat, his foot sending flames licking up his leg. He opened his eyes.

Fellowes sat in a chair while two suited goons stood beside Ewan. It was like something from a comedy show, the hardmen who never speak. He wondered about them, did they go home to wives and kids, kiss them tenderly, tell them it was another boring day in the office? Nothing to mention but shooting innocent members of the public. Except he wasn't innocent, he was up to his neck in it.

He looked at his foot. There was a surprisingly small hole in the bridge of his shoe, the trainer material red, blood oozing from it, more sloshing around inside that he could feel.

He looked around. He was in Paul and Iona's living room, sitting in a chair by the dining table, Fellowes across the other side with his elbows resting on it, fingers templed together. Ewan raised his hands and was surprised he wasn't tied to the chair. But what would be the point? He couldn't outrun them at the best of times, let alone with a hole in his foot. He wondered how long he'd been out. How far Heather had got.

He heard a cough from the sofa across the room. His body stiffened as he saw Iona, face bruised, lip burst.

'What the fuck?' he said to Fellowes.

Fellowes kept his eyes on Ewan. 'We've already established she doesn't know where they've gone. In fact, she doesn't seem to have much sympathy for you lot.'

'She has nothing to do with this,' Ewan said.

He leaned back in his chair with a creak. 'You must have known when Heather called her ex that you were bringing a world of pain down on them.'

Ewan shook his head. 'I knew you were an arsehole, but I didn't realise you were into torture.'

'I don't enjoy it at all, to be honest. But needs must.'

'Who the fuck are you?'

Fellowes smiled. 'You're the investigative journalist, you tell me.'

Ewan thought about what little he'd found online. Wondered how he could rattle his cage and took a leap. 'MI7.'

Fellowes smile faltered. 'No such organisation.'

'That's not what I heard.'

'Conspiracy theories are the last resort of the crank.'

'But sometimes they're true.'

The nearest goon punched him, right cheek, almost knocking him off the chair. He tasted blood, spat onto the floor, looked at Iona.

'Let her go,' he said.

Fellowes leaned in and his face caught the light from outside. Ewan could see pock marks and creases, he was older than Ewan had thought.

'So what is MI7?' Fellowes said.

'Secret government department. MI5 is internal threats, MI6 is international. MI7 is extraterrestrial.'

Fellowes nodded. 'So you admit your little octopus friend is extraterrestrial.'

'No, but you think they are.'

'They? You mean there's more than one?'

Ewan didn't bother correcting him.

Fellowes' features softened and he put his hands out to placate. 'Look, you've got me all wrong. I only want to protect it. Others will come after me, and they won't treat it with the respect I will. I just want to make sure it doesn't come to any harm.'

Ewan felt sick. 'The hole in my foot says otherwise.'

'That was a mistake.' Fellowes nodded at the goons. 'They get a little overexcited. They come from special forces, you see. I don't approve of their methods.'

Ewan swallowed as his foot flared up in pain. He nodded at Iona. 'What about her?'

Fellowes shook his head. 'Mistakes have been made. I hold my hands up.' He did exactly that. 'But these are high stakes, Ewan. What we're dealing with is extraordinary. Life from elsewhere in the universe. Has it spoken to you yet?'

Ewan shook his head then he thought of something. 'How do you know about that?'

'So it does communicate?' Fellowes narrowed his eyes. 'But not with you. I presume with one of the others then. That must sting. Do you feel left out?'

Ewan felt pain washing over him. 'Fuck you.'

Fellowes sighed. 'You know, I come from a scientific background, astrobiology. I got roped into this stuff a long time ago and for years there was nothing. But this has always been my dream, to meet something from another planet.'

'You never answered my question,' Ewan said. 'How do you know they communicate?'

Fellowes had a faraway look in his eyes, like he was remembering a time before all this.

Ewan realised. 'You have another one, that's how you know. Sandy isn't alone.'

'Sandy?' Fellowes smiled. 'You named it.'

'Why do you want this one so much? Did you kill your one?'

The silence said it all. Fellowes looked sad as he stared at his hands. 'Like I said before, mistakes have been made. We didn't understand what we were doing, it was incredibly unfortunate.' He straightened in his chair. 'Now, tell me where they've gone.'

Ewan looked Fellowes in the eye. 'I don't know.'

Fellowes stuck his bottom lip out. Ewan thought about torture. No way he could withstand anything, he wasn't that kind of man. The pain in his foot was too much already.

Fellowes nodded at one of the goons and Ewan tensed his body, gritted his teeth. But the guy walked to Iona and pulled his gun, pressed it against her temple. She was crying and sniffling, stretching her neck to get away.

'Tell us,' Fellowes said. 'Now.'

49
LENNOX

They drove slow along Shore Street, Loch Broom on their left, white cottages gleaming on the right. The sun scudded off the water and blinded Lennox. They reached the small harbour, the jetty and ferry terminal jutting into the blue like an artificial limb, a tiny man-made encroachment on the water. On the other side now were pubs and restaurants, a chippy and a butcher's. But Lennox couldn't take his eyes off the sea.

He felt movement in the backpack, sensed Sandy getting agitated like a dog excited for a walk.

<Ahead.>

Heather slowed the truck at a junction as the road narrowed.

Lennox nodded. 'Keep going.'

Heather nudged the truck forward and they drove another hundred yards, then the road and houses stopped. They were at the tip of a headland, which swept round and away to their right. They were surrounded on three sides by water, only the land behind had any sign of human existence.

Lennox felt a tentacle attach to his wrist as Sandy unzipped the backpack and pulled their body out, expanding to fill the space of the dashboard, gazing outside. Their light display was crazy, yellows and reds and greens sweeping in and out of each other, ebbing and flowing, sparkling in shimmering shapes and designs, spots and stripes, swirls and zooming fractal patterns.

<No longer partial Sandy-Lennox.>

Lennox felt that like a gut punch. 'What?'

The women in the truck turned to him.

'What's up?' Heather said.

Ava's eyes were wide with a look of shock that Lennox didn't understand.

He touched Sandy's head, felt a pulse under his fingers. <What do you mean?>

<Sandy-Lennox no longer partial. Sandy-Lennox-Sandy complete.>

Ava touched Lennox's arm and he jumped.

'I can hear you,' she said.

Lennox turned. 'What?'

<I can hear you. Both.> This was Ava's voice in his head. She sounded part joyful, part terrified.

Lennox stared at her beaming smile. Heather looked bemused at the two of them.

<How?> he thought.

Silence for a moment, then Ava looked at Sandy. <They spoke to me before at the house. Talked to my baby, said everything was OK.>

Lennox placed fingers on his forehead as if he could touch Ava's voice in his brain.

Ava smiled. <This is insane, what is Sandy doing to us?>

Lennox wanted to say that Sandy wasn't doing anything to them, it was already done. And it hadn't been forced, they'd welcomed it. OK, the strokes weren't consensual, but that was an accident and Sandy fixed it. Lennox changed at that moment, something in his chemistry, synapses, metabolism, biology or consciousness or whatever made him who he was. He'd developed and grown, fucking *evolved*.

'What's going on?' Heather said.

Ava threw Lennox a guilty look then turned. 'I can hear them.'

Lennox felt a tug on his hand as Sandy opened the truck door.

<Sandy-Sandy must complete. Sandy-Lennox-Sandy must complete.>

He spoke to the two women. 'They have to get in the water.'

Sandy was already out and scuttling along the grass. There was a large bank of white rocks placed as a storm break and they glided over it with ease, Lennox clambering behind. How could a creature who lived in the water be so comfortable on land too? He felt like a stupid ape, an undeveloped organism with no clue of the possibilities out there in the cosmos. But he was starting to get an inkling.

Sandy slid across the stony beach and paused at the water's edge. They lowered to the ground and throbbed a multitude of colours up and down their body and tentacles. Lennox looked around for any hikers or anglers but there was no one. Ava and Heather got out the truck but didn't follow.

Sandy spread their tentacles into the water and looked back at Lennox.

<Come with us.>

He stripped to his shorts, leaving a pile of clothes as he clambered over the stones to join them.

'Careful,' Heather shouted from the truck.

He waved in reply and stepped into the water, shivers up his legs. He felt as if the brooding brown hills across the water were staring at him, judging him. Sandy was ahead, dipping in and out of the ripples, splashing playfully. He breathed deep then went to dive but before he hit the water, Sandy leaped and hugged him, sucked him into an embrace. Their body expanded to wrap around him and they both went into the water where they zipped just under the surface then dived deep. The light faded as they went further down, until they were only lit by Sandy's light show, a beacon in the gloom.

They swam like this for a few moments, twisting through the darkness like a spiralling torch. Lennox glimpsed fish and other creatures in the murky edges of his vision, smeared by the filter of Sandy's body around him. He breathed what felt like thick air. He felt calm, and wondered if Sandy was doing something to his brain chemistry to stop him freaking out.

Then he saw something below, a glow that grew brighter as they approached. More like a giant jellyfish than an octopus, a huge, hooded mass of lights and sparks, colours that made him feel he was seeing something unreal. There were tendrils hanging down from the main body, shimmering curtains of luminescence, interweaving with each other. As they got closer he realised the colossal size of it, as big as a ferry. Then he spotted other beings amongst the fronds underneath, darting and pushing through the forest of tendrils, the whole thing an ecosystem.

He sensed Sandy was overwhelmed with excitement and joy, as other octopus creatures came to meet them. They danced around each other and Sandy went into overdrive with their light display, stuff Lennox had never seen. Now they were among the tendrils of the giant creature, he could see there were hundreds of smaller octopus-creatures here. He saw some of them enter the huge jellyfish's body, others emerging. They seemed to appear or disappear in a shower of fizzing lights.

He forgot that he had a body, felt like he *was* Sandy, dancing with long-lost friends or relatives in a carnival of lights, patterns and motion that seemed both utterly alien and completely natural.

Sandy swam the two of them towards the body of the main creature, which loomed over them like a brilliant, flowing canopy. As they got closer, Lennox felt something in Sandy change, joy replaced by something deeper, more profound.

<We are home,> Sandy thought, and Lennox felt the power of it.

There was a moment of quiet and he felt something, like the giant creature was considering him.

<Welcome Sandy-Lennox partial.> This was a new voice, deep, calm, resonant, like an adult talking to a child. <Sandy-Lennox-Sandy complete. Thank you.>

50
AVA

Ava needed some air. Heather was checking them into The Ceilidh Place. Ava had initially gone with her to reception but the tourists milling around made her edgy so she bailed and stood outside. The truck was parked along the road, Lennox and Sandy inside. When they'd come back from the water, Lennox seemed dazed. Eventually he started babbling about a giant creature underwater, a collection or ecosystem. Part of her wanted Sandy to show her. But another part just wanted all this to go away. She wanted to go to a hospital, have her baby and hold her in her arms. Have nothing else to worry about except breastfeeding, nappies, sleep, the millions of things new mothers were supposed to worry about.

The baby was moving around less now which probably meant she was locked into position and ready to fire. Head down by the cervix. Ava wished she'd paid more attention to the baby books Michael bought her. But that was the problem, she didn't trust a single thing that came from him.

Her breath was racing, constant anxiety. Acid reflux burned her stomach and she glugged Gaviscon then put the bottle in her bag. She pushed off the hotel wall and walked down the road away from the truck. The sun was on her face and she felt warm.

The town was a grid of narrow streets spread across the small headland by the loch. It wasn't easy to get lost, you always had your bearings from the sea and the mountains across the water. She walked past old couples in matching clothes, bikers in leathers, a tall outdoorsy family. All enjoying the sun without a care.

She turned to the shore, walked along the front and looked at the water, reflected sunlight making her squint. Fishing and sailing boats bobbed out there. It was so beautiful, such a sense of space. She tried to relax her shoulders, imagined what it would feel like to be happy. The salty air was fresh. She walked past a youth hostel then The Ferry Boat Inn, then saw her mum a hundred yards away, walking towards her.

Ava touched the wall next to her. She was suddenly aware of the lapping of waves, the clanks of masts and rigging. She recognised the roll in her mother's hips, the way she took weight off the left side where she needed a knee operation. Always carrying that little edge of pain.

Her mum stared over the loch then turned and saw Ava. She stopped for a moment then hurried forward. Ava smiled, tried to work out what this meant.

'Mum.'

Her mum wrapped her in a hug. Ava felt awkward, not just because of the bump between them.

Her mum stepped back and tucked hair behind Ava's ear. 'Darling. I've been so worried.'

'What are you doing here, Mum?'

'Looking for you, silly.'

Ava shook her head. 'How did you know I was here?'

'Never mind that, I've found you, that's most important.' She looked Ava up and down. 'Look how big you are. It can't be long now.'

Ava put a hand out again and felt the rough wall, tried to steady herself. 'Mum, no one knows we're here.'

'We?' Her mum frowned. 'Don't tell me you're still with those others. The boy kidnapped you!'

'Nobody kidnapped me.' She felt like a kid again, trying to explain some injustice her dad had imposed on her and Freya. Mum always took his side. It had been a distance between them just when she needed her mum most, and it was still a distance now.

Her mum ignored what Ava said and looked at her belly. 'I was just as big with you and Freya, Gallacher babies are not small.'

Ava took hold of her mum's shoulders. 'Tell me how you're here.'

'I'm staying in the Royal Hotel, just back there.' Her mum pointed.

Ava saw a spread of white buildings set back from the road past the junction, large windows, views of the water.

'Why don't we go there now.'

Ava's fingers dug into her mum's shoulders, making her squirm. 'Mum, I wasn't kidnapped or coerced. I ran away, understand? For the first time in ten years I did exactly what I wanted without control from Michael, without having him watch my every move.'

Her mum took Ava's hands and squeezed. 'You're not well, darling. You were in hospital, remember, the stroke. It's made you confused.'

'No.'

'You don't know what you're saying. You need your family to take care of you.'

'The stroke has nothing to do with this, Mum, please just fucking listen.'

Her mum looked shocked. 'Ava, dear, there's no need for language.'

Ava laughed and shook her head. She thought about everything that had happened. She could understand Sandy's thoughts, Lennox's thoughts, yet she couldn't get her mother to believe the truth.

'Trust me, there absolutely *is* need for fucking language.'

Her mum tutted. 'You never spoke like that when your father was alive. And you never spoke like that to Michael.'

Ava went wide-eyed. 'That man abused me for years, Mum, just like Dad abused you.'

Her mum looked confused. 'What are you talking about?'

'Please understand, I was in an abusive marriage. Why won't you believe me?'

Her mum shook her head. 'Michael would never hurt a fly, he's the nicest man I know.'

She gave a slight nod towards the Royal Hotel.

Ava's skin prickled and her stomach tightened. 'Mum, is Michael here, did you bring him?'

Her mum pursed her lips. 'Don't be silly, Ava, he brought me.'

51
HEATHER

She looked around the room. Two single beds and a foldout camp bed, desk and stocked bookshelf, simple rustic décor. Lennox snoring in bed made her think of Rosie, the little snuffle she made when she snoozed. She remembered being on holiday with Rosie and Paul in some crappy Tenerife resort, middle of the day, their little girl asleep while they sat on a balcony looking at the Atlantic between high-rise blocks. The grief never leaves, just comes and goes in waves. The trick was to move with the motion of the waves, not resist, otherwise you'd drown. She took Rosie's photo from her pocket and stared at it for a long time.

She put it away and looked out of the window of their room. Loch Broom rather than the Atlantic but it was all connected, two-thirds of the earth's surface. It was a water world, yet here she was, descended from apes, still walking on land. She'd read somewhere that sharks had been around longer than trees. The human view of earth was so myopic it was virtually blind. Sandy's arrival made her realise that. Humans were nothing in the scheme of things, she felt that in her bones now.

A tense throb started at the base of her skull and she touched her neck. She pictured the tumour spreading through the wet meat of her brain, how it would kill her soon. She tensed in expectation but the pain always took her by surprise, overwhelming her, making her sense of self disappear in its dark depths. She staggered to the adjoining bathroom, hands on the walls for support. She was vaguely aware of Sandy sitting in the bath, water rippling as they flexed, tentacles dangling over the rim.

Their skin changed colour from light brown to cream, grey, light blue.

She fell in front of the toilet and gripped the seat, puked over and over. She felt like her eyeballs might explode out of their sockets, her brain was porridge, her stomach trying to leave her body. She gave herself up to the misery, it would be over soon. She retched twice more as the pain began to fade, the throbs reducing to a dull ache. She felt like her neck might snap from the strain.

Eventually she fell back from the toilet bowl and wiped her mouth, leaned against the wall to recover. These attacks were getting worse, definitely. She tried to control her breathing, stared at Sandy, seemingly oblivious to her in the bath.

She couldn't understand why Sandy was still here. They came to reunite them with others, right? Lennox was frustratingly vague when he came out of the water. Talked about some giant creature or community at the bottom of the loch, something that Sandy was part of. So why had Sandy come back with Lennox?

She felt in limbo between the craziness of their Highland chase and what was to come. They were still wanted by the police, Sandy wasn't reunited with their tribe, Ava hadn't had her baby, Heather was still dying. And Fellowes was closing in.

She thought about Ewan, what he'd done for them. He acted like a selfless father, doing what was best for his family. She felt like she and Ewan were the parents of this ramshackle bunch by default. Her chest was tight and her headache throbbed as she considered what might've happened to him. She was sure Fellowes would get their destination out of him, so it was only a matter of time until he showed. She glanced out of the window, half expecting the SUVs to trundle down the street.

But surely once Sandy was back in the water for good, Fellowes would have no purpose here. It all came back to Sandy. Heather looked at them in the bath, shifting colour like sand in the tide. She walked over. Sandy had spoken to Lennox and now Ava, and

Heather felt left out. She thought about their strokes, how Sandy had both hurt and cured them. And she thought about her cancer. She hadn't cared about her death since Rosie but now she wasn't sure.

She reached out and touched a tentacle, which flinched. She held it firm and the suckers stuck to her skin. She closed her eyes and waited.

There was a loud thump from the bedroom, and Heather pushed the bathroom door open to see Ava standing there, holding her belly and panting.

'Michael's here,' she said.

Lennox sat up in bed and Sandy's tentacle swayed away from Heather's touch. Sandy's eyes opened and Heather stared into them, wishing for a voice in her head. Eventually she turned to Ava, who was leaning against the desk.

'Where?'

'He's here with Mum. I met her by the shore. They're staying at the Royal.'

Lennox pushed up on his elbows. 'Why would she do that?'

'She loves him. She's old school, stand by your man, a woman's place is eating shit, taking crap every day until you die.'

Heather frowned. 'It might just be that she's worried about you.'

'I can't go back to him.'

Lennox swung his legs round to sit up. 'You don't have to, we'll look after you.'

Ava laughed. 'You're just a boy.'

Lennox sucked his teeth.

Ava looked sheepish. 'Shit, sorry, I'm just worried, OK?'

'I don't mean me, I mean Sandy. And Xander, if it comes to it.'

Heather narrowed her eyes. 'Xander?'

'That's what I call the thing down there.' He waved towards the loch.

Ava looked confused. 'Why?'

'Xander is the same name as Sandy. Alexander. I got the feeling they're part of the same ... thing.'

'Why are they here?'

'Didn't say.'

'Why isn't Sandy in the water?'

Lennox frowned. 'What do you mean?'

Heather looked at Sandy. Their tentacles were exploring the taps and plughole, sucker marks on the tiled wall. They turned a tap on and moved under the flow, splashing over the side of the bath.

'They wanted to be reunited with ... Xander, right? So why not stay in the water?'

Lennox looked as if he'd never thought of that. He stared at Sandy, and Heather knew they were talking. Ava's eyes went wide, she could hear too. Heather was excluded from their little club.

Lennox looked at Heather. 'Sandy says they're not finished with you yet.'

52
EWAN

He thought about millions of germs swarming into the ragged hole in his foot, swimming through his veins to his heart and brain. The blinding pain of earlier was replaced by a constant, hard throb that was somehow worse. He bent down in the back of the SUV and touched his trainer at the entry wound. Fuck, that was sore. He tried to arch his foot and the pain shredded up his ankle. His sock was soaked with blood and stuck to his skin.

He'd been trying to get comfortable for the whole ride. He'd told Fellowes about Ullapool, couldn't take the chance they would hurt Iona. It was clear they would kill if needed and that was like a stone in his stomach. He couldn't let anything bad happen to Heather and the rest, but he couldn't work out how to prevent it.

Fellowes was across the other side of the back seat, tapping on a laptop and sighing. The two suits were in the front of the car, silent. The other SUV had raced ahead to Ullapool.

He presumed he would die today. They'd brought him along to make sure he'd told them the truth. But that didn't mean they would let him go if they got what they wanted. They couldn't, he was a journalist. Not a very good one but his instinct had led him here, bleeding in the back of a government car, waiting to get a bullet in the head.

'Tell me,' Ewan said.

Fellowes removed his glasses and pinched the bridge of his nose. 'Tell you what?'

'Who you are and what you want with Sandy.'

Fellowes smiled. 'It's so interesting you named it.'

The car went round a bend and Ewan braced himself. The doors were locked, he'd already tried. He saw a low spread of hills across the other side of a loch and wondered how close they were.

'Look,' Fellowes said, 'I'm a scientist.'

He pointed at the two special forces guys in the front. 'This has given you the wrong idea. I don't do much field work, most of my days are in the office or the lab.'

'And yet here you are, shooting people as if you were taking the minutes of a meeting.'

'I already apologised about that.'

Ewan narrowed his eyes. 'Do you have a boss?'

'Pardon?'

'Do you report this to someone? Fill in a timesheet?'

Fellowes tapped the laptop. 'We have procedures, of course, we're the government. Although you didn't hear that from me.' He tapped the side of his nose like it was a joke.

Ewan swallowed. 'So tell me about the creature you had.'

Fellowes looked out of the window, then at his gun on the seat, well out of Ewan's reach.

'It's very frustrating,' he said eventually. 'Working in an organisation that's so secretive. When we found the NNC, I wasn't allowed to tell anyone.'

'NNC?'

Fellowes straightened his shoulders. 'Excuse the agency acronym. Non-Native Cephalopod. It doesn't really capture its wonder, does it?'

'How did you find them?'

'On a beach in Arran. Only it didn't have a rescue party like your one. There were two cases of extreme stroke in a Glasgow hospital that we think were connected. Those people helped us, were able to communicate with it, but it was dying. I don't think because of anything we did. It was always going to die.'

'Did you experiment on it?'

Fellowes rubbed his neck. 'It's necessary to take chances for scientific progress.'

'You killed it.'

Fellowes looked genuinely pained. Good. Ewan's foot reminded him he wasn't sitting with a friend here.

'People think science is a methodical, clinical practice. But the great leaps forward come at a price, Ewan. They take courage and faith.'

'You sound evangelical.'

Fellowes gave that some thought. 'Maybe I am, about these creatures.' He leaned forward. 'Tell me about Sandy, why do you refer to it as "they"?'

Ewan shrugged. 'That's what Lennox said. They spoke in the plural.'

Fellowes raised his eyebrows. 'Like there are others?'

'Like they're part of a collective. Or maybe they *are* the collective.'

Fellowes nodded. The car went downhill and Ewan saw the loch widening to his left. Glimpses of houses ahead.

Fellowes followed his gaze. 'Is that what's in Ullapool? More of these things?'

'I honestly don't know.' Ewan squirmed in his seat. 'Look, can I please get medical help.'

Fellowes looked at Ewan's blood-soaked trainer. Ewan wondered if he could overpower him, grab the gun, take Fellowes hostage. Threaten to kill him if the other guys didn't unlock the car. But then what? He would have to take Fellowes with him and he couldn't walk. Anyway, he needed to be in Ullapool, to help.

Fellowes threw Ewan a sincerely sorry face. 'We'll get it seen to as soon as we can. Once we have Sandy.'

His tone sounded reasonable. Maybe he didn't want to kill everyone, maybe he *was* just a scientist.

'I was right about MI7, wasn't I?' Ewan said.

They were passing houses now, coming into town. Out the left-hand window it was all water, hills and sky. Ewan thought about what was under the surface of the loch.

'That's not a name we use. But we do deal with possible extra-terrestrial threats, I suppose.'

'Sandy's no threat, that's obvious.'

Fellowes shrugged. 'The people above me are all military. They hear about something they don't understand – that *we* don't understand – and they get scared. Their instincts are to attack, protect themselves. I said that if we don't find Sandy, others would follow, and I meant it.' He nodded towards the front of the car. 'Believe it or not, we're the friendly face of this.'

Ewan felt suddenly exhausted with the bullshit. He wanted Fellowes and his cronies to be swept away in a tide of righteous anger.

'Tell that to the fucking hole in my foot,' he said.

He stared at the gun on the car seat. Why not try? Even if there was no way out of this, taking out this motherfucker would be good. But then what about the others? Fellowes was right, more people would come and that was bad news for everyone.

The car pulled into a petrol station. The view down the loch was stunning, sailing boats rocking in the water by a low jetty.

Fellowes opened his window and Ewan smelled the salty air. He saw the other SUV parked up. Its driver approached their car and leaned in.

'It won't take long to find them, sir, this place is tiny.'

53
LENNOX

The water's edge rippled against his toes. A breeze blew down the loch, ruffling his hair. He touched the curls, thought about Sandy's tentacles, the tangle of fronds and tendrils that descended from Xander in the water. He breathed deeply, salt and seaweed. He couldn't get the vision of Xander out of his head. He felt changed. He imagined being part of that community, gliding through the water like Sandy, slick and fast, completely at home.

Sandy was in The Ceilidh Place with the women. They were deciding what to do about Michael, and Sandy wanted to speak to Heather. Lennox slipped out saying he needed some air. But he knew he would come here. He wished he understood Sandy better. Despite their connection, Sandy still seemed unknowable.

He was in his briefs and T-shirt. The wind down the loch gave him goosebumps. He stepped into the water then dived under, the cold stopping his lungs for a moment, then he was swimming. He felt so feeble, a land animal trying to survive in an alien and hostile environment. He thought about how easily Sandy had adapted to land and he wanted to understand that more.

He looked back and realised he'd gone fifty feet from shore. The water was dark blue and brown, waves getting bigger as he left the shelter of land. He pictured megawaves in the Atlantic turning oil tankers over with ease. What were the waves like on Enceladus, if it was under ice?

His muscles burned a little, he wasn't used to swimming. He stopped, treaded water, looked at the hills on each side, the tiny specks of boats along the shore, pathetic little vessels for this vast expanse.

He took a huge breath and dived, kept his eyes open, looking for a sign of light in the gloom. But he was so tiny, unable to go more than a few yards before coming up for breath. He dived again in another direction, just darkness. Stayed down a little longer this time then kicked his way back up. Gasped in air and looked around. He heard an engine noise. He imagined that Fellowes guy in a helicopter, leaning out like in an eighties action movie. The noise grew louder then two fighter jets appeared at the head of the loch, low and roaring, angling down the contours of the glen, then overhead with an ear-splitting scream and out to sea. Just like at Freya's place. He watched them disappear and thought about how primitive metal machines seemed now. Combustion engines and tin cans flying around like gnats, what was the point?

He filled his lungs and went under again, water stinging his eyes. Nothing but darkness for a moment, then a blue-green light in the distance, a pinprick to begin with, but quickly closer and larger, moving at tremendous speed. It was much bigger than Sandy and a different shape, more like a smaller version of Xander, the size of a bus.

Lennox's lungs were bursting as the thing reached him. A giant jellyfish shape, tendrils and fronds and tentacles, light across their body, no face but a pattern and display that seemed to recognise him. They darted forward and surrounded him. And suddenly he wasn't in a salty puddle off the Scottish coast but in a vast sea, icy cold and piercing blue. Dizziness overwhelmed him and he remembered standing in Figgate Park and feeling the same. His vision spun. He reached out to hold something, felt his hands push through the body of this mini-Xander, the pair of them now somehow on Enceladus.

His brain began to right itself and he saw the water around him, blue in every direction, thousands of creatures like Xander moving slowly through deep currents, each with a huge community in and around them. Below, the water got darker for a while then pulsed and glowed red. His vision telescoped and he somehow understood these were volcanoes on the seabed, a link to the hot core of the moon, spewing lava which flowed across the surface, building into mountains as it cooled. He felt a weird reverence, realised he was sharing feelings with mini-Xander. The volcanoes were like gods but not quite, that was too simple. They were a part of the Enceladons' belief system and life, their ecosystem and faith rolled into one.

He looked above. The ice shelf was a cracked and beautiful sky, a million criss-crossing patterns like a constellation, an infinite number of linked icebergs and glaciers, ice shelves and plates. He had the same feeling from his host, this was to be revered and respected. There was no individuality here, they were all part of the same consciousness, the whole moon was a single entity, an integral community. He watched all the illuminated Xander-like creatures swimming languorously back and forth, blotting out parts of the ice shelf as they went. He sensed kinship with them, they were his comrades in this great expanse.

Suddenly his host shot upward towards one of the bigger cracks in the ice. A jet stream flowed from a volcano on the seabed, like a fountain through the sea to the opening in the ice. They joined it and shot through the ice shelf into space, surrounded by millions of particles of water and ice. He turned and looked at Saturn, huge and orange in the sky. He realised they were in one of the rings, they *were* the ring. And in the expanse of space were more mini-Xanders, floating in space, swaying and drifting.

Then a change. He sensed fear and worry, and his host's body turned to look back. A swarm of tiny dots appeared behind Saturn, growing larger, black against the sunlit surface of the planet. They were like those birds you saw on earth moving in unison, as they descended onto the north pole of Enceladus, swarms of them. He couldn't tell what they were, but they felt like bad news. They formed a black spot on the moon's surface, a cloud surrounding it. They glowed red and orange at the edges of the spot, then sank as the ice melted. They fell into the sea underneath and spread out. He could sense the darkness spreading through the water. He saw more Xander creatures leaving through the ice fissure. There was a panicky flood of them in Saturn's ring suddenly.

His host was happy to see them, but sad too. Lennox looked away from Enceladus and Saturn towards the sun, a small yellow dot in space. Earth was somewhere out there, but he couldn't see it.

54
AVA

She felt dizzy and wondered about her blood pressure. Her anxiety was through the roof.

'We have to leave. Now.'

They were still in The Ceilidh Place and Ava couldn't believe it. They were sitting ducks.

'And go where?' Heather said. She was staring at Sandy, she hadn't taken her eyes off them since she got the message through Lennox.

'Anywhere,' Ava said, waving her hand at the window. 'You don't understand, I can't stay here.'

Heather sighed. 'We can't run forever.'

'Just watch me.' Ava felt hot, leaned heavily against the desk.

'Ava, this can't go on indefinitely. You have to face him sometime or you'll never be free.'

'You don't understand.'

'I know controlling men, we all do. But you're not on your own. You've got us.'

Ava shook her head. She knew there were plenty men just like Michael, thousands treating their wives and girlfriends like dogs, slaves. But this was her personal heartbreak. Michael spent years destroying her sense of herself, her worth. She wasn't going to get dragged back to being an empty shell of a woman.

'Where are the truck keys?' she said.

'Ava.'

'Either you come with me, or I go myself.'

Heather pointed at Sandy in the sink. 'What about Sandy? Lennox?'

Ava shook her head. 'We've brought them here like they wanted.'

'We're not finished.'

Ava folded her arms across her chest. '*You're* not finished. You still have some weird thing to do with Sandy. Maybe Lennox isn't finished, he just wants what they want. But I'm finished. I have to think about my wellbeing. I have to leave.'

Heather chewed the inside of her cheek for a moment. She stood, went to her bag on the floor, pulled out the keys and a roll of money.

'You might need it.'

Ava wanted to cry. Stupid hormones. She hadn't expected Heather to agree so easily. She took the keys and money, tears in her eyes.

'Scotland runs out, Ava,' Heather said. 'There's only an hour or two north of here, then what? Orkney? Shetland? Norway?'

'Maybe.'

'You'll always be looking over your shoulder.'

'That was always going to be true. I'll forever be scared he'll turn up. That's what he's done to me.'

She hugged Heather, felt herself crying then pulled away, didn't want to stay in Heather's arms in case she never left. She walked out and downstairs, nodded to the woman at reception then left the hotel.

The sun was low but the air was still fresh and bright. Two bulky bikers with sleeve tattoos and beer guts sat at an outdoor table with pints. They glanced up as she turned towards the truck.

'Ava.'

Ice in her veins. The voice loud and confident behind her, those two syllables in his mouth making her flinch. It was too late. The truck was fifty yards away, might as well be a million miles.

She didn't want to turn round, as soon as she saw his face, this was real.

'Ava.' This was quieter, closer, assured and controlled.

Ava pushed the point of the truck keys out between her knuckles and turned.

Michael was twenty yards away, walking calmly towards her. He had all the time in the world, knew she wasn't going anywhere.

'Darling.'

He held his arms out to embrace her and she stepped back, raised her fists, showing off the truck keys.

He paused. 'Honey, I'm here to take you home.'

'I'm not going with you.'

'I'm here to look after you. Your mum wants you to be safe. We've been worried sick.'

'Don't mention her,' Ava said, voice shaking.

His face was so familiar yet so alien, like she'd never really known him.

'We're your family,' he said. 'Come home where we can look after you.'

'That's not what you want. You want control.'

'We love each other, Ava, come on.' His eyes widened and he put on an innocent face. 'You're confused and upset. It's the hormones.' He looked at her stomach. 'All this is a mistake.'

'No.'

He heard her tone and his face hardened.

'Honey, I can make all this go away,' he said. 'The police, what happened at the beach, the underage schoolboy.'

'That's not what happened.'

'It's what everyone thinks. But I can tell them you were unwilling and confused.'

'Fuck you.'

'If you don't come home right now, you'll end up in prison.' His voice was flat. 'Of course, you'll never see the baby, I'll make sure of that.'

He was suddenly right in her face, taking her arm, and she saw her own fist swing round and catch his cheek, the edge of the key slicing the skin, blood bubbling to the surface. He didn't stop, gripped her other arm tight, knocked the keys from her hand and began dragging her, his grip burning her skin.

She lost balance and tipped forward. She spotted the bikers watching from their table.

'Rape! Help!' She looked straight at them. 'This man is my stalker, he's going to rape and kill me. You have to help.'

They jumped off the bench and strode over. Michael turned to her and the hatred in his eyes burned like the sun. He kept hold of one of her arms and held a hand up to the guys.

'She's my wife,' he said. 'She's confused.'

The bigger of the two in a cut-off Motörhead T-shirt shook his head as he reached them. He was a foot taller than Michael and several stone heavier. Bald head and bushy beard.

'Let the lady go,' he said. 'She doesn't want to go with you.'

Michael was still pulling her. 'This is none of your business.'

'It's our business now.'

They blocked Michael's way and he tried to step around. Motörhead threw a punch into Michael's stomach and he doubled over. The other guy brought his fist down onto the back of Michael's head sending him to the ground. He lay there curled up, trying to suck in air as he rocked in the gutter.

Ava rubbed her wrists, the skin red.

'Now on your way,' Motörhead said to Michael. 'And don't come back.'

Michael got to his knees and stared at Ava, ignoring the two guys.

'I'll be back,' he said. 'With the police to have you arrested.'

Ava touched her throat and smiled at Motörhead and his mate. Then she turned to Michael on the ground.

'Fuck off.'

55
HEATHER

The door slammed. She didn't think Ava would go like that, after all they'd been through. But Heather couldn't run anymore, that was the truth, she was bone tired. She'd taken on this thing and here they were, she didn't have anything left. Ava was still running, Lennox had his new family. Heather had nothing except Sandy's 'unfinished business'.

She turned and looked through the bathroom door at Sandy. They'd put on a light display while she and Ava argued. Heather presumed Sandy understood. They were telepathic, had shown the other two an alien world. Heather remembered something from a childhood reading Arthur C. Clarke, 'any sufficiently advanced technology is indistinguishable from magic'. Sandy seemed like magic.

She wondered if Sandy knew what Heather was thinking, could map her mind with infinite precision, could sense her hopes and dreams, loss and heartbreak, grief and resignation. The cancer eating away at her every minute. But the tumour was part of her. She hated the military terminology that people used around cancer: 'She lost her brave battle with cancer.' The cancer was part of you, you created it from nothing, so that language meant you were fighting yourself. Turning everything into a battlefield was a masculine, wrong-headed way of looking at things.

She was sure Sandy didn't think like that. But how can we ever know what another being is thinking? How can we comprehend what anyone else is going through? But that was the point of humanity, a search for empathy, putting yourself in someone else's shoes. It seemed futile though. She thought she understood Ava and Lennox at the start of this, but she was wrong. She thought she understood Paul when she married him, Rosie when she was born. But we can't know other people, never enough.

She walked over to Sandy in the bath. Looked into their eyes for something – optimism, knowledge, kindness. The flashes across their body changed from pulsing aquamarine to dark purple, sweeps of orange through it. Two of Sandy's tentacles lifted and swayed close to her face.

She swallowed and held the tentacles, felt the suckers stick to her skin. Her head spun, making her stagger and slump to the floor. Then suddenly she was in an ocean of indescribable blue, moving like an Olympic athlete through the water but much faster, at home in an alien place. She looked down at her hands and was unsurprised to see tentacles pushing water aside. It was magical to be alive in this moment, no worries about who she was or what the world thought of her. Only this moment. Shivers of delight swept through her body, light flashed across her skin. It was beautiful and unique, but also it could be shared with anyone, the barriers between herself and her surroundings were broken down. She imagined the water passing through her as she moved, microbes, tiny fish, bacteria inside her, all a biodome, a collective of organisms working together. And she felt part of something bigger too, she was a bacterium in the organism of the ocean, of the moon, an insignificant piece of an infinite jigsaw, but vital too, without her the picture wouldn't be complete.

She fell out of the ocean and landed back in her body on the bathroom floor. Sandy was in her lap. Heather still held two of their tentacles, while a third wavered at her ear.

<Do we have your permission?>

She flinched at the voice in her head but it was what she'd wanted all along. It felt so right to have this wonderful thing inside her mind. She wished she'd had the same with her loved ones over the years. But then she imagined sharing Rosie's pain and sorrow during her final days. She pictured her life amplified a billion times and felt sick.

She almost spoke in answer, then stopped herself, tried to think.

<Permission for what?>

<Sandy-Heather partial is inefficient.>

Heather stared into Sandy's eyes. They changed from brown to golden, tightening to ovals for a moment then back to circles. She liked that Sandy had referred to the two of them together but was confused about the rest.

<Inefficient?>

The tentacle near her ear went over her head and gently touched the back of her skull. Heather's stomach turned to stone. It was the location of her tumour.

<Sandy-Heather partial neural network has cellular inefficiency. Neural network not functioning to capacity of Sandy-Ava or Sandy-Lennox.>

<It's a brain tumour.>

A moment of silence as Sandy flashed maroon then grey.

<Sandy-Heather partial would like increased efficiency?>

'What do you mean?' She realised she'd spoken that. <What do you mean?>

<We can delete inefficiency in Sandy-Heather neural network.>

Heather swallowed. <You mean cure my tumour?>

<Cellular restructure.>

Heather squeezed Sandy's tentacles tight but stayed silent.

<But what about the strokes, all the other stuff?>

Sandy's tentacles rippled maroon and orange. <Strokes?>

<When you came here, Ava, Lennox and I had strokes. Some others died. And the guy on the beach, he died too. But not Michael. Why?>

Sandy's head elongated a little, ridges across the middle rose up and disappeared. Their skin pulsed light and dark. <Communication signal. Too strong. Calibrated for future connection. Bad mistake.>

<But some recovered. Our strokes disappeared. Why us?> It was a question she'd asked herself since the start of all this. Was it because they had no one else?

<Neural chemistry.>

<What does that mean?>

Sandy shivered a little and two tentacles slid across her hands. <Some humans are more open to communication because of different neural pathways.>

Heather liked the idea of being more open to things.

Sandy's tentacle raised to the side of Heather's head. <Do we have your permission?>

Heather closed her eyes and pictured Rosie in her hospital bed, bald head, wasting away. <Yes.>

The tentacle went into her ear then it seemed to penetrate her whole head. She knew that was impossible but that's what it felt like. She felt information travelling along nerves to her brain, spreading across the surface and soaking beneath the membranes, powering her own synapses to change, telling them how to cure themselves, instructing the cancerous cells to modify. Through her whole body as well, signals to nerves in her fingers and toes that tingled with life. She felt like Frankenstein's monster on the table, charged with power, a new form of energy she couldn't have imagined in a million lifetimes. And it was nothing to Sandy, second nature, the ability to inform parts of yourself how to behave for the efficiency of the organism.

Heather leaned her head against the wall and succumbed. She lost all sense of self, then regained it instantaneously. It felt like Sandy had scrubbed her soul clean and she cried.

She felt the tentacle come out of her ear. She sat there, senses tingling, feet and hands fizzing, the smell of instant coffee from the table across the room, the suckers of Sandy's tentacles still touching her skin, a taste of metal in her mouth and she realised she'd bitten the inside of her cheek. She knew it had worked. She had faith.

She opened her eyes and looked at Sandy in her lap for a long time. <Thank you.>

A little ripple of light down Sandy's tentacles. <Sandy-Heather partial now efficient.>

She laughed through tears.

She heard a noise outside the window and remembered there was a real world out there. She shifted to her knees, Sandy sliding from her lap. She got up, felt her bones ache in a good way, her body somehow new. She wondered if this was what evangelicals felt like when reborn. She went to the window and saw Ava standing with two large bikers, Michael walking away, shouting at her. She realised she didn't want Ava to go, not now, not ever, and headed for the door.

56
LENNOX

The tang of seaweed in his nose, the shush of waves on the shore. He felt pebbles against his back, warm sun on his face. He opened his eyes and blinked. He was on the beach a few yards from his pile of clothes. He rubbed his face, pushed a hand through his wet hair. Stumbled to his feet, started pulling his clothes on, tried to clear his head. He looked around. No one in sight, just a small fishing boat in the water. He wondered if it had nets or lines dropping into the depths. What they could pull up. Not that Xander would let that happen.

Lennox couldn't get his head straight. What were Sandy and Xander? They existed on a different level from humans, giving him visions so clear and precise he felt like he'd been there swimming in the oceans of Enceladus, floating in space. What were those other things that arrived on Enceladus? A swarm or flock of something. He didn't know their intention but countless new creatures arriving in your ecosystem was bad news. And the vibe he got from mini-Xander was an exodus. They were refugees, escaping as quickly as possible.

He had to speak to the others. Had to talk to Sandy. He pulled his socks and trainers on, still trying to shake the fog from his brain. It felt like part of him was still floating in the rings of Saturn. The feelings from mini-Xander rippled through his body. He glanced at the loch. Looking at it now, it seemed massive, overwhelming, but it was just a tiny puddle compared to the undersea oceans of Enceladus. But this tiny puddle stretched to the sea, then the oceans that covered earth. Lots of room.

He scrambled over the storm break and along the road, then turned towards The Ceilidh Place. As he neared the top of the slope he saw Ava with two big guys, Michael striding away, head down, fists clenched.

So he'd found them. The rest wouldn't be far behind. He was amazed how hard it was to disappear in Scotland. He'd never seen this much space in his life, yet everywhere they went they left a trail.

He reached Ava, sitting on the wall outside the hotel, breathing heavily. The bikers stepped up to him, confused at his skinny frame and frizzy hair.

Ava waved a hand. 'He's a friend.'

The bigger of the guys spoke. 'Are you OK?'

Ava nodded and closed her eyes.

'We're over here if you need anything,' he said, walking to a table.

'What happened?' Lennox said.

Ava opened her eyes. 'Nothing.'

'But Michael.'

'Don't worry.' She took in his wet hair, T-shirt clinging to his chest. 'Another swim?'

Lennox nodded. How to explain.

'Without Sandy,' Ava said.

'I met … a part of Xander.'

'And?'

'They showed me stuff.'

'Like Sandy did?'

'More. I think there are loads of them.'

'Loads of Sandys?'

'Loads of Xanders. And other creatures too.'

'In the loch?'

'I'm not sure.'

'Why are they here?'

Lennox bit his lip. 'I think they're refugees, running away.'

Ava's eyes widened. 'From what?'

'I don't know.'

Ava laughed. 'A bit like us.'

'Are you two OK?' This was Heather, stumbling out of the hotel with the backpack on her shoulder. She turned to Ava. 'I saw Michael.'

'I'm fine,' Ava said.

Lennox saw movement in the backpack, nodded at it. 'Did you speak to Sandy?'

Heather took a long time to answer. 'Yes. I think they helped me.'

Ava raised her chin. 'Xander has been showing Lennox something from their home world.'

'What?' Heather said.

Ava tensed up and doubled over, raised a hand like she was trying to flag down a taxi.

'Contractions?' Heather said, interlocking her fingers with Ava's.

Lennox saw the pressure Ava was putting on Heather's hand, knuckles white.

Ava blinked heavily a few times. 'Probably still Braxton Hicks.'

'I don't think so,' Heather said. 'We need to go to hospital.'

'It's nothing.'

Heather crouched down so that her face was level with Ava's. She took her other hand and clenched both fists. 'Listen to me. We've come this far together. I was wrong to let you walk out that door and I'm sorry. I needed to speak to Sandy and I let that get in the way. But I'm here now.' She nodded at Lennox. 'We're both here for you. But you have to let us help you. We need to go to hospital.'

Ava shook her head. 'Women have home births all the time. For thousands of years, that's all we did. It's the most natural thing in the world.'

'Just because it's natural, doesn't mean it's not dangerous.'

'I just need...' Ava winced and buckled like she'd been punched in the stomach, let out a low growl that reminded Lennox of big cats in the zoo.

Lennox saw a wet patch on the concrete between Ava's legs. Drips from her joggers.

'It's happening,' Heather said.

Ava panted, raised her head, closed and opened her eyes. 'OK, I'm having a fucking baby. What now?'

Heather stared at her then turned to Lennox as if he might have the answer.

57
EWAN

Fellowes' phone rang. Ewan's foot pulsed in pain with every heartbeat. Fellowes listened then hung up. He tapped the driver on the shoulder.

'They're at The Ceilidh Place, West Argyle Street.'

Shit.

They drove fast but smooth, turned right then left. Ewan saw a signpost for a police station. As if the local plod could save them now.

Fellowes sighed. 'This will all be over soon.'

'You'll let us go if you get Sandy?'

'Of course.'

Weird spasms ran up Ewan's leg as he craned his neck to look ahead. They couldn't be far. Fellowes looked forward. Ewan felt in his pocket for his phone to call Heather, but of course they'd taken it. He looked at the gun in Fellowes' hand, maybe this was the time to grab it, be a fucking hero. But he sat there frozen, thinking about everything that could go wrong.

They stopped at a junction, two cars trundling up the hill from the shore. Ewan saw the ferry to his left, the gleaming water of the loch, a young couple pushing a buggy, squinting in the sun.

They went over the junction then pulled in alongside the other SUV, blocking the road.

Windows went down.

'Straight ahead,' the guy said, nodding to Fellowes. 'A hundred metres. All three of them outside the hotel.'

'What are they doing?'

'Unclear. There was an altercation between the younger woman and her husband.'

'Her husband is here?'

'He was scared off by two locals.'

'And the target?'

'Not sighted, but they have a bag with them.'

'It could be inside.'

Ewan's stomach clenched up. He knew the doors of the SUV were locked, but what about the windows? He arched his neck to see past the driver. A horn sounded behind, and he turned to see a delivery van waiting to pass. Fellowes tapped on the back of the driver's seat and they took off down the road, the second SUV following. Ewan saw the three of them ahead, Lennox and Heather standing over Ava, who was sitting on a low wall. He saw Paul's truck behind them, the backpack on the ground. What were they doing? Just fucking leave. They were only fifty yards away.

Ewan coughed loudly and shuffled in his seat, moved his back to the window and pressed the button to open it. It slid down. Fellowes hadn't heard, was still looking ahead. It was halfway down when he turned at the electronic whirr, just as Ewan put his weight on his blood-soaked foot and pushed upwards, getting his head and shoulders out the window, feeling a blast of summer air.

'Run,' he screamed at the top of his voice. 'Heather, they're here.'

They turned to stare as Fellowes pulled him back inside the car and threw him across the seat. He saw Lennox and Heather grab Ava's hands and help her to the truck, Lennox lifting the backpack. Part of him wanted them to leave Sandy and run. Why were they still protecting that thing? But he knew why, Sandy had saved their lives, given them purpose.

They jumped in the truck and sped away as both SUVs accelerated, giving chase. They swung hard right as the road ahead ended, skidding round a narrow lane. There was a campsite to the left then the loch and the hills across the water. Small white cottages on their right. The truck couldn't possibly outrun them.

Fellowes stared at him. 'You idiot.'

'Fuck you.'

Fellowes leaned forward and spoke to the driver. 'I don't want the target harmed, understand?'

They were doing sixty, parked cars either side, people on the pavement gawping as they hurtled past.

The road swung right and they followed, away from the loch and alongside a low river. This was pointless, the truck couldn't escape.

They met a car coming the other way which skidded onto the pavement to avoid them. Up ahead the truck barrelled to a junction then hung right and they followed behind. The road opened up as it led them back into the heart of town.

The second SUV came alongside theirs, vehicles in the opposite direction pulling into the side or onto the pavement. They were almost nudging the truck in front, all of them racing down the hill towards shore. The truck slowed as it reached the shore road and Ewan had an idea.

All three guys in the SUV were staring out of the window at the truck as it approached the junction too fast. Ewan swallowed hard and balled his hands into fists, then launched forward with all his weight, feeling his throbbing foot as his body wedged between the front seats. The guys in front pushed at him and Fellowes tried to grab him but he kicked out and caught Fellowes in the face with his foot, leaving a smear of his blood. He jerked his body through the gap and rammed his shoulder into the driver's arm, swerving the car into the SUV alongside them, the two of them barrelling along just a few yards from the junction.

He saw the truck up ahead thudding to a halt in the railings before the water's edge. They hadn't made it round the corner but they didn't go into the loch either.

He had his torso through into the front of the car. The passenger goon pointed his gun at Ewan. He heard the bang before he felt it in his chest, an outrageous roar of anger and pain through him as he elbowed the driver in the face, lunged forward and pushed his hand on the accelerator. They piled over the junction, the other SUV alongside. He grabbed the wheel and turned it, forced the other vehicle into the ferry terminal building with a crunch. Their own car sped along the short jetty, knocking bollards out of the way as they pummelled past the safety barrier and through a final low fence. Then they were in the air for an instant and Ewan saw the view down the loch, an expanse of land and sea and sky blending into one, swirling in and out of the excruciating pain drowning him. They hit the water with a heavy thump and Ewan's head jerked forward into the windscreen.

58
HEATHER

Her head smacked the windscreen and her chest pressed into the steering wheel as they hit the railings and crunched to a stop. She saw the SUVs race down the jetty, the first crashing into a building in a cloud of masonry dust, the second piling into the sea.

Ewan.

She looked across the cab at Ava and Lennox.

'Are you OK?'

They were both conscious, dazed from the crash. Ava grimaced at another contraction, Lennox shook his head.

Heather grabbed the bag from between his legs and jumped out of the truck, ran down the jetty. She looked at the SUV stuck in the ferry terminal building, the driver unconscious. She ran to the end of the jetty, saw the second SUV sinking in the water, just its rear wheels and taillights above the surface.

'Ewan!' She leaned over the edge. The car was twenty yards away. She couldn't swim, but she had a better idea anyway.

She unzipped the bag and Sandy's tentacles unfolded onto the concrete, followed by their body. Heather grabbed a suckered tentacle.

<Sandy, you know Ewan, our friend.>

<Not partial with Sandy. But help Sandy-human partials.>

<That's right. He helped us all.> She glanced at the water, bubbles rising as the back wheels sank below the surface.

<He needs your help. He's trapped in that car.>

Sandy looked at the loch.

<He can't breathe underwater. I need you to bring him here. Can you do that?>

A moment's silence. <We will bring Ewan to you.>

<Quickly, he's drowning.>

Sandy scuttled to the edge and slid underwater. Heather saw their sleek body moving fast to the roof of the car, grabbing it and moving to one of side doors. The car sank lower and Heather wondered how deep the water was.

She thought about the others in the car. She should get Sandy to retrieve them all, but Ewan was her priority. She thought about him shouting from the SUV earlier, what he'd done at Toll Sionnach.

The car had disappeared now, just ripples on the brown surface, seagulls floating, a thin trail of bubbles popping. She thought about Ewan's lungs.

<Sandy?>

Waited.

Nothing.

Fuck, come on.

She glanced around. The truck on the pavement was pressed against bent railings. The SUV nestled inside the crumbling brick of the terminal. Locals and tourists gathered at the seafront, wondering what had happened, how they could help.

<Sandy?>

Come on, come on, come on.

The surface of the water broke a few yards to the left, Sandy's body sparkling in the sunshine, tentacles around Ewan, his face turned upward, eyes closed. Sandy swam fast to the side of the jetty where there were steps to a low boardwalk, two small boats moored there. Heather ran down the steps and leaned over as Sandy arrived. She hauled Ewan out of the water, Sandy pushing from underneath.

Ewan's face was white, wet hair plastered to his head, blood oozing from a chest wound. Heather took a handkerchief from her pocket and pressed hard against it. Did one of the guys shoot him? She got her phone out and called 999, gave their location and hung up. She didn't know where an ambulance was coming from, but she knew it would be too late.

She began CPR, pinching his nose, head back, breathing into him, pressing his chest. She moved down from his sternum, worried about the bullet hole. Every time she pressed his chest, blood bubbled from his wound. Maybe she was doing more harm than good. But she'd seen enough shitty dramas to know you keep going and eventually they cough up a pint of seawater and recover. She kept breathing into his mouth then pumping his damaged chest. She saw Ava and Lennox out of the truck now. More people had gathered on the road, some walking up the jetty towards her. To her right, Sandy crawled from the water and sat alongside, their display flashing and pulsing.

More CPR, more breathing, more pressing on his chest, but Ewan stayed pale and clammy.

Heather looked at Sandy. <Can you help him?>

<In what way?>

<He's not breathing, he might have drowned. And he has a chest wound.> She noticed his left shoe, mangled and blood-soaked.

Sandy glowed. <Make Sandy-Ewan partial?>

Heather heard seagulls calling to each other, the sound of water slapping against the boardwalk. <Please.>

She sat back to make room and Sandy clambered onto Ewan's chest. They reached two tentacles to either side of Ewan's head, inched their body near his throat. The light display dimmed, grey with purple flecks. Sandy sat there for a long time and Heather imagined an ambulance turning up, having to explain. A few people were above her on the jetty, staring. A woman filmed it all on her phone.

'Stay away,' Heather said. 'Get an ambulance.'

She felt so weary. She would never be able to explain this and she resented that she would have to, over and over, to these people, Fellowes if he was alive, the police, other authorities, the press. But none of that mattered if Sandy could bring Ewan back.

<Sandy?> She held Ewan's limp hand. <Is it working?>

No answer, a change in their display, purple getting lighter, grey darker. Their rear tentacles were wrapped around Ewan's legs, squeezing. His face was covered in suckers, one tentacle curled around his neck, Sandy's body pulsing like a human heart. But Ewan's hand felt the same. She imagined him gripping her fingers, coughing up some of Loch Broom, Heather laughing in relief.

<Sandy?>

A few more moments then Sandy released their grip of his legs and head, folding tentacles inward, shrinking their body as they slid off him and onto the boardwalk.

<Sandy, what happened?>

<Could not establish Sandy-Ewan partial.>

<Why not?>

<Ewan already converted energy to initial form.>

Heather felt tears in her eyes. 'What do you mean?'

<Ewan already part of bigger energy. No longer creature. Back to beginning.>

'But why can't you fucking save him? You cured my cancer. Make him live.'

The people on the jetty stared at her but she didn't care.

<That was cell refocus. Ewan energy already converted.>

'Fuck,' she said under her breath. She squeezed Ewan's hand, looked at his grey face. 'Ewan, I'm sorry, I'm so sorry.'

The blood coming from his chest had eased, just a red smear across his clothes. Heather placed her fingers hard into his neck, checking for a pulse. Nothing. She cried as she leaned in and placed her cheek against his. He was clammy on her skin, wet with seawater and tears, already changed into something else, into nothing.

'Heather!'

She screwed her eyes shut, felt a shiver through her body. All this shit was still going on.

'Heather!'

It was Lennox. He and Ava still needed her. Everyone always needed her.

She looked up, still holding Ewan's hand.

Lennox was by the truck, Ava lying on the flat bed at the back. Lennox pointed.

'The baby's coming.'

59
AVA

The pain swept from her groin up her spine and spread through every nerve, lighting her on fire. She gripped the side of the truck, flakes of rust coming off in her hand. She was on an old mattress and wondered about the millions of germs. Looked like she was getting her daughter's immune system up and running from day one.

The pain was constant ebb and flow, then screaming tidal waves, an unbelievable stretching of her body that she couldn't comprehend. Her bladder emptied and she thought she'd shat herself. She wondered how her body could ever recover from this, then another wave of pain jolted her. She stared at the sky, seagulls flapping without a care. She waited for the pain to diminish then raised her head.

'Lennox?'

He climbed into the truck, looking away from her legs. She felt a twinge in her neck from the crash, then was overwhelmed by birth pain. She grabbed Lennox's hand and squeezed like she was trying to break the bones.

'It's OK,' Lennox said.

She gritted her teeth. 'You need to get my joggers and pants off.'

He looked at her wide-eyed. 'What?'

'Just do it.'

Pain swept through her again as she felt Lennox release her hand and take her clothes off. She breathed like she was supposed to, in and out, holy shit, more pain, more stretching, she could feel the baby's head against her uterus. Trying to come and meet her for the first time.

'Ava.'

She opened her eyes and saw Heather crouched over her.

'She's coming.'

Ava grabbed Lennox's fist and squeezed. 'I fucking know that. Jesus.'

'I mean she's crowning, I can see her hair.'

Ava laughed and felt herself wee. 'She has hair?'

'Lots. You need to push,' Heather said, voice calm.

'Ewan?'

'Just focus on this.'

Ava puffed a few times then tried to push but her muscles had collapsed, every squeeze just brought more pain. In a hospital they'd get the baby out one way or another, give Ava enough drugs to make her forget herself. She couldn't believe women still had to go through this after thousands of years of evolution.

She grunted and squeezed, nothing but pain so fierce she thought she might pass out. Fuck this pain, fuck this life, this is insane. Lots of other women around the world were doing this right now and she tried to get some comfort from that but failed.

She tried to raise her head but couldn't. She slumped back on the mattress as she was overcome by pain again. When will this end? She couldn't think of a single thing except how sore she was.

She felt something against her hand, knew it was Sandy. Suckers against her skin, a tentacle brushing her face, another moving over her belly. She opened her eyes as she felt suckers squeeze her fist.

<Ava-Ava-offspring partial in transition.>

The voice in her head made her jump, but she felt reassured. <We need help.>

<Ava-Ava-offspring transition seems normal human process.>

'It fucking hurts,' Ava said. <A lot of pain. I can't push.>

Another wave of burning pain swamped her and she felt her body succumb.

<This is not normal human-offspring transition?>

<I can't get her out, it's too painful. Can you help?>

Sandy's tentacle moved over her belly to her groin. Another tentacle wrapped round her head, a third lay gently on her chest, a fourth curled around her hand. She gave her body over to Sandy, a captain here to guide the ship.

<Sandy-Ava-Ava-offspring partial will transition.>

Her mind flooded with a weird warmth, a positive energy she'd never felt before. It swept from her brain down her arms and legs, through her body to her womb, uterus, vagina. She was a whole person, wonderfully connected to her daughter. She could sense her baby's anxiety and love flowing through her own blood, which was her daughter's blood too, intermingling for a final time. The baby sensed her too, she could feel it, they shared a profound connection that would never be lost no matter what.

An orange light glowed in Ava's mind. Sandy was there, connected in a way she'd never felt before. Nothing in her life had prepared her for this, all past relationships were nothing compared to now.

She realised she hadn't felt any pain in the last few minutes, nothing but contentment. Just chemicals in the brain from Sandy, but who cares if it made her feel like this.

But she worried about her muscles, if she could push. Then she felt something from the other end of the universe infuse her body. Her stomach tensed, groin, chest, it was effortless, the most natural experience, just letting her baby know she was here, always would be, caring for her and making sure she navigated the world. She felt a release, the stretching of her uterus stopped, she was suddenly empty, her body already changing, returning to something like human. She felt Sandy's touch relax.

She heard a baby cry and looked down. Heather held out her

beautiful daughter. It was like she knew her already, that scrunched-up red face, tiny fists, legs kicking out and finding no resistance from Ava's body for the first time.

She took her daughter and held her for a long time and the world around her disappeared.

Sandy's tentacle was jerked away from her hand and they were dragged out of the back of the truck. She pushed onto her elbows, Lennox and Heather at her sides.

It was Fellowes, soaking wet. He had a narrow-grid cage at the end of a metal pole in one hand. He shoved Sandy inside, snapped it shut and slid it a safe distance away from him. In his other hand was a gun, pointing at them.

60
HEATHER

Heather looked at Sandy in the cage and clenched her teeth. She thought about everything Sandy had tried with Ewan, what they'd just done for Ava.

<Sandy, are you OK?>

But there was no answer. She tried again.

Fellowes was dripping on the pavement, suit clinging to him. Heather wondered if wet guns worked.

She looked at Sandy. They were trying to squeeze through the tiny holes in the mesh, but the gaps were too small. The tips of their tentacles wriggled, body flashing with dramatic colour. The tentacles couldn't touch Fellowes, the cage was too far away.

'It's a Faraday cage,' Fellowes said. 'Actually, it's more complicated than that. Stops it from using its telepathy.'

Heather saw that the SUV that crashed into the ferry terminal had its boot open. That must be where the cage had been. She wondered if any of the thugs were still alive.

Ava was on her back, shielding her baby from Fellowes and the gun. Lennox stood in the back of the truck, gripping the edge. Heather saw Ewan's body lying where she and Sandy dragged him out of the water. People were standing at the top of the promenade, some recording on their phones.

Lennox pushed away from the side of the truck, fists balled.

'Don't,' Fellowes said, waggling the gun. 'I don't want to have to use this.'

All Heather's energy had gone. Ewan was dead, Ava had her baby, Fellowes had Sandy. Maybe this was the end.

But she remembered her cancer. Sandy saved her life, tried to save Ewan, helped Ava. They did something for each of them.

Fellowes backed away from them, sliding the cage with the pole. Sandy's tentacles waved around inside, fiddled with the lock. Fellowes flicked a switch in the pole, sending sparks arcing through the cage. Sandy shrunk and pulled their tentacles inward, their body turning grey.

Lennox climbed down from the truck.

'Don't,' Fellowes said.

Lennox took a couple of steps forward. 'Let Sandy go.'

Fellowes backed away towards the crashed SUV, sliding Sandy in the cage.

Lennox followed. 'Let them go or you'll be sorry.'

'I've wanted this my whole life.'

'There's stuff going on here you don't understand.'

Fellowes angled his head. 'Then tell me.'

Heather thought about what Lennox had told her and Ava, Xander out in the loch, visions of Sandy's home moon, an exodus of refugees.

Lennox shook his head.

Fellowes widened his eyes. 'Well?'

Lennox was concentrating hard, like when he and Sandy talked. Fellowes saw it, checked on Sandy who hadn't moved. 'I told you, you can't speak to it when it's in there.'

'I wasn't talking to Sandy.'

Fellowes shook his head. 'I don't have time for this.' He walked across the jetty to the ferry terminal, dragging Sandy in the cage. Lennox followed at a distance.

'Careful,' Heather said.

Lennox glanced back. 'I know what I'm doing.' He closed his eyes like he was getting a message.

Heather looked at Sandy, no change.

Fellowes was almost at the car now. Lennox stepped forward

and Heather saw him smiling. Fellowes looked at Sandy, then back to Lennox.

A colossal rushing noise came from Heather's left. The surface of the loch was bubbling and swirling, seagulls scattering, as a massive oblong portion of the loch seemed to rise into the air. Heather realised it wasn't the loch but another creature, the size of a small ship, water pouring from its sides and cascading into the loch below. A huge shadow spread over the loch's surface as the thing went higher into the air. It was a gigantic jellyfish shape, pink and red, orange and green and a million other colours glinting in the sun, a slippery sheen on their surface, huge tendrils draping from their body to the surface of the loch.

They moved, a sinuous curve shaping and reinventing the air around them as they rushed over the land, the shadow spreading over the fishing boats, the truck and the promenade. The people watching all stepped back or ran up the hill. Fellowes stood underneath, gawping at their underbelly. Heather turned to Ava, who stared wide-eyed. Heather saw an iridescent display like nothing she'd ever seen, swirls and dots and shapes intertwining and coalescing. The air shimmered around them, water still pouring off.

They were all in shade now. Lennox ran to Fellowes and grabbed the pole. Fellowes yanked it away, pointed the gun at Lennox.

One of the tendrils hanging from Xander's belly swung in their direction, then expanded and turned more solid. It looked like a larger, darker version of Sandy, but still attached to Xander, and Heather thought of Ava's umbilical cord still connecting her baby. The creature opened an orifice in a downward tube section and enveloped Lennox, Fellowes and Sandy in the cage, sucking them up like a vacuum cleaner. A few moments later it spat out Fellowes and the empty cage, then it disappeared back into Xander's belly. Xander hovered for a second then narrowed to an ellipsoid, reshaped the air around them again, a shivering hum enveloping their frame. Then they shot straight upwards faster than Heather could comprehend, leaving a wet trail as they disappeared into the distant sky.

Heather blinked in the sunshine and tried to breathe. Lennox and Sandy were gone. The empty cage and the gun lay next to Fellowes, sprawled and unconscious.

61
LENNOX

He didn't know if he was alive or dead, conscious or unconscious, human or something else. This felt different to the mind trips he'd had with Sandy and Xander before, more visceral. He shot away from Ullapool, Scotland, the Earth, through the upper atmosphere into low-orbit space, then higher still.

He was inside Xander. He lifted his hand to his face, like moving in a viscous jelly. He could breathe. He felt his lungs work, wondered if they were full of Xander's body, if this stuff was inside him, getting into his bloodstream, becoming part of him.

Sandy was floating to his side, gently expanding and contracting their body, tentacles swaying in the jelly. It was so good to see them out of that cage. He and Sandy were part of Xander now. It didn't make sense to think of himself as Lennox anymore, he was a compound of a million things – bacteria in his gut, microscopic bugs in his hair, Xander's body passing through his own, Sandy inside his neurons. It finally made physical sense, the idea that Sandy was plural. We all are. And the human idea of being singular, apart, alone, was a ridiculous and lonely way of looking at life.

He could see through Xander's body to outside. He imagined wind whipping his face as they lifted out of the atmosphere. The moon got larger, the sun too, and he worried about radiation, wasn't that something astronauts had to deal with? Beams of energy that changed the make-up of your cells. But he'd experienced plenty of that already, what did it matter?

The stars were brighter than he'd ever seen. He remembered

looking at the sky back in Figgate Park at the start of this. Now he was here amongst the stars.

He had no idea how fast they were travelling, or how they were doing it. There was no jet trail, just easy propulsion through the vacuum. They approached an area of sky where the starlight faded or shimmered as they got closer. They passed through a membrane and were plunged into a darker space, no starlight penetrating. Some kind of shield?

After a moment of darkness Lennox was blinded by light everywhere as Xander slowed. They were surrounded by thousands of creatures like Xander, giant glowing jellyfish, each with their own ecosystem of smaller beings dipping in and out, underneath, between. Lennox just stared. There were millions of interconnected creatures here, in a secret bubble of space. Lennox tried to get his head round it.

<What is this?> he thought eventually.

<Sandy whole.>

Lennox turned to Sandy, who was displaying colours he'd never seen before.

<Xander whole.> This was Xander's voice.

Sandy flashed an iridescent kind of yellow-blue. <Enceladus whole.>

Lennox thought about that.

<Sandy-Lennox partial now Enceladus whole.> Sandy's voice was so comforting, he couldn't remember a time it hadn't been in his mind. He felt a glow at the idea of being a part of something bigger. Him, Sandy and Xander, all part of this horde currently floating in some kind of blind spot.

<This bubble. Enceladons are hiding?>

Sandy waved a tentacle close to Lennox's face. It shimmered and melted away, then reappeared. <Light manipulation.>

The bubble must be many miles across. <Why hide?>

Sandy shrank and Lennox understood Xander would answer.

<Unsure of human reaction.> A pause. <No awareness of other life. No sense of Enceladons. Shock.>

Lennox spotted some creatures with long, spindly arms, antennae twitching as they swam through Xander's tendrils.

<Yeah, shock.>

Sandy flashed green-blue. <Lennox first human to connect.>

<Why me?>

Another pause. He wondered if they were talking to each other without him, or communicating with others in this tribe.

<Happy accident.> Sandy's voice. <Sandy partial one of many partials exploring earth. Examining. Happy Sandy-Lennox partial, now Enceladus whole.>

Lennox thought about Xander at the bottom of Loch Broom. He wondered how many other Xanders were out there, how many Sandys. He thought about all the oceans of the world, the depths that humans knew nothing about.

<Are you coming to live on Earth?>

Their consciousness was completely different to his. He was starting to get a tiny glimpse into their world, their society. But he wanted more, wanted to know everything about this civilisation, these creatures, how they evolved, how long they'd lived on Enceladus, what did they eat, how did they mate, what about culture?

He thought about Sandy-Lennox partial and Enceladus whole. He wondered if there was any differentiation between Xander and Sandy, or if he'd just assumed that. He remembered that thing about Earth octopuses, how they have mini-brains in their tentacles. He understood the words, but what does it really mean? It makes the idea of a self meaningless.

<Enceladus whole coming to earth.> This was Xander.

Lennox frowned. <Those things you showed me on Enceladus. Is that why you left?>

Xander's flesh darkened for a moment. <Other. Not part of Enceladus whole. Not willing to become Enceladus. Destroy all.>

<What are they? Where did they come from?>

Sandy flashed red-orange, tentacles flapping. <Interstellar, you say. Not solar system. Dark. No knowledge.>

<From another star system? How did they get here?>

<Dark, no knowledge.>

<What do they want?>

<Destroy all.>

<Will they come to earth? Will they follow you?>

<Dark, no knowledge.>

Dark, no knowledge. It was fucking dark, all right. Lennox looked around at the exhibition of life floating here. <When are you coming down to Earth?>

A moment of silence, colours swirling around him, through him.

<Now.>

62
AVA

Ava felt the baby squirm in her hands and a glow swept through her.

'Are you OK?' Heather said.

Ava nodded.

Heather glanced at the sky, empty and blue, the gulls still scared to take flight. 'What was that?'

'I guess it was Xander,' Ava said. 'Lennox must've asked for help.'

Heather frowned. 'Did you hear anything?'

Ava hadn't.

Heather shook her head. 'Where did they go?'

Ava looked at her baby, then at Heather. 'I can't believe she's here with me, finally. My Chloe.'

Heather's face softened and she leaned in to get a better look. 'She's beautiful. It's a lovely name.'

Ava stared at Chloe's closed eyes, wrinkled skin, felt the warmth of her. She was so exhausted but at least the pain was gone, just a low-level ache throbbing through her body. She stared at Chloe, tried to get her head round the fact that she'd been inside her a few minutes ago. The umbilical cord was still attached, the placenta still inside Ava, still working to feed Chloe. Ava loved that they were connected for a few more moments.

Heather left a trailing hand and walked to where Lennox had been. The jetty concrete was covered in puddles like a rainstorm had passed through. Fellowes lay with his arms out, legs curled under him like a Victorian lady after a dizzy spell.

Ava sat up slowly, feeling every ache. She shuffled to the edge of the truck to see better, supporting Chloe's head.

Heather went to the cage, touched it, picked up the gun and put it in her pocket. She looked at the sky and Ava followed her gaze. Where were Lennox, Sandy and Xander?

Heather crouched next to Fellowes, touched his neck. Ava looked around, some of the bystanders were inching closer to the pier, many staring at the sky, some holding phones. She wondered if it was on the internet yet, whether folk were already calling it a hoax.

She heard a snuffle and looked at Chloe, closed her eyes as another wave of exhaustion swept over her.

'Well.'

Her shoulders tightened at the voice.

Michael. Standing there smiling like he meant well. She'd forgotten about him and it had been bliss. Now she was right back in the shark tank, her body tense. She covered her groin, feeling exposed.

'No need,' he said, stepping closer. 'I've seen it all before.'

She angled her shoulders to hide Chloe from him, pointless but instinctive.

'Admittedly, this is new,' he said, reaching out to the baby.

'Don't.' Ava felt herself harden, something rock solid at her core.

Michael acted like he didn't hear her. 'Our baby daughter. Margaret, after my mother.'

'She's called Chloe.' It was a mistake to speak. Don't engage, don't give him ammunition. She couldn't believe she had to deal with this.

'I don't think so,' Michael said. 'Chloe is too common. Margaret is much more suitable.'

'Ava?' Another voice she recognised, a similar feeling of dread.

She turned. 'Mum?'

'Darling.' Her mum stepped from the other side of the truck. She stared at Chloe, eyes wet.

Ava felt tears coming, thought about her mum giving birth to her.

'Thank you,' Michael said, wrestling Chloe from her arms before she even knew it was happening. The baby started to cry. She was tiny in Michael's hands and he was holding her all wrong, her head lolling.

Michael didn't even look at Chloe, just stared at Ava. He batted her away as she lunged forward. Then he looked down, saw the umbilical cord, frowned in disgust. He pulled out a penknife, one Ava gave him as an anniversary present, and cut the cord, leaving a few inches dangling from Chloe's belly, the rest flopping between Ava's legs.

Ava had expected that to hurt but there was no pain. But feeling separated from Chloe, she wanted to die. Or kill.

She glanced at her mum who looked confused, as if it had never occurred to her that her son-in-law was a bad man.

'Michael?' she said.

'Let's go,' Michael said to her, ignoring Ava. 'I've got what I came here for.'

Ava slid from the back of the truck, felt her legs wobble, her groin burn. She reached for Chloe but Michael stepped away. This was so easy for him, just like his whole life. He was going to take what he wanted and that was that. She wouldn't let that happen.

'Stop.' Ava turned to see Heather a few yards away, pointing Fellowes' gun at Michael.

Michael laughed and shook his head. Chloe cried. 'Who the fuck even are you?'

Heather stood still. 'Give Chloe back.'

Michael looked at the crowd watching. 'You won't shoot me in front of these people. What if I drop her?'

The world shrank around Ava as her focus narrowed on him

and Chloe. She was still leaning against the truck, trying to stand up. Heather said something but the sound had turned down on her universe, she didn't catch it. Michael replied, smug and confident, like always. They were talking as if this was a negotiation. But this was her daughter's life, there was nothing to discuss.

Heather stepped forward and Michael stepped back. He was just a few feet away. Ava inched along the back of the truck, her hand sliding on the metal, the bloody umbilical cord dangling between her legs. Her knuckles touched something and she turned. A heavy wrench, spilled from an open toolbox. Must've shaken loose in the crash. She lifted the wrench, the cold metal at home in her fist, the weight of it like something holy. She gripped it tight.

She stepped up to Michael and swung the wrench onto the back of his skull with every ounce of strength she had. She heard the crack of metal on bone, blood spraying from his scalp. She dropped the wrench with a clang, took two steps forward while Michael swayed, and gently lifted Chloe from his hands, held her to her chest. Michael stared at her, blood pouring down his neck as he crumpled to the ground, head hitting the concrete with a thunk that made Ava's heart sing.

'It's OK,' she whispered to Chloe. 'Mummy's here.'

She sensed things happening around her. She heard Michael gurgle on the ground, felt Heather's hand on her shoulder, heard her mother speak. Eventually she realised the world had darkened. She looked and saw Xander descending from the sky, casting a shadow over the shore and the jetty. The giant creature came to a stop fifty feet above their heads, flashing blue and green like some crazy fairground show.

63
LENNOX

Lennox floated above Ullapool inside Xander, looking down like a god. He saw Ava and Heather by the truck, Michael and Fellowes on the ground.

A column of Xander's body extended towards the ground and Lennox felt himself slide downwards. Sandy came too, the pair of them drifting through Xander's flesh.

They slowed and Lennox's feet touched the ground. It was strange to be tethered to Earth, to feel gravity. What he'd felt in the space bubble stayed with him, he was part of a community with every other living thing on Earth. He thought about all the other planets and moons and star systems out there, so much interconnected life in the billions of miles of space. If there were already two ecosystems in this solar system, life must be crawling all over the universe. But what about those things that came to Enceladus? Where did they fit?

Lennox looked around. He was standing between Fellowes and the women at the truck. Sandy scuttled to Fellowes' body, touched it with their tentacles.

<Sandy, is he dead?>

Sandy's head swelled. <Fellowes-Sandy partial continues.>

Part of Lennox felt put out, he wanted to be the only one with a special connection to Sandy. But that was crazy, the one thing he'd learned was that everyone was connected.

Xander was still overhead, casting shade on everyone. Lennox heard a low hiss as they slid sideways. They moved until their whole body was over the loch, then lowered to the surface. They sat there taking up half the port like a blockade, colours shifting across their skin, intricate swirling patterns dissolving and reappearing.

Lennox walked over to the women. Ava was resting on the truck tailgate gazing at her baby. Heather stood with a gun loose in her hand. She stared at Michael lying in a large pool of blood and seawater. His eyes were open, staring at nothing.

'Is he dead?'

Heather nodded then stuck her chin out at Lennox. 'What happened to you?'

Lennox looked at the sky. He pulled his earlobe to wake himself up from this dream. 'I went into space.'

'And?' Ava said, looking up.

'It was crazy.'

'More crazy than everything else?'

Lennox looked round. People were gathered along the stony shore, gawping at Xander. 'Yes.'

<What happened?> He was shocked at Heather's voice in his head. She seemed initially bemused too, as if she hadn't meant to do it. So they were telepathic now without Sandy. Holy crap.

<Shit, I heard that.> This was Ava, staring at him and Heather. The three of them, connected forever.

Lennox never wanted them to leave his head. <They're running from something. They're refugees, fleeing for their lives. They've come here to live. There's nowhere else.>

<What are they running from?> Heather thought.

<I don't know. Some other species, maybe, it's not clear. They came to Enceladus from a long way away.>

Fellowes got to his feet, Sandy keeping him steady. He looked confused. He staggered to them at the truck, Sandy alongside. He looked from one to the other, at Michael on the ground. Then at Xander out to sea.

<Sandy, who are those creatures on Enceladus?> Lennox thought. <What do you call them?>

Sandy went to the truck and sat next to Ava. <Different life. Not like Sandy-Xander, not like Enceladus whole. Not like human. Other.>

Heather perked up. <Like robots? AI?>

A pause, Sandy thinking about it. <Unclear. Dark, no knowledge.>

Heather nodded. <Where are they from?>

Sandy wriggled a little. <You name it Proxima Centauri.>

Fellowes turned to look at them. 'Are you talking to it? All of you?'

Lennox felt sorry for him, he just seemed like a lost boy left behind. The rest of them had evolved and Fellowes wasn't a part of it. 'Yes.'

'How is that possible?' Fellowes waved a hand at Xander on the loch. 'And that too? Can you talk to that?'

Lennox swallowed. 'It's all part of the same thing, all one big organism or species. I don't know how to describe it. We're pathetic in comparison. Pissing around in our own little heads, shut off from each other.'

'Why is it here, did it tell you that?'

Fuck that. Fellowes had tried to capture Sandy. He was playing by old, human rules that didn't apply anymore. Everything had changed.

'I guess you don't have a cage big enough for Xander,' Lennox said.

Fellowes gawped at Xander for a long time. Eventually he turned to Lennox. 'You think I'm the bad guy, and maybe I've done things wrong. But I've waited all my life for this. To make contact with something from another planet. Something alien.'

You have no fucking idea, Lennox thought.

Fellowes looked at Sandy in the back of the truck, at Ava with Chloe, Heather with the gun. 'You don't understand, this changes everything. This is the dawn of a new age.'

Lennox hated how he spoke. Big ideas, grand proclamations, but he didn't have a clue. Sandy had spoken to them, not him, there was a reason for that.

Xander made a noise then rose out of the water, stopping fifty feet up, water lashing off their undersides. Sandy came over next to Lennox. A tentacle folded itself into Lennox's hand, suckers pressing against his skin. He wrapped his fingers around it.

Xander gave a low rumble then a high whoosh, like air blowing through a window. There was a moment of silence then similar noises came from higher in the sky.

Sandy's suckers squeezed Lennox's hand as he looked up. Thousands of jellyfish creatures like Xander appeared in the sky, small dots at first, quickly growing and revealing their shapes and intricacies, colours and lights. They filled the sky, bigger and bigger, countless other creatures connecting and intertwining between and beneath them. They continued to descend and spread out.

Lennox saw they were coming down over the water. He turned to the hills behind Ullapool and the sky was clear. But over the water, thousands of Enceladons continued to drift closer to the sea.

He smelled the same odour as the first night he met Sandy. But he didn't feel faint and didn't lose balance, just stared at the creatures in the sky. He looked round at the bystanders along the promenade, they weren't affected the way Lennox had been with Sandy that first time, something was different now.

The Enceladons landed on the surface of Loch Broom and out to sea as far as the horizon. Their light displays were mesmerising, seemingly communicating with each other, colours and patterns flowing from one to another as far as the eye could see.

Fellowes stared at them all, slack-jawed.

Xander lowered themself into the water to sit alongside the others and joined in the light display.

Sandy squeezed Lennox's hand. <Enceladons-Humans whole.>

Lennox looked around. Heather stared at the loch full of Enceladons, then turned to him and smiled. Ava looked up from Chloe in her arms and did the same. They all looked at Sandy, who was glowing and pulsing, indescribable patterns and colours, the most alive thing Lennox had ever seen.

The three of them had all been alone at the start of this, isolated and separate. Now they were three parts of something much bigger, three tiny elements of a new future. They were changed, they weren't just human anymore, they were something else, something better.

<Wow.> This was Ava in his head, in their joint mind.

Heather grinned. <What now?>

Lennox turned to Sandy and squeezed their tentacle.

<Good question. What now, Sandy?>

ACKNOWLEDGEMENTS

Endless thanks to Karen Sullivan, who saw the potential in this story, and everyone else at Orenda Books for their tireless work and dedication. Thanks to Phil Patterson and all at Marjacq for their unstinting support. I also owe a debt of gratitude to Creative Scotland, for their belief in this book and their financial assistance. Thanks to everyone who has supported my writing over the years, it would be impossible without you. And loads of love, as always, to Tricia, Aidan and Amber.